John Popplewell Renaissance

by
Anthony D Roberts

For Andrea.

All rights reserved
Copyright © Anthony D Roberts

Anthony D Roberts is hereby identified as author of this
work in accordance with Section 77 of the Copyright, Designs
and Patents Act 1988

This book is published by
Grosvenor House Publishing Ltd
28–30 High Street, Guildford, Surrey, GU1 3HY.
www.grosvenorhousepublishing.co.uk

This book is sold subject to the conditions that it shall not, by way of
trade or otherwise, be lent, resold, hired out or otherwise circulated
without the author's or publisher's prior consent in any form of binding or cover other
than that in which it is published and
without a similar condition including this condition being imposed
on the subsequent purchaser.

A CIP record for this book
is available from the British Library

ISBN 1-905529-35-X

Cover design by Bluestone Design Group Ltd

THE AIR ATTACK

The battle-scarred destroyer ploughed her way through the rolling sea as fast as her steam turbines could propel her. The sun, which hung high in the clear blue sky, wasn't due to set for hours. Yet, what was needed right now was darkness. Darkness and speed. And for no more German aircraft to turn up and attack the ship.

The captain of this ship, Philip Ambrose, was at his action-station on the bridge, an open-topped conning position which was exposed to the elements. He felt the deck shudder and shake each time the ship slammed into a large wave. A stiff breeze suddenly whipped around Philip's face and this carried a little sea-spray from one of the breaking waves. He dabbed away the spray from his face with a neatly folded handkerchief, and then glanced to either side of his ship for the reassuring sight of the other two surviving British destroyers which were also tearing their way through the sea. This was a desperate race for survival: three exhausted, battle-weary greyhounds, neck and neck, bolting for the safer seas beyond the range of prowling German aircraft. Philip re-adjusted the chin-strap on his tin helmet and focused his attention on the cloudless sky around them. His was not the only pair of anxious eyes scouring the sky that afternoon. The rest of his bridge crew, and gun crews, also frantically searched for signs of further enemy aircraft.

"Sir!" exclaimed a signalman, who pointed to twelve German dive-bombers that were fast emerging from the far distant sky astern of the fleeing flotilla. As the aircraft approached, Philip counted them over and over again, hoping there would be fewer with every count. This was the largest number of enemy aircraft they had encountered all day, and Philip felt like his moment of reckoning was almost upon him. His stomach turned cold and the anxiety of the moment weighed heavily within him – like an anchor tied to the bottom of his ribcage.

Through his binoculars, he saw the approaching aircraft divide into three groups, each group taking a ship as a target. He then leaned over to the row of communications pipes and lifted the flap on the pipe to the wheelhouse.

"Coxswain," he said calmly, "this is the Captain. Dive-bombers approaching. Stand by for some heavy manoeuvres."

"Yes, Sir," the reply floated out of the pipe.

Philip ordered the anti-aircraft guns to open fire and, within seconds, every weapon that could be brought to bear erupted in a cacophony of rattles and booms. The whole flotilla hurled a furious barrage at the enemy. Undaunted, the first aircraft flew through this curtain of fire and began its dive, accompanied by its usual, characteristic scream: a scream designed to strike terror into its victim. But Philip and his crew knew best how to react. They simply ignored it and went about their business. A signalman with binoculars was tracking the dive of the first bomber. Philip glanced at the other two destroyers as he considered his manoeuvres. He then leaned into the communication pipe.

"Coxswain, standby..." he said.

"Bombs away!" exclaimed the signalman.

"Hard a starboard!" Philip barked down the communication pipe.

A fraction of a second later, the ship turned sharply, leaning heavily. The bomb exploded harmlessly in the sea close to the port side of the ship, throwing up a huge plume of water that drenched some of the exposed gunners as the ship ran close by it.

The ship was brought straight again just as the second dive-bomber entered its dive. Once again, the same gunners were soaked by a similar manoeuvre, this time as the second bomb exploded off the starboard side. But the third bomber was obviously more experienced, because it entered its dive close behind the second aircraft and instead of aiming for the ship it aimed its bomb at the sea that lay directly in the path of the turning destroyer. Philip stared at the bomb as it descended in surreal slow-motion and he realised that they did not have the vital seconds needed to avoid it.

The bomb entered the ship through the boat-deck, shattering the sea-boat from its davits and knocking the wreckage into the sea. The bridge crew instinctively crouched for cover from flying debris. But not Philip. He stood bolt upright, with an impassive expression as splinters flew all around him. Outwardly, he appeared fearless. Inwardly, he was in turmoil.

As the bomb crashed its way down through the decks, it severed the main steam supply to the engines. Then it exploded, instantly consuming the engine room in an inferno of volcanic ferocity. Philip felt the deck lift in the air and shake with the sudden violence of the explosion.

He leaned across to the communications pipe for the engine room, lifted the flap and placed his lips close to the pipe.

"Damage control report, Chief Rogers." There was no reply. "Chief Rogers?" But as he spoke, his cheeks and lips felt the pull of a vacuum in the pipe. For a split second he was confused by the sensation. Then it dawned on him that the engine room fire was sucking in air from wherever it could. The engineers had stood little chance.

Philip glanced up at the sky and saw the aircraft turn away and gradually disappear into the distance. The guns of the flotilla fell silent, leaving the sky littered with the small puffs of sooty smoke where anti-aircraft shells had exploded. Philip realised that his ship was the only one damaged in this encounter.

The destroyer slowed to a stop as thick, black, acrid smoke billowed furiously out of its gaping wound. Smoke drifted in a great cloud towards the stern of the ship, engulfing the crew of the main guns who were soon struggling to breathe. Panicked, they jumped overboard into the gentle swell of waves.

Sailors of all description poured out through doors onto the upper decks, desperate to escape the devastation below. Many were bent double as they struggled for breath, their eyes stinging and streaming with tears. Their poisoned lungs coughed and rasped. A couple of engineering ratings staggered out of one door, dragging an injured shipmate between them. Their faces were blackened by smoke and their hands were blistered red from the flames. The wounded man's left trouser leg was shredded and a bloodied and broken limb was exposed. He was delirious with pain.

Philip saw that the situation was degenerating into chaos. He turned to one of his officers. The man, who was in his mid twenties and relatively new to the ship, was shocked and frozen to the spot.

"Lieutenant Markham," Philip called out.

"Y-Yes Sir?" The Lieutenant snapped out of his trance.

"Go and organise the men down there. Make sure a Senior Rate takes charge of the wounded and get the rest of the men fighting that fire. And see if you can find the First Lieutenant."

"Sir," the officer replied, then darted across the bridge and slid quickly down a ladder without touching a single rung.

Lieutenant Markham barked a few orders here and there and very soon several crewmen managed to rig two fire-hoses, which whipped across the deck like large snakes and wrestled to escape the grip of the crewmen struggling on the end. They discharged a torrent of salt spray down into the gaping hole in the decks.

Then a fuel tank ruptured, and a column of crimson flame burst out through the bomb damaged decks, reaching as high as the funnel-top and knocking several men over with the force of the blast. At that moment, all water pressure failed and the fire-hoses drooped lifeless and limp, dribbling pathetically. The crewmen discarded them hurriedly and retreated to a safer area of upper deck. This was a major setback; and voices were carried on the sea breeze with cries of "…pissing in the wind…" and other colourful statements of opinion which could briefly be heard above the decibels of destruction.

Philip recognised that the loss of water pressure had dashed any hopes for salvage. He was also acutely aware that there had not been enough time to flood the magazines to make them safe. So, he thought it was probably just a matter of time before one of the magazines, or another fuel tank, exploded, killing many more of his men.

Lieutenant Markham climbed back up the ladder onto the bridge. Soot and blood was streaked down his soaking wet uniform. He looked a pitiful, bedraggled sight.

"Sir," he said, "the water…"

"I know," Philip interrupted, "I can see. Tell the men to muster on the forecastle. We're going to abandon ship."

"But, Sir! There are still men trapped…"

"It's too late for them, Markham," snapped Philip, "The magazines aren't safe, and could go up at any moment. The ship is lost. Now, do as I order."

"Yes, Sir," Lieutenant Markham answered and slid back down the ladder.

The ship was beyond salvage, and Philip knew it. The destroyer had become the destroyed and it was likely that some men were going to be left behind to die. It was a grave choice he'd had to make: abandon those men who were trapped below, or risk the lives of more men by staying and trying to attempt a rescue. It was no longer about saving the ship: it was about saving what was left of his crew. Philip knew that the trapped men were as good as dead whichever way he looked at it. There was no hope for them.

He turned to his signalman.

"Hollis. Signal to Captain 'D.' Abandoning ship. Request assistance.'"

"Yes, Sir," replied the signalman, who grabbed his hand flags and began furiously semaphoring the signal.

Whilst the signal was being relayed, the emotional straight-jacket that Philip had spent so much of his life weaving began to strain at the seams as he struggled to contain his rising anger and frustration. As the ship rolled gently in the swell of the sea he gripped a guardrail tightly, as much to steady his composure as to steady his posture.

As the order to abandon ship began to disseminate amongst the crew, a couple of sailors released three emergency life-rafts overboard. A dozen or so men jumped into the water and swam to them through a thick oil slick that seeped from splits in the weakened hull of the ship. Covered in this black slippery sludge, the men clung on nervously as the floats drifted in the swell. With stinging eyes and a slippery grip they hoped they could hold on for long enough and prayed that they would drift away from the wreck of their ship. Thankfully, they did.

Above the noise of the fire, Lieutenant Markham could be heard ordering other men not to jump overboard but to go to the bow of the ship, where many men, including the wounded, were already mustering, anxious, exhausted, but still disciplined and ready to transfer to the two ships of the flotilla that had been lucky enough to out-manoeuvre the dive-bombers. The two other warships were soon within a few hundred yards of the dying destroyer, making their way towards the survivors.

Some of the men hanging on to the floats waved arms and yelled to attract the attention of the ships. One of the destroyers changed course, slightly, and headed directly for them: scrambling nets hung over its sides in readiness to help their rescue.

The other ship, the flagship of the Flotilla Captain, tentatively approached the burning vessel bow-to-bow and it came to a stop with forecastle alongside forecastle. Fenders squeaked and creaked as hull rubbed against hull. Men quickly jumped across from the abandoned ship to relative safety.

Within a few minutes Philip stood alone on his ship's forecastle. He turned to face the quarterdeck, stood to attention and saluted – a final gesture to the dead and trapped crewmen he was leaving behind. The feelings of despair and regret at the day's events were overwhelming as he stepped across between ships. Curiously, though, he felt no hatred towards the German pilots who had inflicted such suffering.

He quickly composed himself again, by repeating a single thought over and over again in his mind: he had no choice but to abandon the ship – this was war.

Philip readily acknowledged that the operational effectiveness of the flotilla and the safety of survivors were of paramount importance. But he knew this would be little comfort to the families of those who were still trapped below decks. He knew that they would know it was his decision, and his decision alone that ultimately condemned those trapped men to a watery grave.

Shafts turned and water churned as the rescuing destroyer eased away from the wreck, quickly picking up speed as it made for comparatively safer waters. Philip squeezed his way through the crowd of men packed onto the forecastle, acknowledging various members of his crew as he went along. He paused by one sailor, who was holding a bloodied dressing to his forehead.

"How are we bearing up, Johnson?" Philip asked. The sailor did not reply. Philip reached out his arm and touched the sailor's elbow and followed it up with a gentle "Mmm? Johnson?"

The sailor, avoiding eye contact with Philip, replied in a clear and composed voice, "I'm as right as nine-pence, Sir. Just glad I ain't one of them poor sods left trapped below."

Philip was taken aback by the sailor's frankness. But rather than confront it, Philip stepped away.

"Good man, Johnson," he muttered. "You did well today." Philip caught the eye of a number of men who simply glowered back at him. He then added, "You all did well."

It was not the best of circumstances to give morale boosting comments, and so he resolved to address his men after speaking with the Flotilla Captain.

As he made his way through the throng of men, his thoughts wandered into surreal detachment: he felt conscious of his crew's likely perception of him – one of him being born into the right family, going to the right school and so on; one of being given command of a ship because of his family connections rather than his ability to command. That was their likely perception. But in truth, he was far from aristocracy and far from wealthy. He was the son of a village doctor; he was a grammar school boy who'd won a scholarship to university. True, that when he joined the Royal Navy, he was recommended for a commission and he quickly rose in rank, but this was on merit, not money or connections. He was given command of a ship *despite* his background.

Philip continued to move through the crowd on the deck. Eventually, he found himself at the foot of a ladder which he climbed up towards the bridge to report to the Captain. He knew the route well. Philip's ship was exactly the same. Well, it used to be. After climbing a second ladder he arrived on the bridge and presented himself to the Captain, a stocky, ruddy faced man, whose flamboyance and eccentricities were quite intimidating to most people.

On seeing Philip enter the bridge the Captain opened his arms in a grand gesture of welcome, "Philip!" he declared and grasped Philip's hand firmly, before shaking it with a sincerity that Philip knew from experience was false. "Bad luck, old chap. You look like you could do with a drink."

"Thank you, Sir," muttered Philip. For some reason, his usual confidence was suddenly absent from his voice and, with the discomfort of an embarrassed schoolboy, he stared intently at his shuffling feet. Philip then realised he was beginning to look foolish in front of the bridge crew. He raised his eyes to meet those of the Captain and saw the Captain staring at him hard and thoughtfully. Then, placing a hand on Philip's shoulder the Captain relaxed his gaze and spoke softly. "You can go down to my day cabin, Philip. I'll send a steward to get you a drink. I'll be another ten minutes or so and then I'll join you. That is, unless you want to watch and say farewell to her."

Philip straightened his posture and suppressed his emotions with iron fortitude. She wasn't gone, yet.

"Thank you, Sir. But I'm fine. As soon as she's gone I'll need to assess my crew – casualties and the like. Bit of a morale boost needed."

"Good," the Captain nodded quietly, and then turned his attention to that of his bridge. He ordered loudly, "Let's get this over with."

The destroyer swung around, the arc of white bubbles in her wake contrasting against the dark grey-green of the sea. With a loud hiss, a torpedo was loosed in the direction of the burning wreck. As it dived into the water, Philip let out a sigh. In a few seconds she would be gone forever.

TRAPPED!

John regained consciousness to find himself engulfed in a pitch darkness that could rival that of any deep coal mine in his native Yorkshire. His foggy memory began to slowly return to him and he gradually remembered where he was and what had happened to him. The last thing he could remember, with any clarity at least, was climbing down the ladder into the Tiller Flat. This was the compartment in the stern of the ship, containing the rudder head and steering machinery. And now he was laid on the deck in total darkness and with pains in his left wrist and forehead. A fleeting image of being flung across the compartment entered his mind's eye and he recalled that the ship had been pursued and attacked almost continuously for hours on end. It occurred to John that the ship had been attacked again and, this time, finally hit.

He listened, because he could see nothing in the darkness, and he immediately realised that the ship was in serious trouble. The propeller shafts had stopped turning, and the noise and vibration familiar with the ship being propelled forward could not he felt. Instead he could hear, and feel, the low rumbling of fire. A sudden explosion somewhere deep in the ship shook the deck-plates and he heard the groan of stressed metal buckling in another compartment not very far away. The ship was obviously dead in the water. Then, suddenly, he heard the sound of spraying water, and he realised the compartment was slowly flooding, possibly from ruptured pipes, possibly from a leaking rudder head. The outlook did not appear promising to him.

"Bugger!" was all he could think to say.

He crawled along the deck plates and tried to find his bearings. When he reached a ladder below a hatch, he pulled himself up and leaned his body against the ladder, wrapping his right arm around a rung for extra support. Using his injured hand, he felt for the lump that was developing just above his left eye. He gently rubbed around it, but he felt no cut or tear – a good sign. It hurt, but not so much as to cause great discomfort. Tentatively, he climbed the ladder, holding his injured left hand above his head – he didn't want to bang his head if he reached the hatch too quickly, particularly as it was only a few feet above his head. When he reached the hatch he tried to push it open. It didn't budge. Not that he expected it to. In the panic and confusion above decks, the crew must not have been able to unclip the hatch that kept him secured at his action station. John was trapped and, it seemed, destined to die in this battle. He descended the ladder and propped himself against the lower rungs.

As the ship rolled gently in the swell, the rising flood water streamed from one side of the compartment to the other and back again. He felt its coolness enter his boots and swirl around his ankles.

Narrowing his eyes, he strained to see anything in the blackness, but he could see nothing. For a split second John thought his concussion may have blinded him – hence the darkness. Adrenaline rushed through his body at the thought of being blind for the rest of his life. Surely it couldn't be that bad, he reassured himself, there wasn't any blood coming from the lump on his head. Then the adrenaline rush gave way to a giddy panic as the seriousness of his predicament began to dawn on him. His hands and knees began to involuntarily shake, only slightly, yet unmistakably and he found it difficult to steady them. He suddenly felt very frightened and very alone.

"Bugger!" he breathed to himself. "How the soddin' hell am I going to get out of this?"

He didn't want to die. He wanted to get out. So he concentrated on thinking more rationally about attracting the attention of potential rescuers.

"Spanner!" he suddenly exclaimed out loud to himself. "Why didn't I think of it earlier?" Of course! If he could find a wheel spanner, or something similar, he could bang on the underside of the fastened hatch to attract attention. "Right then, where are they?" He tried to recall where he had seen a wheel spanner. He recalled that one was somewhere nearby – or at least it had been earlier.

Moving sideways, sliding one foot along the deck plates, followed by the other foot, he tentatively made his way through the sloshing water towards a valve wheel where he had earlier hung a wheel spanner. In the darkness he raised his left arm until it was out-stretched in front of him – he didn't want to bang his head on something again. He used his other arm to steady himself on a guardrail as the ship rolled in the swell.

After shuffling a couple of yards, John's injured left hand came into contact with a large steel object, which he thought he recognised as part of the hydraulic system. He ran the back of his fingers down its casing, and his wrist came into contact with the side of a valve wheel. Gently, he slipped his hand down around the wheel – the last thing he wanted to do now was be too rough and knock the wheel spanner off into the bilge. He touched the spanner, grabbed it and unhooked it. The pain of holding it made him wince, so he quickly swapped hands. John gripped the wheel spanner tightly in his right hand and made his way back to the ladder, employing similar shuffling tactics as before.

When he reached the ladder, he grasped the rungs tightly and let out a sigh of relief. Still gripping the wheel spanner he slowly climbed the ladder. Once at the top of the ladder, he used the wheel spanner to hammer repeatedly against the underside of the hatch.

Paint chipped away from the hatch and tiny pieces fell into his half-opened mouth. He spat and spluttered to clear them away from his mouth whilst wiping other paint chips from his perspiring brow. He continued his hammering.

"Down 'ere!" he yelled as loud as he could "Help! Man trapped below!"

John slowed the hammering as his arm tired. After thirty seconds or so, he stopped banging. Motionless, he listened for signs of activity above. John could sense the rumble of the blaze elsewhere in the ship and hear the spray of the water within his own compartment, but little else came to his attention.

John resumed the hammering and shouting, stopping occasionally to listen for any signs of life above decks. After about ten minutes of this, John concluded that a rescue was unlikely and he descended to the foot of the ladder. At least the water was rising slowly, he noted to himself. That was a good thing, wasn't it?

Yet it grew clear to John that he should prepare himself to die. He wondered why it was that your life only flashed before your eyes when you had a close encounter with *sudden* death. Here he was, staring into the jaws of his own inevitable extinction and all he could muster was the occasional abstract reflection in slow motion – such as the loss of his ditty box. It only contained a few sentimental knick-knacks: a faded photograph of his parents on their wedding day; his father's medal from the Great War, and the final letter he had received from his late wife. But it mattered a lot to him and the thought of its loss irritated him.

Then a curious thought crossed his mind. His late wife would shortly become his widow. That is, she would have become his widow had she not already been dead. And then, suddenly, John became nervous at the possibility of meeting her again after these six, long, dead years. But that, of course, was only if there *was* an afterlife – which there wasn't, because John didn't believe in one. He believed that death was death. The end. There was nothing after death. But that belief didn't halt his brief fantasy.

Sensing that this might not be an altogether constructive use of what little time he might have left, John resolved to change the subject. He rubbed his eyes to remove some more paint flakes, and suddenly noticed that a very small flicker of orange light had appeared at the opposite side of the compartment, near the ship's hull.

The light looked like a spinning flame. It was a couple of inches in diameter, and about waist height. It didn't look like any sort of fire he'd ever seen before, and John had seen many over the last year or so. This particular fire was suspended in mid air, with no base or fuel to feed it. John thought it looked a little bit like a very small Catherine Wheel. He was transfixed by its radiance. As he stared, the flicker began to grow, and within ten seconds it was almost three feet in diameter. John blinked several times as it dimly illuminated the compartment with its orange glow. Dark pockets of shadow were cast behind machinery. Instinctively, John waded through the water, now above his knees, and crouched in the watery shadows to hide. The water seeped right through his overalls and he could feel the swirl of the water around his waist and groin. As he peered over the top of one of the hydraulic pumps he could see that the flame was changing shape. It continued to spin like a Catherine Wheel, but it became straight-edged on each side, as if moulded by invisible butter paddles, and it expanded upward and downward. The bottom of the flame stopped with a straight-edge, just above the swirling flood-water. The top of the flame stopped growing when it almost reached the deck-head, but the top remained rounded, which made the whole thing look like an arched doorway filled with a spinning flame. John's jaw dropped.

"This is mad," he whispered to himself.

"No, John," replied a voice. "It is The Pathway."

Momentarily stunned, John looked around expecting to find the source of the voice. He thought he was the only person in the compartment. He rubbed the lump on his head, closed his eyes tightly and then pinched himself. He re-opened his eyes but the flame-doorway was still there.

Eventually he ventured his thoughts, "Wh-Who's that?"

"It is I, your opportunity for rescue," replied the voice.

As the words were spoken, a silhouette of a man revealed himself inside the flame-filled doorway. The dim light obscured John's vision, so he could only make out the vague silhouette of a short, broad man wearing some kind of brimmed hat and what appeared to be a knapsack on his back. As the man stepped out of the doorway and into the water, he leaned forward, looking around for John. John kept very still.

"It must be that bang on the head," he murmured to himself, "or I'm dead."

"Where are you, John?" the figure called out hurriedly. "Show yourself, please. We have little time."

"What for?"

"We have little time to get you out of danger, so, come along, please, John, time is extremely short."

John's curiosity got the better of his apprehensions and he emerged from behind the machinery and moved towards the figure.

"Who are you? You're no matelot."

"Come, quickly, John. Come, hurry," the figure said, and beckoned with an outstretched arm.

"Am I dead, or what? – or is it my eyes playing up?"

"Neither. However, you will be dead in precisely one minute if you don't follow me back through The Pathway."

"Oh aye?"

"Yes, John. I know this is difficult for you to understand but, even as we speak, a torpedo is heading this way. Your ship is wrecked. Your Captain has abandoned you. You have no hope of survival in here. Hurry, follow me if you want to live." The figure gestured towards the flame-door of the Pathway.

"What, into that fire?"

"Its not fire, John. It's The Pathway. Trust me. It's not as dangerous as it looks."

A vision of a streaming torpedo flashed across John's mind, and so he tentatively moved towards The Pathway. He took a deep breath and steeled himself for some more pain. The figure stepped up first and held out an arm for John to help himself up with. As John lifted his left foot into The Pathway he realised that there was no heat coming from the flames. He felt no pain, only the sensation of pins and needles in his lower leg and foot. It was only mild, but it was definitely pins and needles. John hesitated a moment before pulling himself up into The Pathway. As he stood inside The Pathway, both of his lower legs and feet now felt the sensation of pins and needles. It took a moment for John to accustom to it.

"Don't worry John, you'll soon acclimatize to the sensation. Now, come inside, quickly."

John stepped closer and eyed his rescuer up and down. The style of dress was unfamiliar to him. The dark green trousers were tight fitting and stopped short of the ankle, where thick brown socks were folded several times. Dark brown leather boots looked large and heavy. A thick brown leather jacket covered a woollen pullover that matched the trousers. And resting on the thin, greying hair of its middle-aged owner's head was a broad-brimmed hat, now very crumpled and a little tatty.

John gazed deep into The Pathway. It was a tunnel of spinning flame – or at least that's how it appeared to him – but with no heat. He opened his arms, reaching out to either side of himself to see if he could touch the sides of The Pathway. John felt a faint tingling sensation in the tips of the fingers of both his hands, but he felt nothing tangible like a wall. His short experiment complete, John let his arms drop to his side.

"So, I'm not dead then?" he asked.

"No."

"Alright, then. What about you?"

"I am very much alive, also. However, if we want to remain alive it would serve us well to leave your ship immediately. Come." And with that, John's rescuer turned on his heels and walked briskly down the Pathway.

John hurried after him as best he could, whilst carefully watching each and every step of his own along The Pathway. "Wait up, wait up. Where are we going?"

"Along The Pathway."

"Oh, aye? Well, I think I've got that bit already, whatever-your-name-is."

"My name is Marcus."

"Well, how-do, Marcus," John paused and offered a hand-shake. "I'm John Popplethwaite."

Marcus turned and looked at John's outstretched hand. He appeared momentarily uncomfortable with the invitation, before briefly shaking John's hand and returning to his brisk walk.

"I already know your name, John," Marcus replied over his shoulder.

John was left standing, his arm still outstretched. He rubbed the lump on his head – as much for reassurance than for any other reason. He hurried to catch up with Marcus.

"Why me?"

"Ask me another question."

"Alright. Where are we going?"

"Somewhere safe, John, somewhere safe."

"Why won't you give me a straight answer? You're not one of them solicitor sorts are you?"

"Of course I'm not."

"Then gimme a straight answer," John said. Marcus paused and turned to face John.

"Very well. I shall try, but I cannot promise."

"Alright. How come you know my name?"

"I was briefed before I embarked on your rescue," Marcus said and glanced at where they had come from. "Ah. Good. The Pathway's door to your ship has closed. We're safe for the moment." And with that, Marcus resumed his hike along The Pathway. He pointed to a dark blob that was growing in the distance. It looked like they were approaching the end of The Pathway's long tunnel. "Can you see that?" he said. "We're nearly there."

John saw that another doorway had opened. Through that doorway, he could just about recognise a tree-filled landscape, a cloud-free skyline and another figure, which he couldn't quite see clearly.

"Marcus," asked John, seriously, and slowing to a stroll. "Tell me where we're going. Please, I need to know. Is it Heaven or Hell?"

Marcus stopped walking and slowly turned to face John.

"It's neither, John. I'm simply taking you to my commanding officer."

"And who's he?"

Marcus stared blankly at John.

"Alright, then. *Where* is he?"

"He's at headquarters, of course," replied Marcus. John stared impassively back. Marcus then sighed in resignation.

"Very well. I shall reveal our destination on condition that you agree not to disclose me as your source."

"Alright, I promise, just tell me."

"He's at Overbank Hall."

THE BOY BULLIES

The boy sauntered up the lane leading out of the village. It was a beautiful, bright afternoon and several birds exchanged a cheerful chorus as they wheeled around in the sky above the golden fields at the edge of the village. The boy couldn't see the birds clearly, though, because the glare of the sun was too intense for him. He turned off the lane and began walking along the rough track towards old Mr Thwaite's farm, his most recent and longest lasting home. Stones crunched beneath his new hob-nails. He was a boy who was happy in his own company and content with his own thoughts. And the thoughts currently occupying his mind were of the recent illness and death of Mrs Thwaite, and its likely effect on his future.

"Oi! Gunner!" yelled a voice behind him. He spun around as he recognised the voice of one of the school's regular bullies. He'd managed to avoid the bullies for a while now, and he thought that maybe they weren't interested in him any more. There were four of them and they were just behind him, at the junction where the track left the lane. They must have followed him from school. They began to walk towards him, menacingly. He protectively grasped hold of his satchel and gasmask box. A feeling of heavy anxiety gripped his stomach.

"Gunner, gunner, you're gunner be a gonner," they chanted. The boy began to back away from them and tried to ignore them by turning his back on them and carrying on with his walk home.

"Come on, lads," yelled one of them, breaking into a run. "Let's get 'im."

"Leave me alone!" the boy shouted and ran off up the lane as fast as his nine year old legs could carry him. But the bullies closed in on him rapidly. He knew he couldn't out-run them – they were all bigger than him and a couple of years older too. His best chance would be to outsmart them. He saw the gate to a wheat-field and the woods beyond and so he made a dash for it. Soon he was galloping across the field, parting his way through the ripened wheat with his arms outstretched like an imaginary diver or swimmer. The sun beat down on his bare neck and beads of sweat began to form on his forehead. The bullies followed, gaining all the while.

"When we get yer, we're gunner bash yer fer runnin'," gasped one of them.

"No, you're not!" yelled the boy as he crashed through the undergrowth at the edge of the woods and disappeared into the trees without slowing his pace.

The bullies stopped at the edge of the trees. They couldn't see through the foliage and paused to consider their next move.

"Stan, George," the ringleader ordered, "you go down that way. Billy, you come with me." The bullies split up and slowly pushed their way through the undergrowth and into the gloomy shadows of the trees. The woods had grown over a rocky outcrop and it was for this reason that the woods had never been cleared for agriculture. The bullies clambered tentatively over obstacles, careful not to lose their footing on the large weathered boulders and careful not to snag their clothing on the thick, twiggy branches.

Meanwhile, the boy wasted no such time as he hurtled through the woods, striding over a fallen branch and skidding across the top of a huge flat rock that lay between the trees. Eventually, he sensed some distance between himself and his pursuers and so he paused momentarily to reassess the situation.

He could hear his own breathing as his lungs gasped for air; he could feel his heart drumming as if trying to burst from his chest. He could hear a high pitch buzzing from within his ears, and he could hear his bullies some way behind him. He could also sense from their conversation that they were separated across the woods, unsure of each other's location. When he realised that he had the advantage, he became less anxious. He knew these woods better than anyone he knew. And he also knew that his bullies were street boys who rarely ventured into these woods.

Then one of the bullies came into view, clambered slowly over a particularly large boulder and slid clumsily down the side. The boy took a good look at the bully. It was the one called Stan. The boy considered his options. He could hide and wait for the bullies to get bored, but then again…he hated bullies and was reasonably confident that he could maybe take this one on. Before the bully spotted him, the boy hid behind a large oak tree.

The bully approached the tree completely unaware that the boy was close at hand. The bully stopped by the tree and took a deep breath as if about to shout something to his mates. But he never got the chance. A large stick swung out from behind the tree and struck him squarely across the stomach. He collapsed, winded and totally stunned. The boy jumped from the cover of the tree and kicked the reeling bully.

"I said leave me alone!" the boy yelled and ran off into the trees. The other bullies heard the shouting and quickly converged on their suffering friend.

"He… he… there," the bully struggled and wheezed and pointed in the direction of the boy's escape route.

"Right," the ringleader said, "I'll show him," and ran into the trees to continue his pursuit. "You lads wait here."

"Awh. Can't we just leave him?" one of the other bullies called after him.

"Just wait. I'll be back in a bit," the ringleader called over his shoulder and continued his pursuit, "Oi, Gunner! Yer really gunner get it now."

The boy didn't reply as he charged headlong through the trees. He knew that to shout a response would give his position away again. As he ran under the shadow of a craggy outcrop, a flash of inspiration came to mind. He stopped, looked all around and then darted for cover behind an enormous boulder. He crouched down and began to pull several fist-sized stones from the ground. He had accumulated half a dozen or so when he heard the snap of twigs close by.

"You wait 'til I get you, you gunner."

On hearing the voice, the boy tentatively raised his head above the cover of the rock to survey the scene. But the bully saw him and leapt the last few feet over to the boy.

"Got yer!" exclaimed the bully as he threw himself at the boy. "Now yer really gunner get it!"

The boy stumbled backwards and fell on to his backside. He raised his arms to protect himself and to push the bully away.

"Leave me alone," he shouted angrily.

The other bullies heard the commotion and gleefully ran to join their ringleader. They converged a few yards away from the huge boulder, behind which their ringleader had hold of the boy. But the bullies could not see their ringleader. Instead, they saw a bright, phosphorescent white light emanating from behind the boulder. And from behind the same boulder a high pitch scream of terror pierced the tranquillity of the wood. The bullies paused and glanced at each other, nervously. None of them had the courage to investigate.

Then the light dimmed and disappeared and the ringleader staggered out from behind the boulder, clutching his head and wailing with inconsolable tears.

"No! No! Mum! Tell 'em to go away!" the ringleader cried and shook his head, as if to rid it of something. "Please! Go away!" he pleaded and then collapsed to the ground.

The other bullies ran over to help their friend, but by the time they reached him, he was already curled up, traumatised and sobbing uncontrollably, wailing for his mother.

The boy, meanwhile, had fled the scene and soon burst out of the far side of the wood and into the stubble of a recently harvested field. He didn't look back until he was across the field and had rejoined the track to the farm. Nobody followed him.

His heart was still thumping when he reached the farmyard gate; his nerves were still sharpened by his encounter. A dog-bark initially made him jump, but then he recognised the Border Colley dog that scurried out to greet him with its customary protocol of busy inspections, tail wagging and hand licking.

"Woah, eh-up, Deefer," the boy said, and began to relax as he entered the farmyard, accompanied by the dog.

The yard consisted of a central cobbled quadrangle flanked by stone barns and outbuildings. A stone farmhouse stood at the far end. Mr Thwaite, the tenant of the farm, emerged from one of the outbuildings. He was a rake-thin man of middle age and wore a crumpled off-white shirt with sleeves rolled up above the elbow, and his dark trousers were held up with frayed braces. The long wisps of unkempt greying hair, unshaven chin and a generally untidy appearance suggested the absence of womanly encouragement. He carried a scruffy old towel, which he was using to dry his hands and forearms.

"Now, then, Boy. Yer late," Mr Thwaite said, flatly.

"Sorry, Mr Thwaite."

"I heard yellin' and screamin'. Nowt to do with you?"

"Honest, Mr Thwaite. It's them lads from school."

"Hmm. I've already sorted out them chickens I were on about, so you'll have to wait 'til next time," he added. "What were they doing? Them lads."

"Dunno. They just chased me. They do it to everybody."

"Hmm. Dan McGarrett and his lads are down Lower Stag field, getting their engines ready to plough. You'd best look lively if you want to earn yer keep, Boy."

"Aye, Mr Thwaite," replied the boy, and dumped his satchel and gas mask box next to the wall of the outbuilding.

"I could hear somebody roaring like a lass. Did yer bash one on 'em?"

"They wouldn't leave me alone."

"Hmm." Mr Thwaite put his hand gently on the boy's shoulder. "It's done with now, Boy. Best get down that field, eh."

"Aye, Mr Thwaite."

"Good lad," the old man said. And with that the boy ran across the yard and through a small gate next to the farmhouse. Deefer followed him. Mr Thwaite folded the towel, picked up the boy's things and went into the farmhouse.

The boy and the dog ran along a narrow path, lined with high overgrown hedgerows on either side. These cast a cooling shadow that gave the Boy the sensation of running down a tunnel. At the end of the path was a farm track which led down a short steep hill. At the bottom of the hill, in one of the fields, were two steam traction engines, one at each side of the field. Two men were dragging a steel rope across the field from one traction engine to the other.

As the boy clambered over the gate to the field, one of the men noticed him and raised an arm in a wave. The boy returned the wave, jumped down and trotted down the side of the field to meet the men at the traction engine to which they were dragging the steel rope. Deefer jumped up over the wall and began to sniff around the field.

"What time do you call this, Boy?" Dan smiled. "We've already started."

"Sorry, Dan."

"Don't be sorry to me. Its old man Thwaite you should be sorry to. You have to earn your keep round 'ere, you know. Now, go fetch me that tool roll and help me get this cable fastened up."

The boy darted around the back of the engine and emerged a few moments later carrying a heavy canvas tool roll, which he handed to Dan.

"If you look sharp, Boy, while I'm doing this, you could have a pot mashed for us."

"Aye, Dan," replied the boy and walked over to the footplate of the engine, where he opened a small cabinet which revealed a metal teapot, several tin mugs and a small jug of milk. The boy picked up the teapot and, using a rag to protect his hand from the heat, filled it with water from a tap on the engine and then held it under a steam drain-valve. He cracked open the drain-valve and the water in the teapot crackled and gurgled as the steam from the drain boiled the water.

The tea was soon made and the boy was just about to take a sip from his mug when Dan called him over.

"I've been thinking, Boy. How long you been with old man Thwaite, then? A year? Bit longer?"

"Dunno. Ages."

"Well, you don't think you'll be living with him forever, do you? I mean, he's struggling to cope as it is, you know. And now *Mrs* Thwaite's no longer about to look after him, well..."

"Er...What d'you mean?"

"What I mean is... well, you know we're short of a lad... and Mrs McGarret says it's fine if you want to live at our place. She misses not having a young 'un around the house since our Arthur joined up. And besides which, you mash a good pot. What do you think?" The boy paused for a moment in careful consideration.

"Do you travel far?"

"A fair bit. But we rarely stay out over night, though. You'd only come with us at weekends, and when you're not at school. And you could even stop on at the village school if you like. What do you think?"

"What will Mr Thwaite think? Who's going to help him if I go and live with you?"

"Well, it's only a matter of time 'til Churchill takes his farm off him, anyway. But if you think you can make all the difference for him..."

"Well, yeah. I mean, no. I mean... I was told to live with Mr Thwaite. And he's good to me – never shouts; never beats me."

"But you think I might?" Dan sounded surprised.

"No. No. It's not that. I have to live with him, see, 'cos I was told to."

"But that was before Mrs Thwaite passed away. He's finding it tough on his own now."

"Yeah, I know, but he's not on his own. He's got me."

"You could earn real cash. That'll help old man Thwaite, wouldn't it?"

"'suppose."

"Well, then," Dan said, then finished his tea and poured the tea dregs onto the ground. "Just think about it."

"Aye. Thanks."

Dan's attention was caught by Mr Thwaite and a visitor walking down the farm track towards them. Mr Thwaite raised an arm in greeting. Dan raised his arm in acknowledgement.

"Got a visitor by the looks of it. Wonder what's up?"

"Boy!" shouted Mr Thwaite. "Send the boy!"

"What you been up to, then?" asked Dan.

"Nowt. Honest!"

"Well, I wouldn't hang about. He looks serious."

The boy looked across to the visitor and Mr Thwaite, and his heart became a little heavier when he recognised the visitor.

"See you later, Dan," the boy sounded sombre. He clambered over the gate and walked up the track to meet Mr Thwaite and the visitor.

The visitor was a short, broad, middle-aged man, who was wearing a brown leather jacket over a woollen pullover, a pair of tight fitting, dark green trousers, thick brown socks that were folded several times, and heavy brown boots. And resting on the thin, greying hair of its owner's head was a broad-brimmed hat, now very crumpled and a little tatty.

"Good afternoon, young man."

"Eh-up, Tobias," the boy answered. They began the walk back to the farm house.

"How are we keeping, then, young man?" asked Tobias.

"Alright."

"I'm terribly sorry about all this, but I've received orders to move you on. I'm afraid it's no longer appropriate for you to stay here. For security reasons, of course."

"Oh," the boy sounded saddened, "It's not 'cos of them lads is it?"

"I should say not. By all accounts you have acquitted yourself admirably whenever you have been confronted by those beastly ruffians."

"Eh?"

"He means," explained Mr Thwaite, sadly. "It's not your fault, Boy. But you've got to move on."

"Oh," the boy answered and then looked down at his feet. He was in pensive mood as they walked back to the farm. "What about you, Mr Thwaite?" he eventually said, as they walked along the narrow, hedgerow path.

"I'll be right, lad. Don't whittle about me."

"Can I go and live with Dan McGarret? He needs a boy to help him with his plough engines."

"Sorry, son. You go where Tobias says."

"Awh! But I like it round here!"

"It's most regrettable that Mr McGarret is not on the panel of approved homes, I'm sure. However, we are already preparing your new home for you," Tobias replied, and then opened the gate to the farm. They all filed into the farmyard.

"I'm sorry, Boy," Mr Thwaite said, and placed a gentle hand on the boy's shoulder, "but we both knew this could happen sooner or later, didn't we?"

"But…" the boy looked up at Mr Thwaite's sad face.

"I know, son. I know," Mr Thwaite replied. "Any road, you'd best go pack your things." The boy walked slowly into the farmhouse, his arms hung sulkily.

"It's not fair!" he muttered. "I wanted to stay."

OVERBANK HALL

The old and decaying Gazebo was classical in theme. Three sides of the stone building were supported by Roman-style columns and the fourth side was supported by a smooth stone wall. A statue of Venus stood next to one corner column and a stone bench was set against the stone wall. Any occupant of the bench would at one time have had an excellent view of the lower part of the estate, but now the view was partially obscured by large, overgrown rhododendrons. In another corner of the gazebo, ivy had colonised one of the columns and part of the roof. This prolific climber now hung in a loose curtain of foliage through which the late afternoon sun cast a dappled shade. Fallen leaves, which had accumulated on the stone floor next to the bench, had lain undisturbed for some time, and the nearby cobwebs had become partially clothed in the fluff from old dandelion seeds and some of the dead leaves.

The stone steps at the front of the gazebo led down to a gravel path, which in turn led down through the rhododendrons to a lake just a few yards away. The lake, a man-made feature of this shallow-sided valley, covered an area of several dozen acres. Three ducks could be seen gliding serenely across the still water, cutting V shaped bow waves as they paddled in formation. Another overgrown rhododendron partially obstructed a second path that ran from the gazebo into a mature wood. A babbling stream could be heard close by the gazebo but it could not be seen beneath the dense undergrowth.

This was a strangely tranquil scene, drawn by history and coloured by decay.

In the centre of the gazebo the first flickering of The Pathway appeared, quickly opening into the full doorway. The sound of conversation drifted from The Pathway and Marcus appeared in the doorway.

"... and that's how he came to lose the horse," he said, and stepped down from The Pathway into the gazebo.

"Oh aye?" John replied, but he then fell into an astonished silence when he emerged from The Pathway and stepped down into the centre of the gazebo. His surprised eyes took in the vista before him. "Bugger me!" he exclaimed. He stepped this way and that, and excitedly looked out between the columns. The smell of the gazebo's decay and the damp vegetation evoked vivid memories of his childhood. In particular, memories of the overgrown ruin of a cottage that he and his friends used to play in at the edge of the village where he grew up. John paused by the statue and ran a finger over her mouldy shoulder before examining the dirt on his finger. The gentle babbling of the nearby stream gradually induced his body to relax a little and he suddenly became aware of how tense and stressed he had recently been. He wandered over to a nearby rhododendron bush and stared intently at its large, rubbery foliage.

"Is this Blighty?" he asked, cautiously.

"We are in England," confirmed Marcus.

"But how..?" John asked, but Marcus held up his hand to silence John's questioning.

"You ask questions that I cannot answer."

"Alright, then. Which way now?" asked John, gesturing to both paths.

"This way," Marcus answered and marched along the second path, pushing past a large rhododendron before disappearing into the woodland beyond. John hurried after him.

"Where we goin'?"

"Shush. Keep close and keep quiet."

"Why quiet?"

"Because," Marcus lowered his voice for dramatic emphasis, "we are not quite out of the woods, yet – in more ways than one."

"Oh?" John had no idea what Marcus was talking about but he thought it best not to ask further questions if there was a real need for quiet. He had to hurry to keep up with Marcus, who scurried through the woods at a rapid pace. The woodland path ran parallel to the lakeside. As they rounded a bend in the contour of the valley, John caught sight of a large 18th century country house in the distance. It was more of a large manor house than stately home. It was built of the same stone as the gazebo and had large open gardens with four large, neglected flower beds bordered by lawn and paths. A disused stone fountain was the garden centre-piece. The garden covered the area between the house and the lakeside, where a small wooden jetty was to be found at the bottom of a short flight of stone steps. It all looked very quiet.

"Overbank Hall?" enquired John.

"Correct," replied Marcus.

As they continued on their woodland walk, the hall disappeared from view behind a screen of trees and when it emerged back into view, John could see several people walking around outside. The figures were too far away to be recognisable.

"Friends of yours?" he whispered to Marcus.

"In a manner of speaking, they are my comrades," Marcus replied.

Through the trees John caught sight of another stone building. It was a small chapel and the woodland path ran close by it. John assumed it must be some kind of family chapel.

Less than a hundred yards of rolling lawn lay between the chapel and the house. But, just as they left the cover of the wood an alarm bell rang out from the house. The figures outside the house scurried in through the nearest doors into the house. John and Marcus stopped in their tracks. Marcus turned, grabbed John and dragged him back towards the cover of the wood and roughly shoved him into the heart of a large rhododendron. Marcus then threw himself into the bush after John.

Crouching under the canopy of the vegetation John suddenly felt a pang of concern.

"I thought you said they were friends of yours."

"Shush. They are," answered Marcus in a curt whisper. "Look." He raised a finger, pointing up through the canopy of the bush. At that moment John heard the sound of voices up in the sky, coming from the same direction that they had just come from. As he stared up through the broken view, he glimpsed the fleeting images of figures floating past, high in the air. He couldn't quite work out what they were – but they were flying towards Overbank Hall. The voices were clear to hear as the figures passed overhead, but they spoke too quickly for John to understand what was being said. He repositioned himself closer to the edge of the canopy and parted a few leaves to give himself a clear view of the hall.

Angels! He was looking at the backs of Angels flying towards the hall. Five of them, to be precise and all were in formation. They were translucent, red apparitions, and were at least seven feet tall with enormous feathered wings that hung heavily from their shoulders. The wings arched high above their heads, with the lower tips of their wings tapering to a point just below the back of their knees. John's heart skipped a beat and he felt his throat dry up as he stared incredulous at the sight. It then occurred to him that the apparitions were floating and yet not flapping their wings; and the colour of these celestial creatures seemed most peculiar to him, too. He had expected angels to be white, but these were plainly not. But they were definitely partially transparent, because he could see things through them. The apparitions descended onto the lawned area next to the flowerbeds and John could clearly see the stone fountain through one of them. These apparent angels walked up the garden and then paused to face the hall. And it was at that moment that John saw their faces. They were not in the least angelic. They were in fact fierce and they sneered.

John tensed and turned to whisper to Marcus, but was interrupted by a howling scream so loud that he stuck his fingers in his ears to try to muffle the noise. He turned back to the hall and saw the red celestial creatures were howling at the building before them, shaking clenched fists high above their heads, and shaking their heads violently with their noise-making. The howling screams lasted for only a few seconds, but it was more than enough to make the hairs on the back of John's neck stand on end. He glanced at Marcus, who looked mortified by the shock.

"Demons," whispered Marcus. "Be very, very quiet."

John looked back at the hall, where the demons were strutting up and down the garden, gesturing at the building and shouting demands and obscenities at the occupants. One of the demons stood further forward than the rest and appeared to be the more dominant one. John could clearly hear the demon's voices in the distance and this time he could understand them. They were speaking, or at least yelling, in English.

"We warned you to keep away," shouted the dominant demon, "Do not interfere in our affairs. Give him up now and we may be merciful."

In reply to the intimidation and threats of these demons, a group of five white angels suddenly appeared from behind the roof of the hall. As far as John could see from his hiding place, the white angels seemed to be the genuine articles: similar in shape and size as the demons, but more formidable looking and, yet, with peacefully contented faces. They flew over and landed between the demons and the hall. The five white angels stood calmly with their arms folded, and stared impassively at the demons. The demons fell silent. The dominant demon was clearly taken aback by the unexpected presence of white angels and took a step backwards, glancing behind himself for reassurance from his accomplices. All of the five white angels took one large co-ordinated step forward. The demons shuffled backwards across the lawn. Another couple of steps forward from the white angels sent the demons shuffling further backwards.

The dominant demon shook a defiant fist at the white angels.

"You can't protect these creatures indefinitely," it pointed to the hall. "We'll get our way sooner or later. And when we do..." the dominant demon let out a howling scream and took to the air. The other four followed suit. The departing formation retraced its flight path back towards the wood where John and Marcus were hiding. The pair of them let go of the parted vegetation, letting it spring back into place. They crouched as low as they possibly could, keeping perfectly still as the demons flew overhead. Once again, John could hear their rapid chattering, but soon their voices faded to silence as they disappeared round the corner of the valley.

Marcus gave an enormous sigh of relief, which also contained a little anger mixed in with it.

"Demons!" he exclaimed to John. "Nobody briefed me on running you past demons... Maligns, possibly. But not demons. And when did we acquire a detachment of Galearii at Overbank Hall?" He looked at John as if expecting an answer.

John stared back at him. "One for your commanding officer?" he replied, suppressing the urge to laugh out loud at the incredulity of the whole encounter. "Come on, Marcus. They're gone now aren't they?"

"Hhmph! They could have alerted me of the risks much earlier, I'm sure," Marcus muttered as he scrambled out of the Rhododendron bush, clasping his hat to his head with one hand. He paused by the path, dusted himself down as best he could and held out a helping hand to John, who emerged from the bush shortly afterwards.

They flitted across the rolling lawn to the hall. Marcus kept a wary eye on the sky all the while. As they reached the hall, a modest looking side door opened and a head popped around it.

"Marcus!" the head exclaimed, throwing open the door. "Am I glad to see you." A small man of the same age and style of dress as Marcus trotted out to greet them.

"Hello Tobias," Marcus said, shaking Tobias's hand warmly and firmly. "John, this is my brother, Tobias." John offered a handshake to Tobias.

"Eh-up, Tobias. Nice to meet you, I think."

"Likewise, John." Tobias grasped John's outstretched hand and shook it firmly, "Shall we go inside?" he said and ushered Marcus and John to the hall.

"I wasn't aware that we were expecting demons," Marcus commented, "or Galearii."

"Solomon had the foresight to order a detachment of Galearii whilst our Commanding Officer was absent."

"He's absent?" Marcus sounded surprised. "Again?"

"He's on his way back from London, apparently," Tobias replied. They entered the hall through the side door and stood in a very small and dimly lit reception corridor. Its magnolia plasterwork was stained and badly scuffed. John assumed that it was possibly a servants' access. A short oak bench was against one wall and it was beside this that Marcus threw his knapsack, before dropping his weary body onto the bench whilst he talked with his brother.

"It was a close run thing," he said. "The compartment was flooding more quickly than I had first thought."

Whilst the brothers were chatting, John's attention wandered and he soon found himself running a finger along the wall opposite the bench. There were two other doors running off the corridor, both of which had small frosted-glass windows above them. John could hear voices and the clattering of steel pans and crockery through one of the doors. He could faintly smell food. He walked over to the door, breathed in a huge lungful and began to salivate – fried onions!

Tobias noticed that John was no longer participating in their conversation.

"I think John may be a little hungry after his ordeal," he said. Then he noticed John's damp overalls, "and you look like you could do with a change of clothing," he added.

"Hmm. Food first I think," replied John, "I haven't had a proper meal in ages."

"Wait here and I shall return in a moment," Tobias said and disappeared into the kitchen. A moment later he returned with a plate of stew, with three mouth-watering dumplings and a crust of bread on top. He handed this to John, along with a fork.

"Oops," Tobias rolled his eyes in mock admonishment, "I almost forgot," he said and disappeared again into the kitchen. John sat down and quickly ate one of the dumplings. He looked sideways at Marcus. A broad smile appeared on Marcus's face, presumably in anticipation of his own food, but it soon fell away when Tobias returned with a large mug and placed it on the bench beside John. "A cup of tea for you, John," he said, "although it may be a little stewed... and cool. I believe the pot may have been brewed some time ago."

John smiled whilst he chewed ravenously. He swallowed and thanked Tobias.

"As long as it's wet, Tobias. Cheers," he said.

Meanwhile, Marcus could not contain his disappointment, "And to what should I ascribe the delay in the delivery of my meal?" he demanded.

"The absence of injuries to your arms and legs suggests the delay in delivery may be one of your own creation," retorted his brother.

Marcus huffed and folded his arms, "Charming. And after all I do for you, brother."

"You know where the kitchen is, Marcus. I'm sure Chef will only throw a few things at you."

John smiled at them both and wondered how it might have been if he'd had a brother of his own. But of course he didn't have one; he was an only child. John looked at his plate and saw his last dumpling and some gravy. He offered his plate to Marcus. An enormous smile beamed back at him as a grateful Marcus accepted his offer with thanks.

"Very well, then," Tobias said to John. "You really should get showered and changed into clean clothes before Marcus takes you to see Mr Forsyth."

"Me?" exclaimed Marcus, "Why does this task fall onto my shoulders when the responsibility for this phase of John's Renaissance is yours?"

"I have other, more urgent duties to attend to, brother. My apologies for not pausing to discuss them with you, but events require my urgent attention," Tobias said and looked at his watch. "Oh my, and time is now desperately short. Gentlemen, I must dash." Tobias nodded to John and added, "I bid you a very good evening, John," and he then hurried off out through the outside door. After Tobias had gone, John turned to Marcus.

"So, who is this Forsyth bloke?" he asked.

"He's our Commanding Officer, of course."

MR FORSYTH

John stood in the centre of the room, now showered and changed, and wearing a pair of brown cotton trousers with braces and a white collarless shirt. Upon his feet was a pair of old brown leather slippers. Marcus stood alongside him, fidgeting and shuffling his feet. John's hair was still damp and his head felt a little cool. John looked around the room and saw the large, black, ornate fireplace which stood dark and empty. The room, with its peeling "art nouveau" flowered wallpaper was probably originally used as some kind of drawing room, but now it was Mr Forsyth's office. Sparsely furnished, it contained a few basic items of furniture. A large oak writing desk and matching brown leather chair were in the corner near the shuttered windows. The desk's leather inlay was half hidden under an untidy pile of documents and papers. Next to the desk stood a bookcase with a small number of old leather-bound volumes, which filled only half the shelves. And in the corner nearest the only door into the room stood a high backed leather armchair and a large, very old, globe, which was set in a thick, dark wooden frame.

Mr Forsyth's portly frame hurried into the room, sweating profusely. He wore a tight-fitting British Army Brigadier's uniform that looked like it needed a good clean and press. The crumpled jacket and creased-up trousers strained to contain his middle-aged spread. He paused by the window and threw open the shutters, allowing the late glow of the setting sun to flood in and cast a long shadow of the desk across the room.

"Let's have these open shall we," he said and then sat himself behind his desk. "Sorry for keeping you waiting, I've just returned from London. Caused a bit of a rumpus, so I hear, but it's nothing I can't handle." He removed his cap to reveal a thin covering of fast-receding brown hair, and then wiped his large perspiring forehead with a scruffy old handkerchief which he then screwed up and forced into a trouser pocket. Finally, he took a good long look at John. "So, you're John Popplethwaite."

"Aye, Sir," John replied.

"Quite. Well, welcome to Overbank Hall."

"Thanks, Sir."

"Preparations for your arrival have already been made," continued Mr Forsyth. "You should restrict your movements to authorised areas within the Hall. Avoid those areas that are restricted to 'authorised personnel only' and under no circumstance must you leave the building unescorted. Marcus will make sure you are catered for in the meantime."

"Sir."

"Now, you've probably had quite an ordeal: they usually have, you know. And you will probably want to rest for a while. Has anyone examined that bump, yet?"

John had almost forgotten about the lump on his head and gave it a gentle rub with his hurt hand, which still ached and was beginning to feel a little stiff.

"Oh, I'm fine Sir. It doesn't hurt much, really."

"If you say so," continued Mr Forsyth. "You have a long day ahead of you tomorrow. Your Renaissance Briefing begins at 8 am sharp. And if there's anything you need for your mission," he glanced at John's clothing, "such as uniforms and kit, don't worry. We will sort everything for you. Yes? Good. Now, I suggest you get an early night." And he stood up to leave the room. This rather abrupt end to the exchange caused John's sense of humour to momentarily lapse.

"Woah! Hang on a minute, Sir," he said, and then realised that he sounded insolent. He inwardly winced in anticipation of an almighty reprimand. Mr Forsyth stayed calm, although the irritation was plain to see upon his face.

"Yes?" Mr Forsyth eventually said, flatly. John thought that he was probably in trouble anyway, so he continued.

"Sorry, Sir, but shouldn't I be reporting back to Chatham? And what about my survivor's leave? And what are you on about, mission?" he knew he was now ranting but he couldn't stop himself, "I mean, come on, what is this place and what am I doing here? And what were all that flying demon stuff about earlier?" he added, jabbing a finger at the view of the garden through the window. "Just tell us what's going on." He paused for a deep breath and then added, half-apologetically, "Please. Sir."

Mr Forsyth glanced across to Marcus, who returned a look of mild bewilderment and shrugged his shoulders.

"Talk to me," John pleaded as quietly and calmly as he could. "Please."

Mr Forsyth stared at John for several moments whilst he considered his reply.

"You have your father's temperament. And his build."

"Err," faltered John.

"But your face looks a good mix of both your parents, yes?"

"Err," John was taken completely off guard. How on earth would Mr Forsyth know what his parents looked like? "Err."

"I knew your parents, you see. Your father was a fine chap, and he was a good NCO. One of the best I had."

"Oh aye?" John replied. A few seconds of silence followed as they stared at one another before John continued. "Did you know him, you know… during the war?"

"Why, yes, yes, of course. We served in the same company of Fusiliers from, what, 1913 right through to Mons. That was when most of the company bought it, during the retreat."

"Including my dad."

Mr Forsyth cast a momentary glance at Marcus, but Marcus was, by this time, deep in his own thoughts and he didn't even notice Mr Forsyth's glance.

As Mr Forsyth considered his reply, he avoided eye contact with John for maybe ten seconds before eventually replying.

"Well, missing presumed killed, I think the term is. With emphasis on presumed."

"Eh?" frowned John, slightly baffled by the statement. "You mean he survived, or do you mean they presumed correctly?"

"I'm sorry, John," Mr Forsyth looked directly at John and replied, solemnly. "Your father is most certainly no longer with us."

"Oh."

"But…" began Mr Forsyth.

"But what?" said John.

"Let's just say that he wasn't killed that day, nor was he taken prisoner."

John frowned and took a moment to digest this. Slowly, he realised the only other logical option would be that his father… No… surely not.

"I can't believe he'd have deserted!" he exclaimed.

"No, no," Mr Forsyth said with a suppressed smile. "Of course he didn't desert. But your father's official military service definitely terminated that day...," he paused, "along with my own, as a point of fact."

John remained utterly confused, and so tried to encourage further answers by breaking the pause with a slow, questioning "Aye?"

Mr Forsyth glanced across to Marcus again before continuing, but Marcus's attention was elsewhere and he now seemed oblivious to the conversation that was taking place.

"Take a seat, John," Mr Forsyth gestured toward the leather armchair. He then opened a draw in his desk and took out a bottle of whiskey and two glasses. He poured a generous measure in each and handed one to John. "It's only whiskey." He propped himself against the edge of the desk and took a sip from his glass. John sat in the armchair and sipped from his own.

"It was only a few weeks into the Great War and I was still a young officer. We'd been marching for most of the previous day and night. It wasn't straight marching, though, because we were in retreat. Every few hours we had to deploy and beat off a German attack and, after beating them off, we'd carry on marching. It was nearly midnight on the second night and I was out checking the men in the various outposts. I'm not precisely sure exactly where we were as I was dog-tired and things were getting a little hazy in my mind by that time. We'd lost a lot of men in the skirmishes with the Germans, including our commanding officer and we were pretty short manned. One particular out-post, which was nothing more than a few shallow trenches, was manned by your father and a dozen or so other men. We came under artillery fire, just after I arrived. We were at the edge of a wood and we could see the Hun advancing in great masses across the fields towards the battalion on our left flank. To our right, a squadron of Hun cavalry crossed in front, so the platoon opened up with "rapid" rifle fire. We hit a few, and the fact that we were doing something improved our morale tremendously and took away a lot of the nervousness. Some of the cavalry dismounted and began to return fire; and we shot each one that dismounted. It was at that moment that a cloud began to manifest itself on the battlefield between the cavalry and us. It was an inexplicable luminous cloud. It contained a curious red glow and the silhouettes of figures were moving around inside. I couldn't make them out and at first thought they must be German.

One of the men pointed out that it couldn't be because the Germans were making progress down our left flank. Anyway, we stopped firing and continued our retreat. We were already moving through the woods when one of my other NCOs realised that your father and another man hadn't been ordered to retreat. I couldn't believe we'd forgotten them, so I ordered the men to continue the retreat and I went back for them. I shouldn't have, really, and maybe I wasn't thinking clearly. I just felt responsible for him. As I reached your father, alone in his scrape-hole, the cloud drifted over us. It engulfed us and… well… that's how the pair of us were rescued from the Great War and we were given our Renaissance."

"You weren't taken prisoner?"

"Oh no, we weren't captured."

"So, how do you mean, rescued?"

"…with the intervention of what later became the legend of the Angels of Mons."

"Oh aye? I thought that was just propaganda?"

"Yes, it was, partly. To cover up real events. A blatant propaganda campaign based upon a grain of truth, and smeared by several works of fiction published in the press. After all, who would believe any genuine eyewitness accounts amid a sea of fictional encounters with angels and Richard the Lionheart's crusaders?"

"So what happened with the cloud?"

"The cloud delivered our rescuers, just as The Pathway delivered yours."

"You said the pair of you were rescued. What about the other man?"

"Alas, we were unable to locate him. Poor chap was probably killed."

"So why only you two?"

"Oh we weren't the only ones. There were a number of other rescues during the Great War."

"Oh aye? So why is it some get rescued, like us, but others end up dead?" asked John. Mr Forsyth carefully considered his reply.

"Are you a religious man, John?"

"Err."

"All of the answers to all of man's questions, both in the past, the present and the future are all contained within the holy scriptures. Unfortunately, there isn't a single man alive who can correctly interpret the true meanings of all those chapters and verses."

John cast Mr Forsyth a puzzled look.

"I don't know what you're on about."

"What I mean, John, is that I don't know why some are chosen to live whilst others are left to die. But your name is on the List of Chosen; and this is why you are now *here* and not at the bottom of the sea."

"Oh." John was still puzzled and took a large gulp of whiskey. "Alright. So, we're not dead."

"No."

"But my father is."

Mr Forsyth paused before replying.

"Yes, John. I'm sorry."

"Can I go home, now? I've had enough."

"Oh, no, John. You can never go home. Ever."

John slowly leaned forward and gazed pensively at the slippers on his feet whilst he considered his next question.

"You said something about official military service being finished?"

"That's correct."

"I don't get it. How come you're still in the Army, then?"

"Before my own rescue and Renaissance, my family name was Rotheton. Now my name is Forsyth, and Forsyth is in the Army."

"Rotheton?" John said, a note of recognition in his voice. "What, you mean, as in Lord Rotheton? I mean, as in Rotheton Park?"

"The Rothetons of Rotheton Park. Yes, John."

"My mum," said John, "She…"

"…was in service at Rotheton Park. Yes, John. I remember her."

There was a long silence.

"So, I'm not dead, but I can't ever visit me mum again," John said, and frowned.

"Your flesh may not be dead but your life, as it was, most certainly is over. Your next of kin – presumably your mother – will receive a telegram to say that you are dead: 'killed in action'. Technically, I think that is reason enough to assume that your service is terminated, yes? And correct me if I'm wrong, John, but you are only entitled to survivor's leave if you survive. As far as the Royal Navy and the rest of the world are concerned, you were killed on that ship."

"But why, though? I mean, why save me? I've never done owt wrong. Well, not that bad, any road."

Mr Forsyth gave John a hard stare.

"You have been chosen for a special mission, John."

"Mission?" John reacted with subdued incredulity – the whiskey was having its mellowing effect. "What do you mean, 'mission'? I'm supposed to be dead, aren't I?" Mr Forsyth ignored the interruption and continued.

"It is a secret mission, John. Of immense importance. It's likely to involve danger, maybe even the ultimate sacrifice. That is why you have been chosen."

"Oh aye? Chosen by who?"

"You were chosen by authorities at the highest level you can imagine."

"Well, Churchill's lot got it wrong."

"Churchill is not the highest authority, John. In fact, we as an organisation operate outside the boundary of all government authority and military control. And in many ways, we have a kind of authority over Churchill and many other Allied governments."

"Well, whatever it is, you've gone and got the wrong bloke for your 'mission' – unless it's just greasing, painting or deck-scrubbing."

Mr Forsyth cleared his throat, and answered in a prickly tone.

"Yes. Well, you can be as self-deprecating as you wish. But your name appears on the List of Chosen, and I have my orders."

"Well they must be wrong. Look, I'm nowt but a lowly sailor who has enough trouble finding his own way back on board after a run ashore! You need an officer or somebody like that."

"I've no wish to argue the point with you, John," Mr Forsyth replied, irritably. "Unfortunately, it's not about rank. We are all chosen for our respective missions because we have the inner qualities, the talent and the determination to beat the malign forces of evil. I appreciate that the prospects of your mission may at first appear daunting, even awesome, but you'll quickly adapt to your new circumstances. You have no choice but to. There is no escaping the mission for which you have been chosen. You cannot escape it any more than Jonah could escape the whale."

"You saying I'm press-ganged?"

"In a manner of speaking, I suppose we all are," Mr Forsyth replied, and then his attention was momentary lost in a pensive thought. "I'm sorry that I can do so little to reconcile you to the loss of your family, your friends and your lifestyle," he continued, and then grinned. "This is the beginning of your *Renaissance*, John!"

"Oh, aye?" John sounded unconvinced. He glanced over to Marcus, hoping for words of reassurance and sanity, but Marcus was not paying attention. His mind was elsewhere. "Go on, then. Tell us what this mission is, then?"

"You'll be briefed in good time," Mr Forsyth said, and then turned to Marcus. "Won't he Marcus?" he said in a slow, loud voice. Marcus snapped out of his daydream.

"What? Sorry? Didn't quite catch that Sir," Marcus spluttered as he scrambled to gather his thoughts. "Sorry, Sir, can you please repeat that?"

"Never mind, Marcus. But first, John, you really should try to get some rest, yes?"

"Oh, aye, I'll get loads won't I after listening to this lot," John said sarcastically and rose from his chair. Mr Forsyth then ushered John and Marcus out the door. But just as they went out into the corridor, it occurred to John that there was still a question he'd forgotten to ask. "Just one last thing, Mr Forsyth. Who's in charge of this higher authority, then?"

"Jesus Christ, John!" Mr Forsyth said in an exasperated tone, "Do I have to spell everything out to you? Now get some rest!" and with that remark Mr Forsyth abruptly closed the door on them. John turned to Marcus and said, defensively,

"I only asked."

THE BOY's NEW HOME

It was the blackout. There were no street lamps lit, and the empty, terraced streets looked eerily pale under the macabre illumination of the full moon that hung in the cloudless night sky. The moonlight reflected off some of the shiny, well worn cobbles as if it were reflecting off small rectangular puddles of water.

Tobias emerged from around a shadowy corner and scurried along the street. Every few seconds he glanced around, nervously. A faint murmur of conversation drifted from many of the houses as he passed them. And from somewhere in the night sky, there came the distant low droning of German bombers on another flight to unleash their destruction somewhere upon the British Isles. Tobias tentatively crossed the street, anxiously scanning the night sky above him, and stopped outside one of the houses. It was indistinguishable from the others except, perhaps, for the silence within it. He looked up and down the street again and then knocked firmly on the door. Several minutes elapsed and he knocked again, this time with a greater sense of urgency. The door opened part-way and a short, weary-looking woman in her late twenties filled the narrow opening, obstructing his entry. Wrapped in her nightgown, and with her dark hair ruffled, she had clearly been roused from her bed. She folded her arms in a rather matronly fashion and stared disapprovingly at Tobias, who looked uncomfortable.

"Good evening Agnes."

"Bit late for evening don't you think?" she snapped back. "What do you want now?"

"May I enter and converse with you over a civilised pot of tea?" he said as he glanced up and down the street.

"If you must," she said and stood back just enough to allow Tobias to squeeze himself past her and into the house. "In the kitchen, then," she added as she closed the door.

"Thank you," he said and removed his hat. Agnes followed Tobias into the kitchen, a dimly lit room dominated by the old coal-fired cooking range that looked like it hadn't been blackened with polish for a long time. On the wall beside the range there were two shelves that held various items of old and chipped crockery. Beneath the blackout curtain that hung at the window, sat a large square ceramic sink, yellowed and crazed with age, and with a large brass tap fastened to it. In front of the range was an old wooden clothes-horse upon which several items of boy's clothing were slowly drying in the warmth; they were still damp and steamed ever so slightly. The only items of furniture in the kitchen were a small, square, wooden table with three matching chairs, all now bleached with age and badly scuffed through constant use. The table was set against the wall opposite the range.

"Sit down, then," Agnes said. Tobias deposited his hat onto the table, removed his knapsack and placed it onto the floor. He pulled out a chair; its legs grated on the stone floor. As he sat down, it wobbled and creaked quite worryingly. Agnes placed a part-filled kettle on the range.

"You're lucky," she said without looking at Tobias.

"Mmm? In what way?" he asked.

"Range's still lit." She reached for a teapot on one of the shelves and added a couple of spoons of tea from a ceramic jar on the same shelf. She then took two old mugs, blew the dust from them and placed them on the table.

"Oh, I see," he replied, "for the tea."

"'Been doing his washin' haven't I."

"Oh... er..." Tobias faltered; his face betrayed the fact that he was not quite sure what she meant. "Have you?"

"Look at me hands!" She held them out. "Red raw with all that scrubbing."

"Oh."

"Black bright, that lad were. Looked like he'd been down 'pit."

"Which is why the boy has been placed into the expert hands and delicate care of yourself."

"Temporary," she said.

"Temporarily," Tobias confirmed.

"So, you've come to tell me when I can go back to London?"

"Er, no. At the moment I regret to say that I do not know when you can return to London."

"Well you'd better find out!" She raised her voice, but then when she realised the increase in volume she paused and glanced at the ceiling, as if aware she might have disturbed someone upstairs. She leaned over towards Tobias and lowered her voice to barely above a whisper. "Look, I've only managed to get leave 'til Monday, next. The Admiral wants me back by then, so you'd best get somebody sorted by then."

"I'm sorry Agnes, but we've had some problems with…"

"Look, I don't care," she declared, "I'm not one of you, remember? Never was. I weren't chosen like everybody else. I shouldn't be doing this sort of thing for you at all, anymore. I've got a proper job, now. You promised. You promised that I wouldn't be needed again; and look where you brought me to," she said and cast an arm around the kitchen. "Hell's backside, that's what this place is."

"I'm sorry, Agnes. We are doing everything we can."

"Well, it's not enough. Do some more."

"I appreciate the formidable circumstances you now find yourself in, particularly when one considers the experiences that you had to live through last year."

"Look, don't start bringing all that stuff up again," she said and turned away from Tobias. She grasped the handle of the boiling hot kettle and muttered in a mimicked 'Tobias' voice, "formidable circumstances," whilst she poured hot water into the teapot. She then picked up the teapot and placed it on the table next to the mugs. "Did you or did you not say I'd have a normal life again?" There was a pause.

"Yes, I did."

"And you said I'd never be needed again."

"Yes, I did."

"And you said I'd never see you again."

"Yes, I did."

"But you came back for me again."

"Yes I did."

"And now you don't know when I can go back. You went back on your word, again, Tobias," she said and glared at him, "You *lied* to me!" Tobias's face betrayed his mind's frantic search for a reasonable explanation for this accusation.

"It would appear," he eventually replied in a rather slow and deliberate voice, "that current circumstances could imply that I indeed misled you with my previous assurances: however let me assure you in the strongest possible terms that I believe my conduct has always been characterised by the highest levels of integrity and honesty. I recall that I myself was assured by Mr Forsyth that you were to be specifically proscribed from any future field activities and that your rehabilitation back into mainstream British Society was to be full and permanent. My commitment to assisting you in acquiring your secretarial position within the War Ministry should be sufficient testament to this."

"And within months, that promise means nowt any more."

"It…"

"It means that you do as you're told; that *they* tell you what to say and *they* can change their minds whenever they want."

"It means that…"

"It means *nowt*!" Agnes raised her voice, again.

"It means," Tobias replied firmly and leaned towards Agnes to emphasise the importance of what he was about to say. "It means that when this child was in desperate danger and need; when our own organisation became compromised by the Maligns; when all customary avenues appeared closed to me; there was one person of incorruptible character whom I could trust to shelter and protect the boy in his hour of greatest need."

"Well, I don't know about protect… from muck maybe…" replied Agnes, flattered by Tobias's comments.

"Which is why you agreed to help."

"Temporary."

"Of course, temporarily."

"But you still can't tell me how long temporary is?"

"Well, I have no wish to allude to idle forecasts, especially if I am unlikely to be able to meet such a forecast," Tobias explained, "and particularly in the light of today's incidents." But Agnes simply stared blankly at Tobias, who continued. "We had demons in the grounds of Overbank Hall again today."

"Oh?" Agnes replied, surprised by the revelation, "Everybody alright?"

"Fortunately a detachment of Galearii was available to disperse them."

"Really?" she said with a raised eyebrow. "And you came to see me in the middle of the night to tell me that?"

"Er, no. But in the light of today's developments I've been ordered to instruct you to transfer the boy to a different safe house."

"Good. This one's awful."

"First thing tomorrow morning…" Tobias hesitated, "and, well…" Tobias looked a little uncomfortable as he spoke the words, "its location is familiar to you, but it may cause you some emotional discomfort."

"Oh?" Agnes replied, and a look of nervous apprehension appeared across her face. "Where?"

"Well, its… it's in Scotland… and, as I said, it's in a place that you are already familiar..." Tobias stammered. Agnes raised both eyebrows in sudden astonishment, and within a fraction of a second all the colour drained from her face. She pulled out a chair and sat down. Tobias continued. "Having considered the merits of various locations…"

"No," she said, quietly, "not there again. Find somewhere else."

"Worry not, Agnes," Tobias tried to sound cheery. "Statistically speaking, lightning rarely strikes the same place twice."

"I don't care. I'm not going," she said, emphatically. Tobias looked at Agnes, seriously.

"Agnes, in the last twenty four hours eight of our safe houses have been visited by Maligns. Four were openly attacked and one was completely demolished during an attack that took place under the cover of an air raid; four staff have been killed." Agnes rested her elbows on the table, placed her head in her hands and closed her eyes.

"Don't send me there. Please. Not after what happened last time."

"Agnes, it has been a dormant safe house for a long time, now. So it's likely to be the safest we have. But should there be any other way, I would choose it..."

"Yeah?" She looked up. "Well, what about my flat in London? We could use that."

"The risks are currently too high. Major air raids are likely to begin over the capital any time soon: ideal cover for Malign operations, as you well know. Your designated replacement as guardian will hopefully be able to relieve you in Scotland within your period of leave."

"Days, not weeks, then?" she asked.

"I cannot promise. I understand your replacement will be a recent recruit and requires some training."

"Training! That could take months!"

"Time is a scarce commodity in these troubled times," replied Tobias, "and circumstances are presently desperate. The training of recruits is currently but a few days' duration." Agnes stared at Tobias.

"So who is it?" she asked. Tobias shook his head.

"I'm afraid I don't know, yet."

Agnes placed her head in her hands and sighed deeply. Tobias reached over and with a genuine, but awkward, sympathy he gently placed a hand on her shoulder.

"Agnes, you are not compelled to assist. As you say, your name is not on the List of Chosen. You can still go back to London, alone, if you so wish… if the mission is going to be too much for you to cope with."

"What, and leave the lad in the lurch?" she snapped, "I thought you said you didn't have anybody else to look after him?"

"Well, we don't. Not at this precise moment in time."

"In which case you already know that I can't just drop you in it now that I'm here, can I," she said. Tobias smiled gratefully and poured tea into the two mugs.

"Thank you, Agnes," he said, and pushed a mug across the table to Agnes. "Milk?" he asked. She shook her head.

"So, it's the same house?" she asked after a pause.

"Yes."

"You say it's still empty?"

"Yes."

"Since we left?"

"Yes."

"And our story?"

"Erm… story?"

"Well I can't just waltz back in like I'd just nipped to the shops, can I? It's been nearly a year!"

"I see." Tobias thought for a moment. "Well, Mr Forsyth wasn't particularly specific with my orders."

"Right. Well, we'd best think of one then hadn't we?" She grasped her mug and slurped at the hot black brew. "Well, I've been working in London, so I could just tell the neighbours that. But what about William? What do I say about him not being with me?"

"You may wish to tell them the truth… Well, that he's dead, anyway. It's perfectly plausible, particularly as it's true. An air raid, perhaps?"

"Well I'm hardly going to admit that he was killed whilst setting fire to that ship in the middle of the Firth of Forth, am I?"

Tobias lowered his gaze for a moment. "But all the evidence,

Agnes... the Maligns that were with him…"

"He didn't do it, I tell you!" she insisted. "You and I both know…"

"But Mr Forsyth said he saw..." Agnes flashed Tobias an angry stare.

"I don't care what he said he saw," she snarled, "it wasn't William."

"Agnes, can we concentrate on the details of *this* mission?"

A moment passed whilst she calmed herself.

"The boy could be a nephew," she continued, "that's easy. But transport. What about transport? Has Marcus got The Pathway working properly, yet?"

"Marcus is still endeavouring to make The Pathway secure again. However, until that time, transportation for you will consist of rail passage."

"I think we should have a car as well."

"A horseless carriage?"

"Look, if we can't use The Pathway, we'll need more flexible transport than just the train, just in case. And don't fob me off with any vague promises, Tobias."

"Agnes, such is the importance of this mission, I shall personally ensure the delivery of your very own horseless carriage. However, tomorrow morning you must take the train to Scotland."

Suddenly, the staircase creaked, and both Tobias and Agnes turned to see the boy descend the last few steps. He was bleary eyed and was wearing a pair of faded, blue and white striped pyjamas that were too small for him.

"Hello, Love," said Agnes softly. She rose from the table and crossed the kitchen to the boy. "What are you doing up at this time?"

"Heard voices," he replied.

"Yes, well, Tobias just popped in for a cup of tea and now he's going, aren't you Tobias?" Agnes looked at Tobias and indicated with her eyes for him to leave. Tobias hesitated for a moment.

"That's right, young man," he said, "I'm very busy as you know, and er…," he rose from the table and looked at Agnes, "I shall endeavour to rectify the, er… outstanding transportation issues as swiftly as possible." He picked up his hat, pulled his knapsack onto his back and made his way to the door. Agnes followed and opened the door to let him out. Tobias glanced at Agnes and the boy. He then put his hat on and said, "Good evening to you both and have a safe and pleasant journey tomorrow."

Tobias stepped into the street, looked both ways, and above, and then scurried off into the shadows of the night.

Agnes closed the door, locked it and bolted it firmly. She turned to the boy who was slurping from Tobias's mug of tea.

"Right then my love," she tried to sound light and unconcerned with the conversation she'd just had with Tobias, "let's get you back to bed shall we?"

The boy continued to slurp tea, but managed to murmur an acknowledgement. He placed the mug back on the table.

"You from London, then?" he asked. "You sound more like you come from round here." Agnes was surprised by the boy's observation.

"How long have you been listening?" she enquired. The boy shrugged. "Well, I'm not from London. I just live there. And no, I'm not from round here either. Come on, love," she said, "back to bed." The boy slowly climbed the bare wooden stairs, obviously tired and so Agnes helped him up the stairs by supporting his back. He leaned on her as he climbed.

"What did you mean when you said you're not one of them?" he asked. "You're not a Malign are you?"

"'Course not!" she laughed. "I just wasn't chosen like the others."

"What do you mean?"

"It means, nosy nine year olds wouldn't understand and shouldn't ask."

"Aw go on."

"Bed," she said. The boy reached the top of the stairs and stumbled into one of the two bedrooms. It was very dark, but he managed to flop onto his bed. Agnes pulled the sheet and blanket over him and kissed him on the forehead.

"Get some sleep, now, love. We've got a busy morning. We've got a train to catch, so you need to get your sleep."

"Is Scotland far?"

"It's a nice long train ride away. Now, night-night, love."

"Who was William?" There was a pause. She said nothing, but kissed the boy's forehead again and left the room. As she descended the stairs, her eyes welled up and a single tear rolled down her cheek.

NIGHTMARES OF YOUTH

John paused at the foot of the grand staircase and viewed the climb. His mind was in a whirl. The combination of whiskey and the exhaustion of the day's events were beginning to take their toll. The stairs were wide with shallow steps. Down the centre of the staircase a faded and threadbare carpet was held in place by discoloured brass carpet rods. An ornate, wrought iron banister with a polished mahogany rail ran the entire length of the staircase and along the upstairs landing.

John grasped the banister rail and began to climb.

Marcus saw John begin to sway slightly and so held out his arm to help steady John's climb.

"Well, it has been quite a day for you, don't you think, John."

"Mmm," agreed John.

"Tomorrow will be another busy day, I think, so you should get as much rest as you can."

"Mmm," John agreed again.

They reached the top of the stairs and walked down a corridor. The old floorboards creaked noisily under foot. Along the wall, the patterned old wallpaper was curled at the edges and, in places, it was coming away from the wall altogether. They stopped at a door and Marcus pushed it open and ushered John inside. It was a modest sized bedroom, for a mansion-sized house. It was modestly furnished too, with a simple wardrobe, and a single bed. At one side of the bed stood a bedside table and lamp, and on the other side was small dressing table on top of which stood a decorated china wash basin and matching jug. Beside the window was a wooden rocking chair with a folded towel on the seat. The fusty, stale air betrayed the under-use of the room.

"This is your room for tonight."

"Mine?"

"Yes."

"My own room?"

"Why, yes."

"Oh, I thought… you know… a messdeck… or dormitory… you know…"

"Remember, you're not in the Navy any more."

"Mmm. I need some air," said John, and he crossed the room to the sash window and opened it fully. He leaned his head out and took in a large breath of the fresh night air. "Ahhh… that's better."

The bedroom overlooked the gardens and the lake beyond. The moon's reflection shimmered on the lake as a gentle breeze rippled the water. All was quiet as John took in the view of the grounds. Marcus interrupted with a deliberate cough.

"Sorry, Marcus. I were miles away."

"Yes. Well. I'll take my leave of you. Breakfast is at seven. I shall collect you ten minutes beforehand and escort you to the dining area."

"Escort?"

"Yes. Escort. And as Mr Forsyth said, it would be appropriate if you refrained from wandering the hall on your own. Many of the staff will be unaware of your presence. It would be unwise to provoke a security situation, wouldn't you agree? Remember, the staff will be busy enough with their own duties without having to deal with a face they don't recognise."

"Busy? Looks quiet out yon' window," said John, but Marcus brushed off the remark.

"Seven o'clock, sharp. Sleep well, John," Marcus said, and then added, "Oh, the chamber pot under the bed is for decoration. Please don't use it. There is a lavatory down the corridor, on your left hand side." Marcus then left the room, closing the door behind him.

John cast one last look out of the open window, and closed the curtains. Then, after eying the bed for a moment, he allowed himself the luxury of a theatrical collapse onto the soft, welcoming mattress before he kicked off his slippers. He climbed under the sheets and drifted into a deep sleep. He hadn't even bothered to undress.

John woke with a sharp jerk of his body. He was no longer in bed. He was in a trench, standing alone, rifle in hand, with a tin helmet upon his head. This was simply outrageous! He'd only just fallen asleep! As he examined himself he realised that he was dressed in the uniform of a British Army private and it was perfectly clean, as if newly issued. Not even a splash of mud was on his boots.

John visually explored his surroundings. It looked like an authentic First World War trench, with smoke and mist drifting across the landscape. He could hear faint voices in the distance. English voices, but he could see nobody in the trench. Apart from the murmuring voices it was otherwise quiet. No gunfire, no artillery. Just voices. He walked a short distance along the trench towards the voices. Nervously, he peered around each corner of the zig-zag line of the trench, expecting to see soldiers. But it was empty. The closer he thought he was getting to the voices, the more they seemed to be avoiding him. He reached a dugout and paused momentarily, listening for the voices. They were almost inaudible now. He peered nervously into the dugout. It was silent. No sign of life. He removed his helmet, hung it on a nail outside the entrance, and ventured inside for a look around. Nobody was there. More strangely, there was no sign that anyone else had been there. There was no kit, no rifles, no food, no field telephone, and no rubbish. There was no evidence of occupation whatsoever. Nothing. Just the damp air. A shiver ran down his spine, so he left the dugout for the open air of the trench. The voices could still be heard, chattering in the distance.

Forgetting to collect his helmet, he continued along the trench towards the voices. As he peered around each corner he became less and less nervous about what may lay around them. Still, there was no one. Nor was there any evidence that anybody had been there at all. He rounded another corner and saw a second dugout, with a tin helmet hanging on a nail outside the entrance. John stood still and felt the top of his head with the palm of his hand. He knew the helmet was his.

Suddenly, the emptiness of the moment was broken when a giant of a German soldier, well over six feet tall, appeared from out of no-man's land, and leaped into the trench. The German soldier landed with a heavy thud that shook the ground.

This foe was dressed in a grubby infantry uniform, complete with rifle, helmet and spike. A heavily waxed moustache partly obscured a pale and greasy complexion. The soldier was terrifying as he sneered and growled at John, exposing half filled rows of crooked yellow teeth. The stench that wafted into John's nostrils was one of overpowering filth and decay. John stared into the soldier's intense, volcanic, blood-red eyes. Anger and hatred seemed to erupt from them. John was petrified.

Immediately, the soldier assaulted John with a bear-like ferocity, using the back of one of his over-sized hands to give John a hard slap across the face. The strength of this blow was enough to knock John backwards down the trench and he landed awkwardly on his back, sprawled across the duckboards. John dropped his rifle, scrambled quickly to his feet and began to run. He could hear the thud of the soldier's boots on the wooden duckboards as chase was given. In his desperation to escape, John ran blindly along the trench, round corner after corner.

The faint voices were no longer chattering. Now they were laughing. A mad, giddy laugh that grew steadily in volume until it reached a deafening crescendo.

Rounding a corner John reached a dugout with a tin helmet hanging on a nail outside the entrance and a rifle abandoned on the duckboards. John slid to a breathless stop at the side of the helmet and quickly looked around. No soldier.

Then the smell returned. John's heart felt like it missed a beat as he slowly turned to face his pursuer. The soldier looked at John curiously for a moment, before resuming his assault.

Another back-hand slap from the soldier sent John reeling. Staggering from the blow, John tripped over his rifle and landed on the duckboards against the trench wall. He began to pick himself up and tried desperately to back away from the soldier, but he was too slow. The soldier towered over John, rifle in hand with bayonet fixed and aimed at John's stomach. Before John had time to react the soldier thrust forwards and John was impaled on the bayonet with an audible tearing of garment and flesh. The soldier gave out a deep guttural roar as he lifted John clear into the air on the end of the rifle. As John looked downwards he felt peculiarly detached from the situation. He felt no pain as he watched his legs flail and twitch. His tip-toes vainly tried to make contact with the ground.

This was the nightmare of his youth.

And here the nightmare ended, as abruptly as it had begun. No death. Just a sweat soaked awakening in the bed in which he dreamt it.

John quickly threw back the bed sheets and swung his legs out of bed. He lifted his shirt and checked his stomach for injuries. There were none, of course. There never were, but nonetheless he always checked.

A breeze caused the curtains to billow into the room and the cool air made John shiver. He went to close the window and, as he stood poised to pull down the sash, he looked down from the window and saw Mr Forsyth in the garden, huddled in conversation with a soldier. John couldn't see the rank of the soldier, nor could he hear more than a murmur of conversation. Mr Forsyth held a large brown envelope under one arm. They broke off their conversation, and the two of them saluted each other smartly before bidding each other goodbye. Mr Forsyth came indoors, and the soldier walked over to the side of the house, where John saw a waiting car on the gravel driveway.

John closed the window, drew the curtains and returned to his bed, where he lay on his back and stared at the cracked plaster ceiling. The events of the last twenty four hours had been one long, non-stop rollercoaster. As he relived the events over and over again in his mind, he drifted slowly back to sleep. This time it was unbroken by dream or nightmare.

John was eventually stirred by the brilliance of the morning sunshine that filtered through the thin fabric of the curtains. A shaft of light shone through a gap between the curtains, like a spotlight on a stage, and dust particles danced within its beam.

As John emerged from his slumber and slowly opened his eyes to the brightness of the morning, his first thoughts on seeing the shaft of light were of The Pathway. Would he be travelling along another one today?

Glancing at his watch, he suddenly realised the time was almost seven o'clock. He jumped out of bed and quickly washed his face using the jug and washbasin on the bedside table.

There was a knock at the door and Marcus called.

"Good morning, John."

"Mornin'."

"Err.." asked Marcus. The door creaked open a few inches.

"Come in, Marcus. Come in."

"Thank you, John." Marcus entered the room and began to look around the room in an inquisitive, almost intrusive manner. "Did you sleep well?"

"Aye. Like a prince."

"Good, good. And are you ready to go to breakfast?"

"Yep."

Marcus led John downstairs towards the mess hall, from where the smell of cooked bacon and toast made John's empty stomach rumble very loudly.

"The mess hall sounds very busy, this morning," observed Marcus as they approached. "Which means it is quite likely that one or two other missions have been recently concluded."

"That's alright. I don't mind, as long as I get breakfast," replied John.

"No, John," Marcus said, and paused outside the door, "I mean it is possible that you will be surprised by who is probably having breakfast today and, well, please do not be alarmed by their presence."

They entered the mess hall and John was, indeed, greeted by an unexpected sight. There were probably fifteen servicemen and civilians sat at the tables. But there were not just the usual Allied servicemen. In amongst the British and French uniforms were those from Germany, Italy, and Soviet Russia. All were chatting away at their tables, some quietly and others not so quietly. One table erupted into laughter as a German airman comically animated an evidently humorous tale about something or other.

"Er," John began.

"Remember, John, your new life is not the same as the one you were accustomed to before yesterday," Marcus said, and then added, "All will be explained in your Renaissance Briefing."

"Oh, aye? I'll try and remember that."

Marcus led John to the serving counter, behind which a jolly catering lady smiled her good mornings and served them both a plate full of beans, sausage and scrambled eggs. John commented on the generous portions and thanked her each time she spooned food onto his plate. Then, they made their way towards a vacant table near the rear of the room. A German Airman leaned over from another table, stopped them, and offered out his hand to John.

"Hello. You look new. Yes?" he said in a deliberately thick German accent. "I'm Walther. Or should that be Walter, now I'm back at headquarters?"

"Oh, aye?" replied John, "I'm John." He balanced his tray in one hand and returned a hurried handshake. "At least I think I am."

"Don't worry," chuckled Walter. "You'll soon settle in. I was rescued about eighteen months ago from my crashed Dornier. I was very confused when first they brought me here. But now I am alright." He acted out a comical, nervous twitch and chuckled again before he realised Marcus was glaring at him, unimpressed by the entertainment. Walter coughed apologetically into his hand and settled into a more serious tone. "Sorry, Marcus. I was only joking. Seriously, John, I was very reassured by my Renaissance and I am very proud to have been chosen to fight the Maligns."

"Oh, aye? Your English sounds pretty good, for a Jerry. I mean, without the uniform I would never have guessed you was a Jerry."

Walter chuckled again and turned to Marcus.

"Marcus, he teases me, yes?"

"Walter, he only arrived last night. He hasn't even had his Briefing. So, I'd be grateful if you would refrain from your teasing." Walter flashed an apologetic look.

"Sorry, old chap," Walter now spoke in flawless English, "I was just having a joke with the man."

Marcus sighed, wearily. "Always the joker. Thank you, Walter, but I'd appreciate it if you would refrain from toying with the newly chosen. It becomes rather tiresome after a while."

"Sorry, Marcus. But maybe he should have been warned of us before coming in for breakfast."

"No doubt you are correct, as usual, Walter," Marcus said with another weary sigh, "I just hadn't expected you to all still be in here."

"What don't I know, yet?" asked John.

"All will be revealed at your Briefing, John," said Marcus, "Walter was simply teasing you. It is his particular way of welcoming the newly chosen. Come, let us find a seat before our breakfast grows cold."

"You can sit with us, if you want," Walter offered.

"A generous offer, Walter, but no thank you," replied Marcus, curtly. He pointed to a small group huddled around a table in the corner. "We shall eat at the vacant table next to the other newly chosen."

"Never mind, John," Walter said with a genuine sincerity, "it was a pleasure to meet you." John and Marcus crossed to an empty table.

"My apologies for Walter's behaviour," Marcus said, and rolled his eyes. "He has a peculiar sense of humour when it comes to the newly chosen. It is his way of being friendly."

"Oh, aye?" said John. "So is he English or German, then?"

"The List of Chosen is not restricted just to Englishmen, or to the Allies," replied Marcus. "These headquarters command all who are chosen from across the whole of Europe."

"So he's German, then," said John.

"We have Headquarters on each continent. Here, we deal with European affairs, and that includes *all* the European countries, including Germany."

"So, he is German, then?"

"Walter was born a German, but now he commands a team of

multinational and multilingual soldiers," explained Marcus. "He is a very experienced and capable man. And the men in his team are very versatile and very good."

"Versatile?"

"Yes, John," Marcus said proudly. "His team is so good, they can even deploy as either a British Army unit, or as a unit of the German Wehrmacht."

"You're kidding me?" exclaimed John.

"I kid you not, John. They have done so on several occasions. Now, come, eat up. Remember, you have much work to do today."

RENAISSANCE AND BRIEFING

The old man shuffled slowly into the room, tightly gripping his walking stick for support. His tall, yet slightly stooped frame was frail, skeletal and wrinkly. The arthritic deformities of his emaciated, bony fingers were clearly visible through his age-speckled skin. The man was a shuffling bag of bones. His thinning, grey, shoulder length hair hung heavy and lank, like it needed a good wash; and his large, round ears held back his locks from his face. The old man wore a similar style of clothing to Marcus and Tobias – a dark green woollen pullover, dark green trousers that stopped short of the ankle, and thick brown socks neatly folded above heavy brown boots.

A murmur of excitement rippled through the room. The dozen or so people, John and Marcus amongst them, were sat in two rows of chairs. The people were a mixture of military and civilian men and women. Some of them exchanged excited glances before giving their undivided attention to the old man. When Marcus saw the old man he nudged John and stood to his feet. John and the others followed. The old man did not look up at the group; he simply lifted his stick a few inches from the floor and waved it weakly in acknowledgement. John thought the man looked in his eighties, or nineties.

"At ease, men," the old man said. His tone of voice had the depth, confidence and clarity of someone with a great deal of natural authority. "Thank you Marcus, you can go now." Marcus glanced at John and then back at the old man. "Go and find something else to do, Marcus. You're dismissed." No one was in any doubt that this old man was firmly in charge of the proceedings and was anything but frail of mind. Marcus stood up and looked at John. The embarrassing disappointment in Marcus's face was clear for all to see. He leaned closer to John and spoke in a hushed voice.

"I have every confidence that you will judge this training to be of the utmost usefulness during your mission. The knowledge you will derive from Solomon today will yield significant benefits for you."

"Oh, aye?"

"Thank you, Marcus," interrupted the old man. "I would like to begin now."

"My apologies, Solomon. I shall depart immediately." Marcus politely squeezed his way to the end of the row and headed for the open door in the corner of the room. When the door had been closed behind Marcus, Solomon addressed his audience. John had his first real glimpse of Solomon's sharp, piercing blue eyes. They sparkled with an energy and enthusiasm that his body seemed scarcely able to contain. He had the eyes of youth in the body of the aged.

"Good morning all," he said.

"'mornin'" they mumbled.

"As Marcus so eloquently alluded, my name is Solomon and I'm here to answer your questions and to impart a few practical and procedural activities that will hopefully extend your life out in the field. This does not constitute formal training. There was a time when we could spend weeks training our operatives. But in the current emergency we can spare but a few hours for pre-mission briefings. Any questions so far? Good."

Another murmur rippled around the room.

"Now, before I begin, a few house rules. If you have a question, please don't interrupt me. You may put your hand up if there is anything specific you do not understand, and I may invite you to share your question with everyone. But if you have only comments or opinions that you would like to share or debate, please keep them for the tea breaks or meal times."

Solomon shuffled over to a large leather armchair and carefully lowered himself into it.

"Ah, that's better. Well, where do you think we should begin? Eh?" Nobody answered. "Come on, don't be shy."

One man in an RAF Sergeant's uniform raised his hand.

"At the beginning?" he suggested.

"An excellent idea. But where is the beginning? For each of you it is likely to be in as different a place as there are points on a compass. But as the purpose of your being here is to prepare you for your mission in the war against the Maligns, I suppose a good starting point would be to define the war and tell you about the Maligns. Now, the war that you are all familiar with is between the Allies and the Axis powers. Are we all agreed on that point?" There was a murmur of agreement. "So what about the war between good and evil?"

"Well, isn't it the same?" the RAF sergeant piped up.

"Not at all. There are evil men and there are good men on both sides in every war. Although, I grant you, there are more evil men on the Axis side in this particular war."

"So, what are you saying?"

"I'm saying that we are now outside of the Second World War. We are – you all are – now engaged in a much more fundamental struggle between the forces of good and evil. And this straddles both sides of the dividing line between Axis and Allies. "

"Oh, aye?" John said, rather sceptically.

"Yes," Solomon continued, "You see, there is an evil, malignant movement which penetrated the borders of all the combatant nations long before Hitler came to power. It was the prime motivation that led to the violence and suffering of this century. The prejudices of the Nazi and Fascist parties are simply convenient facades. This malignant movement is injurious, malevolent and destructive in influence – it is based upon wickedness and, in short, it intends to destroy the world for its own wicked ends. The principal individuals are very cunning and conduct their activities covertly. They have assimilated themselves into most societies, and they are not easily detected. They are at work even within elements of the British government. The Maligns, as we prefer to call them, have subordinates who have more overt roles to play in influencing the progression of the war – just think of any of the major personalities engaged on the Axis side and most will probably have links to the Maligns.

"And them flying demon things. Where do they fit in?" interrupted John.

"Well, let's just say that they are some of God's heavenly creatures who fell from grace and opted for the cause of the Maligns."

"You mean we're fighting Satan and his hordes of Hell?" asked the man sitting next to John.

"In a manner of speaking, yes, I suppose we are."

"And what happens if we bump into Old Nick himself?" the RAF sergeant asked.

"That is most unlikely," replied Solomon.

"How come?" asked John.

"Ah, well," explained Solomon, "imagine the world is a chess board, and we are the pawns in a terrible game. Then ask yourself this: How often does a chess player climb onto the board and behave as a piece?"

"So we won't meet the devil," John said.

"No," Solomon replied.

"But we'll meet them flying demon things," John added.

"Yeah, but we'll not have to worry about them, will we?" the RAF sergeant said, "because we have angels to protect us."

"Well that is true," Solomon said, "but only to a certain extent. You see, celestial creatures are not permitted to physically interfere with the actions of man. They've always had the ability, but were never given the authority. So, this means all the angels, including the Galearii from yesterday, cannot touch or interfere with anything from this physical world. Their ability to help you is, therefore, limited to things of a celestial nature."

"Like fighting them demons," said John.

"Yes, John. But be warned, demons frequently act outside of their authority," Solomon added. "After their fall from grace they realised that they could use their powers to touch and interfere with the physical world, despite not having the authority to do so."

"And I suppose they do it a lot, now," observed the man sat next to John.

"I'm afraid they do," confirmed Solomon.

"So where exactly do us 'pawns' fit in, then?" asked the RAF sergeant.

"Our strategy is to frustrate the Maligns in all their purposes wherever and whenever we find them. And that will be the core objective of every one of your missions. Some of you will have missions that are quite modest in ambition: intelligence gathering, for example. You will be the passives. Others among you will have more risky missions: ones in which you seek out a direct confrontation with the Maligns. You will be the actives. Each mission is as important as the other; and equally dependent upon each other. Neither mission type can function for very long without the other. However, I have no wish to digress on this point. This training is not to tell you how to conduct your individual missions. No. You already have all the tools and skills tucked away in your mind and in your soul. Your success or failures are already written in your destiny."

"Is that right?" a sceptical voice chipped in.

"Absolutely," replied Solomon, "our victory is already assured. It will come about in the end. We just don't know how or when. But it will. He gave us His Word and it is written."

Another murmur rippled through the group.

"No, let us return to the here and now. What is the most important thing you will want to know once you embark up on your mission, regardless of what your mission orders happen to be?"

The RAF sergeant raised his hand again.

"Well, I'd want to know where the Maligns are," he said.

"Correct," replied Solomon. "The most important life-prolonging skill is identifying who and where the Maligns are. And then, of course, there is keeping your own identity from them if yours is a passive mission. So, how do we do it? Well, there are a number of ways: talking in tongues; conversing and behaving as if you're a Malign; and of course let's not forget how to use our wit and ingenuity."

A man sat next to John raised his hand.

"So, if Maligns look the same as ordinary people, how do you spot one before he or she spots you?"

"You could ask them 'Are you a Malign?'" another man answered sarcastically. A few people sniggered and giggled at this, and a smile opened across Solomon's face.

"You may laugh, but he is closer to the truth than he realises."

"What? Ask them? But then they'll know who you are," the RAF sergeant said.

"Will they?" replied Solomon. "Remember that on the face of things a Malign may appear ordinary, civilised, generous; even avuncular. But dig a little deeper and you will find the cause of their malign intent; something that led them to the arms of the Maligns. They may be consumed by a jealousy, bitterness, hatred, vanity, malice, greed, a lust for revenge for something. And this deeper emotion impairs their judgement. So if you pretend to be a Malign, they may well believe you are one of them, too. After all, Maligns wear no badge of identification."

"So what do we say to 'em to find out?" asked John.

"Well, if you meet someone you suspect is a Malign," continued Solomon, "you could say something like 'Malign the Lord. His end is near'. That is probably the most commonly used greeting amongst Maligns. There are others, of course."

"And what are we meant to do if we find one?" asked the RAF sergeant.

"That would entirely depend upon your orders. If you are on a

Passive mission, you may simply be required to report your findings. Or infiltrate their team."

"Team?"

"Yes, team. Maligns tend to work either alone or in small teams of maybe a dozen or so individuals, frequently with demon support."

"What if it's an active mission?" the RAF sergeant asked.

"You may be required to take the Malign into custody or, in some cases…kill them."

"Assassination, like?" asked John, incredulous at the notion.

"Well, that would be subject to your individual mission orders. And if those are your orders, then, yes."

The room fell silent for a moment.

"Let us move on, shall we?" Solomon said. "Let us suppose you encounter a Malign and there is a confrontation in which the Malign is vanquished. What do you do with your Malign, whether dead or alive? Do you call the police? Or do you…" There was a knock at the door and Marcus entered the room.

"Excuse me, Solomon. My apologies for interrupting your briefing."

"Yes, Marcus. What is it, now?"

"Mr Forsyth would like to see John Popplethwaite, immediately."

"Can it not wait? We have only just begun to open into our stride."

"He said immediately, Solomon. It would appear that he has just received John's order papers."

"Already?"

"Indeed."

"Well, then, John. It would appear that you are dismissed," said Solomon. "Good luck with your mission."

A few minutes later, John was once again standing inside Mr Forsyth's office.

"Well, John, I have them right here." Mr Forsyth picked up a large brown envelope from his desk. "How are you feeling this morning? Ready for your mission?"

"Ask me again in ten minutes."

"Ah, it'll be nothing to get too worried about, I'm sure. First missions are usually fairly straightforward. Break you in gently, eh? Sit down, sit down. Let's get down to business then."

John sat in the large leather armchair, whilst Mr Forsyth opened the envelope. After perching a pair of gold-rimmed spectacles on the end of his nose, Mr Forsyth carefully read through the order papers, occasionally scrutinising the enclosed documentation. Eventually, he removed his spectacles.

"Well, John. Firstly, you have my congratulations. You have been promoted. Your new identity is Chief Petty Officer John Drummond." He passed John some identity paperwork and a brown leather wallet.

"Oh aye? Does that mean I get a pay rise?"

"Remember, John Popplethwaite is dead. And no King's service means no King's shilling. Chief Drummond, however, really is dead I'm afraid. Died as a child, but you don't need to know the rest. We have acquired his identity for you to use, but you don't get his pay."

"Oh."

"Don't worry, John, you won't be without funds. Inside the wallet there should be twenty pounds in various notes and coins." John glanced inside the wallet and stared wide-eyed when he saw the money inside. He'd never carried so much money in his life.

"By, that's a lot."

"Yes, and it's not for wasting on frivolities like beer or rum or women. It's there to enable you to complete your mission."

"Aye."

"Good," Mr Forsyth said and returned to his reading. "Now, your orders are to go to Scotland. The exact address is here in this envelope, so you don't forget." Mr Forsyth looked over to John. "It's near Edinburgh. That's near the Firth of Forth, so you should have no trouble finding it."

"Aye, 'course," John replied, "I've sailed up round there many a time."

"Yes, quite. At that address you will be met by one of our operatives. Your mission is to act as guardian for a child in her care until such time as you are relieved."

"Guardian?"

"Yes, guardian."

"Eh?" John was puzzled by this revelation. "You're kidding me. Babysitting somebody's bloody kid? Give over."

"Let me assure you in the strongest of terms that 'guardianship' is not a term we use for babysitting. Guardians provide physical protection, not advice on schooling. Evidently the Maligns want to get at that child for some reason and it's your job to protect him."

"Oh."

"Oh, indeed, John. This is an active mission. It seems your earlier observations may prove to be correct."

"Eh?"

"You appear to have been chosen because of your physical attributes, after all."

"Cheers," John said, "I'll make sure I take a pair of boxing gloves."

"Don't be facetious with me, John. Remember, I'm still your commanding officer. And this is a serious mission you are to embark upon." John's cheeks reddened, slightly, at the admonishment.

"Sorry, Sir."

"Marcus will escort you to the station."

"Thank you, Sir."

"Now if you don't mind," Mr Forsyth said, curtly, and walked towards the door, "we both have duties to attend to and you have a train to catch."

Outside in the corridor, Marcus stood with his back against the wall whilst he waited wearily for John to emerge from Mr Forsyth's office. He stifled a yawn and his heavy eyelids began to droop. The sound of the opening door startled him and he stood bolt upright. He quickly looked around to see if anyone had noticed him dozing.

"Ah, Marcus," said Mr Forsyth, "I'd like you to meet Chief Petty Officer John Drummond. He'll need a change of kit and a lift to the station."

"Yes, Sir," replied Marcus. "Congratulations, John. It'll be my pleasure to escort you."

"Cheers, Marcus," John said and turned to Mr Forsyth. "See you later then, Sir."

"Goodbye, John," Mr Forsyth said and returned to his office. He closed the door behind him with a heavy clunk.

HOMECOMING

Terra firma!

Philip walked down the gangway from the Flotilla Captain's ship to the concrete jetty. He was the last of his surviving crew to disembark. The others had gone ashore hours earlier and had probably already begun their survivor's leave. Philip was relieved when he had learned that the crew were to be dispersed amongst the other vessels of the fleet. It marked the official end of his command and it felt as if an enormous weight had been lifted from his shoulders. His own leave had just begun, and he felt a child-like excitement whenever he thought of his long-awaited reunion with his beloved wife and children.

A sailor, who was standing at the foot of the gangway, saluted him, smartly.

"Good luck, Sir," the sailor said. Philip smiled and saluted him in return.

"Why, thank you, Bains," he replied. "And good luck to you too."

Philip glanced up at the rust-streaked vessel and quietly thanked her for his rescue. He walked across the dockyard with a sense of relief that he hadn't felt for months. It somehow didn't quite feel real, so he had to remind himself that he had two weeks leave ahead of him and he was going home!

He noticed that his subconscious mind, which was so used to coping with living at sea, continued to believe that his legs were absorbing the subtle deck movements of a ship at sea. It made him smile. Similarly, his subconscious continued to hear the low hum of ventilation fans and machinery, even though this was obviously not possible as he was now some distance from the ship. Clearly they were sensory illusions, but nonetheless they felt real. Philip had experienced them on a number of occasions during his sea-going service, and he fondly recalled the words of a gruff old sailor who once told him that a ship is more than just a big tub made of metal. With a good crew at her helm, a ship could be brought to life. Not physically alive, of course, but alive with her own personality and characteristics.

And then Philip pictured his own ship, now resting on the sea bed, cold and lifeless; the dead fingers of a perished crew steering her on her final voyage of corrosion and oblivion. A flicker of guilt passed across his heart.

The dockyard was a hive of activity, and sailors and dockyard workers of all sorts scurried past whilst attending to their respective duties. A nearby dockyard crane blared out its warning klaxon and began to crawl along its rails in the concrete. Philip stepped out of its path and walked past a stoker who was engrossed in repairing a leaking steam hose that snaked its way along the jetty. A fog of steam drifted from a damaged flange on the hissing hose and it felt warm and damp against Philip's skin as he passed through it. The stoker strained on two spanners as he tried to tighten the nuts and bolts of the flange, but a spanner slipped from a nut and he fell forward, grazing a knuckle on the concrete. He then erupted in expletives and hurled the spanner to the ground with a clang before sucking his graze. Philip paused and turned.

"Are we alright?"

"Oh, sorry, Sir, wrong size spanner, Sir," the sailor replied and grinned sheepishly. Philip suppressed an amused grin.

"Carry on, then."

"Sir."

Philip continued his walk towards the dockyard gate. He walked past the history of the yard. There were storehouses from the 18th and 19th century, and Edwardian stone offices fortified with sandbagged doorways and sailors bearing rifles. He walked past an old, tired-looking lorry, being emptied of its cargo, which was still partially covered with a grubby tarpaulin. Eventually, Philip reached the imposing oak gates set within the red brick, dockyard boundary wall. He returned the salute of the sailors standing guard, and then left the dockyard through a smaller, pedestrian doorway in the wall next to the main gate.

Outside the dockyard, to his pleasure and surprise, three figures stood on the bustling corner across the street. He paused momentarily, to behold his family. His wife and two young children were buffeted by the passing crowd. Nonetheless, they saw Philip come through the pedestrian door and immediately began waving to him. Philip acknowledged their attention with a modest nod of his head and a broad smile. He paused for a break in the traffic before quickly, and smartly, he crossed the street to meet them.

"Hello, Philip," she said. He took hold of his wife's soft, porcelain-white hand and kissed her gently on the cheek.

"Hello, Grace," he replied and then turned his attention to his young children. Keeping his back straight, he bent his knees and lowered himself effortlessly to their head-height. "And how are my little ones?"

"Very well, Daddy," his daughter beamed back at him.

"Hello, Daddy," greeted his son.

"Not at school today?" Philip asked.

"No, Daddy," his son replied. The child's large eyes glinted with excitement, "School was bombed!" Philip did not physically react.

"Oh, my. How unfortunate," he replied, "no algebra for you today." He stood up and, with a raised eyebrow, he glanced at Grace.

"Oh, it's nothing," she said. "It's just an unexploded bomb in the street. School's been closed until it's removed."

"I see," he said. "How long have you been waiting here?"

"Only about an hour," she replied, "Dorothy Markham telephoned me. She told me that Gerald had just arrived home on survivor's leave."

The crowd continued to jostle and push past the four of them, and Philip decided that it would probably be wise to move on. "Shall we?" he said and offered his hand to his daughter, who grasped it tightly. His wife took his other hand and, with his son leading the way, they moved off in the direction of home. After a couple of hundred yards the crowd thinned and Philip felt more able to converse without having to raise his voice. "Any thoughts on what you'd like to do whilst I'm on leave?"

"Ooo, lots..." began his daughter.

"Beginning with," interrupted Grace, "a few days away from this place. We're going to leave this war behind us. The children are not at school, so I thought we might visit your mother."

"And why not, indeed. A relaxing stroll in the countryside enjoying the last of the summer sunshine sounds just the ticket."

"We've already packed some things," his son proudly informed him.

"Even some of your clothes, Daddy," added his daughter.

"If it's OK with you, Philip, we thought we'd take the train this evening."

"My, we are organized. You should work for the Admiralty."

The family continued their walk across town, past bomb damaged buildings and a queue of women clutching their ration books outside a corner grocer's shop. Eventually, they turned into an avenue of late Victorian town houses. Down at the far end was a pile of rubble that was once a house. The street, like the rest of the town, had a grim, neglected air about it. Only a few of the houses that had had windows blown-in from the blast of the bomb, were lucky enough to be boarded-up with scraps of old wood. The others had to contend with torn blackout curtains drawn across shattered windows to provide makeshift protection from the elements. Undamaged windows still defiantly displayed their large brown 'X's taped across them. Fortunately, Philip's home had escaped relatively unscathed, with only a large crack across an upstairs window.

"Oh, my," Philip said. He paused to glance at his children. They simply smiled back at him, innocently. After a moment he winked at them and, gestured to the sight before them. "Has your mother been cleaning again?"

"Well, one tries…" she replied. The children ran ahead and so Philip and Grace were able to link arms as they walked the last few yards to their home.

"When did this…?"

"A few days ago."

"Mmm. You know, the countryside around Mother's is beautiful in winter. And the village school would be quite acceptable. And safe."

"Do you think she'd mind?"

"As long as you don't offer to clean."

Philip's jocularity quickly left him when he realised a staff car was parked outside their home. As the children approached the car, a Wren driver opened a door and climbed out. She stood on the pavement and waited for Philip and his wife to reach her. She saluted smartly.

"Leiutenant-Commander Ambrose, Sir?"

"Yes. What do you want?" Philip said, curtly.

"Sir," she said and passed him a small brown envelope, which he duly opened, "Sorry to catch you at home, Sir. But when I got to the ship I was told you'd already gone ashore." Philip's face dropped as he read the note.

"You'd better wait here. I want five minutes with my family," he said and ushered his family into the house. They stood quietly for a moment in the living room before his son interrupted the silence.

"Daddy, what's that lady want?" Philip looked into his wife's eyes before replying.

"I have to go and see an admiral, son."

"Oh, Philip!" Grace whispered.

"I'm sorry, dear."

"But your survivor's leave."

"Don't worry. It's probably nothing much."

"But Daddy, you've only just come home," exclaimed his daughter.

"Yes. And the sooner I go and see him, the sooner we go and see your Grandmother." Philip squeezed his wife's hand before kissing her and the children. "And if I'm not back in time, make sure you catch that train and I'll meet you at Mother's," he added. He closed the front door behind him with a heavy-handed slam that made everyone jump. His family stood in stunned silence for a moment before Grace spoke.

"Well, we don't want to keep your father waiting when he returns, do we? Let's get everything ready, shall we? You never know, he may have to meet us at Grandma's."

The Wren opened the passenger door and Philip climbed into the car. The Wren drove to an office building, somewhere within the heart of the dockyard. The journey was in silence. On one occasion the Wren looked across to Philip as if about to engage him in conversation, but she saw that he was in no mood for idle chit-chat. He just stared blankly ahead.

The car pulled up outside a sandbagged doorway and Philip got out. Without even thanking the Wren, he slammed the door shut and entered the building, remembering to return the salute of the rifle-bearing sailor only after he had passed him. Once inside, Philip vaulted up a flight of stairs, three at a time. The top of the stairs opened into a reception area where several Wrens were clattering away at typewriters. One of them, a Wren Officer, looked up and saw Philip approach. She stood to greet him.

"Leiutenant-Commander Ambrose?" she enquired. Philip was quite surprised she knew him by name. Did she know him from previous visits? Or was it just a lucky guess?

"Yes."

"Please take a seat," she said. "The Admiral will see you in a moment." She walked over to a door, knocked on it lightly, opened it a little and peered around it before muttering, "Leiutenant-Commander Ambrose is outside, Sir."

The Admiral replied with a soft, slightly effeminate voice. The Wren closed the door and returned to Philip, who was about to sit down.

"The Admiral will see you now, Sir," she said.

Philip was led into the office, a formerly splendid room but now simply decorated. The panelling and plaster ceiling had long since been muted by successive coats of magnolia and white, and it had become heavily smoke stained from the habit of its most recent occupant.

The admiral was a figure made slender by worry. His eyes, though not sunken, showed the dark-marks, bags and heavy lids of sleep deprivation. The fingers of his right hand were stained by tobacco. Smoke from the cigarette that was hung from the Admiral's lips swirled around his eyes, making him squint as he raised his head to see John enter the room. He rested the cigarette on the overflowing ashtray, rose from his desk and shook Philip's hand. He gestured to an elaborately decorated china teapot with matching cups and saucers.

"The tea's fresh, Philip. Would you care to join me?"

"Thank you, Sir," replied Philip. The Wren poured the tea, passed a cup to the admiral, then one to Philip and then she left the room.

"I've just read all about your, er… exploits. Bad luck wouldn't you say?"

"If you say so, Sir," Philip replied, flatly. The admiral returned to his desk and slurped his tea from the comfort of his large chair. He lit a fresh cigarette from the embers of the old one.

"Ahh, there's nothing more refreshing than a steaming hot cup of tea and a cigarette, wouldn't you agree?"

"I do like a good cup, myself, Sir, yes," replied Philip, but he didn't take a sip. Philip simply looked at the admiral, and waited to hear what he had to say.

"You're probably wondering why I asked you to see me," the admiral said. Philip didn't reply, and so the admiral continued. "You fought a very gallant action, you know, Philip. You must be very proud." Philip didn't answer, but took a sip of his tea instead. "Your conduct, and that of your ship's company, hasn't gone un-noticed in the corridors of Whitehall."

Philip looked at the admiral through narrowed eyes. He wasn't sure whether the admiral was referring to the action fought against the

Germans, or Philip's decision to leave some of his men trapped on board.

"I wouldn't at all be surprised if the odd gong came of it," the admiral added. Philip assumed the admiral was referring to the action against the Germans.

"My men, their widows, and their families will be most appreciative of His Majesty's gratitude, Sir," Philip said and he recalled the faces of some of the men he had condemned to die.

"Yes... well... anyway..." the Admiral frowned at the remark, "one step closer to victory, eh, Philip?" Philip took another sip of tea without breaking eye contact with the admiral. The admiral placed his cup onto his desk, puffed on his cigarette for a moment and then leaned forward. "Philip. The Captain of the Kiveton was seriously wounded when they were attacked a couple of days ago. He's in hospital and likely to be recuperating for some months. "

"I'm sorry to hear that, Sir. How's the ship?"

"She suffered only minor damage. She's alongside for repairs. But we need her operational and back at sea within days, and that would mean encroaching on your survivor's leave." The two men looked at each other for a moment. "It's not an order, Philip. I'm giving you the option of another command, straight away. But only if you want it."

"Because you can't think of anyone else who can step into the breach at such short notice?"

"Because when one falls off a bicycle, Philip..." There was along pause.

"I left those men to die, though," Philip said, flatly.

"To save the rest of your men," the admiral added. "And if you hadn't, you all could have been lost. If I'd been in command, I would have made the very same decision."

"I just wish I could have helped them."

"I know," replied the admiral, "but this is war, Philip. And there was nothing more you could have done. And besides, we're desperate for good men like yourself to keep things together if we're going to beat the Hun."

There was another pause.

"So where is she being repaired?" asked Philip.

"I'm not sure. Somewhere on the Forth, I think. Hang on and I'll..." the admiral said, puffed on his cigarette, and began riffling through papers on his desk.

Philip stared into his cup of tea for a moment. He then drank it down in one gulp and placed the empty cup on the desk.

"I'll need to make a stop along the way, Sir. To say goodbye to my family."

"Of course," the admiral said and looked across at Philip. "Congratulations, Philip," he added and offered out his hand. Philip rose from his seat and shook hands with the admiral.

"Thank you, Sir."

A few minutes later, Philip emerged from the admiral's office and closed the office door behind him with a heavy-handed slam that made the Wren typists stop their typing for a moment. The Wren officer looked across and smiled. Philip smiled weakly in return, before he descended the stairs to the awaiting staff car.

A SURPRISE VISIT

John was now staring at himself in a mirror. He was dressed in his new uniform. The transformation into a Chief Petty Officer gave him a feeling of pride, and boosted his confidence. He straightened his tie, again.

"You have the bearing and posture of a natural non-commissioned officer," Marcus said.

"Aye? How do you work that one out?" John replied. "A uniform doesn't make the man you know."

"No? I'll wager that you feel it does."

"Well," John had difficulty hiding a smile, "it's a right good fit. I'll give you that."

"An excellent fit worthy of any Savile Row tailor," Marcus replied, "and enough to make any mother proud." He then glanced at his watch, "Come, John. We have only half an hour before your train's departure time."

"Alright, alright. I'm coming," John said as he grabbed his half-filled kitbag. He followed Marcus outside to a waiting staff car. The gravel crunched beneath his shoes, and as he reached the car he suddenly realised he was thinking about his mother. Would she have received the official "Killed in Action" telegram yet? Would she ever get to see it? Or would the nurses keep the news from her, until she was fit enough to cope with the trauma of another loss? John took hold of the car door handle and paused for a moment.

"Is everything alright, John?" Marcus asked as he went around to the other side of the car.

"Mmm?"

"Your countenance has become somewhat pensive."

"Just thinking about my mum," John said. "She always said Dad came to see her after he got killed. Nobody believed her though. Everyone thought she were mad."

Marcus was taken off guard by this statement.

"And do you believe she was correct in her assertion?" he asked, after a moment of thought. John paused, looked at the ground and then sighed.

"Don't suppose it matters any more," he replied. "She went mad in the end anyway."

Marcus looked away, embarrassed and uncomfortable with the direction of the conversation. John opened the car door and climbed inside. Marcus rolled his eyes, as if admonishing himself for his own tactlessness, and then he too opened his door and climbed inside.

"Hello, Perkins," said Marcus, relieved to be able to change the subject.

"Marcus," Perkins replied.

"Railway Station please."

"Right-ho." Perkins started the engine and drove the staff car slowly away from the house. "Becoming a bit of a habit, don't you think?"

"Sorry?"

"Using the staff car again. Pathway on the blink again is it?"

"The absolute concealment of The Pathway's destination may not currently be as secure as it once was. But it is definitely not 'on the blink'."

"Is that why I'm going by train?" asked John.

"You know that I can neither confirm nor deny the reasons for your rail journey, John, even if I know them. Your orders are your orders."

At the end of the gravel driveway, the car paused at the gate whilst the guards lifted the barrier-gate. The car then drove out of Headquarters, turned onto a tree-lined country lane and sped off towards the nearby town.

The valley containing this quaint, provincial town of stone-built factories and terraces meant that the railway station was located on the edge of town. Smoke and steam could be seen rising from a scruffy looking engine at the platform just beyond the station buildings, and the hissing of steam became audible as the car pulled up a short distance from the busy station entrance. Marcus and John both climbed out of the car. John looked across to the station and then back to Marcus.

"I'm afraid this is as far as I go," said Marcus.

"Oh aye?"

"Good luck, John."

"Aye, cheers Marcus." They shook hands firmly. John slung his kitbag onto his shoulder and crossed the road into the station. He had just finished crossing the road when the staff car pulled away and drove off in the direction of Headquarters. John caught a fleeting glance of Marcus in the car and they exchanged one final parting gesture, a wave of the hand.

The ticket office queue wasn't actually as long as John had initially expected, given how busy the station seemed. Within a few minutes he was clutching his ticket and climbing the steps of the old wrought iron footbridge that led him over the tracks to his waiting train. The rust-streaked paintwork was flaking from the ornate ironwork, and the decaying planks of the bridge's decking seemed soft underfoot. John trod carefully along the bridge and down the steps at the other side.

"Come on!" shouted the train guard. John looked across and realised the guard was shouting at him. "We don't have all day y'know."

"Am cumin'. Am cumin'," John called out. He leaped the last few steps and trotted up to the door that the guard was holding open for him. The guard glanced at his watch. John threw in his kitbag and stepped aboard. The guard closed the door behind him. John leaned through the open window and flashed the guard a disarming smile. "Cheers, mate."

"Well…" the guard replied, disarmed by the smile, "I do my bit for the war effort. Now you go and do yours." And with that the guard raised his flag and blew his whistle. The engine's whistle peeped in reply and then the train lurched and clanked and pulled slowly out of the station, gathering pace with every passing yard.

John shuffled along the corridor of the carriage, looking for a vacant compartment. He soon found one, dropped his kitbag on a seat and sat himself next to it. He laid a forearm protectively across his kitbag, rested his head back against the corner of the seat and closed his eyes. But he couldn't sleep. He couldn't even relax. The moment allowed him too much time to dwell on events of the past. He couldn't stop himself from dwelling, and so he gave in to the urge and let his mind flit from one image to another. The ship; his shipmates; Headquarters; his mother in hospital; his long-dead wife; and his ditty-box at the bottom of the sea with the ink of her last letter diffusing into the water.

His thoughts were broken by the guard sliding open the compartment door and asking to check John's ticket. The ticket was checked and punched and the guard left John alone once again.

The train lurched and rounded a bend in the line, which brought the full brightness of the summer sunshine directly into his compartment. John closed his eyes to shield them from the sun. The pattern of the sun on the inside of his eyelids reminded him of The Pathway. The warmth of the sunshine radiating into the compartment felt comforting, and comfortable, and eventually John was induced into a doze.

He was woken a short while after by the opening of the compartment door. It was the guard.

"You headin' for Edinburgh?"

"Aye," replied John, stretching his arms up with a yawn.

"Change at the next station for the Edinburgh Express."

"Next stop? Oh, Aye. Cheers." John stifled another yawn and smiled at the guard, who nodded a humourless acknowledgement before leaving. John looked out of the window and vaguely recognised the approaching landscape of his home city: grey, industrial, and dirty; a forest of smoke-billowing chimneys dominating the skyline.

Within a few minutes of their arrival he was standing on the station concourse examining timetables, when he suddenly thought of his mother being visited by his "dead" father. What if he *had* visited her, after all? Could John do the same? Without a second thought, he slung his kitbag onto his shoulder and approached a station porter to negotiate the temporary deposit of his kitbag at the station.

Outside the station, John hailed a taxi from the nearby rank, and instructed the driver to take him to the mental hospital where his mother was a patient. But then, he thought that he might be made accountable for the money he had spent on the mission, so he apologised to the taxi driver and walked across the cobbled street to the bus and tram stop that was just a few yards away. Fortunately, the trams were regular and in less than fifteen minutes the tram arrived at its terminus at the city limits.

The entrance to the mental hospital was a further hundred yards or so beyond the terminus, and the driveway up to the hospital buildings cut across a rolling meadow that was fringed by mature sycamore. John recalled that as a child he'd pretended it wasn't really the driveway to a mental hospital: instead it was the driveway to the grand stately home where he pretended his mother had gone to live.

At the head of the driveway was the grand entrance to the once Victorian asylum, adorned by its clock tower and flanked by a thick canopy of sycamores. John could see an ambulance and a couple of parked cars next to the entrance. A nurse emerged from behind the ambulance and, walking in a busy-yet-not-rushed way, she entered the main hospital building.

John approached the entrance. A feeling of trepidation beat hard within his chest. He took a deep breath and walked in through the open door. After no more than five or six paces down the corridor a voice called out to him.

"Can I help you?" the nurse emerged from a side room.

"Erm... I've come to visit Celia Popplethwaite."

"And you are?"

"Er... a friend of her son. Can I visit her, please?"

"Popplethwaite...mmm," the nurse considered for a moment. "Oh, yes. I'm not sure whether you'll get to see her today, though. But we can ask Matron. Follow me." John followed her through some double doors and along a wide corridor painted entirely in white gloss paint, which was now scuffed and scratched after years of use. Here and there, a tile from the linoleum-tiled floor was also missing, revealing the pattern of the adhesive on the concrete beneath. John recalled the place being much less run-down in his childhood than it appeared now, but then again there was a war on.

"She's popular with visitors today," the nurse said, casually.

"Oh aye?"

But before the nurse could reply, a door to a side room further along the corridor opened and a man's head peered round the door. He looked anxious. John could hear wailing coming from inside room.

"Nurse! Your help please," the head said.

"Yes, Doctor," the nurse replied and then turned to John. "At the end of the corridor turn right. It's the first ward on your right. Loxley Ward." And she then scurried over to the doctor and disappeared into the room. The door closed behind her.

John stood for a moment and looked up and down the length of the corridor. There was no one else around, so he continued on his way. When he reached Loxley Ward, he peered in through the glass panel of the entrance door. He could see the ward desk situated a few feet away in the centre aisle of the ward. But there was no Matron. No nurses either. He scanned down the ward. There were only four patients in the ward, though there were beds for at least eight.

And then John saw his mother, Celia, at the far end of the ward, sitting in an armchair. She looked really old and frail, and a good twenty years older than her actual 52 years. She was still dressed in her nightshirt. John's heart quickened for a moment at the prospect of seeing and speaking to his mother again after such a long time. He pushed the door open slightly, but stopped when he realised that she already had a visitor with her. A giant of a man, in British Army uniform, was sat with her. John backed away into the corridor and eased the door back into place. He stood beside the door and carefully peeked in through the window. The visitor, who had his back to John, was preparing to leave: he stood up and briefly placed a large hand gently upon her shoulder. And when the visitor turned to leave, John saw that he had a heavily waxed moustache that partly obscured a pale and greasy complexion. The visitor smiled a sneering, satisfied smile, exposing half filled rows of crooked yellow teeth. John pulled quickly away from the window, suddenly breathless at this revelation. The man from the nightmare of his youth was alive! How could this be? John's hands felt clammy and his stomach turned cold. What should he do? What should he do? The butterflies in his stomach were in full flight when the rush of adrenaline took hold.

He should run.

And so he ran. And he ran faster than he had ever run in his entire life. As he careered out of the main entrance, he almost knocked over the nurse who had given him the earlier directions.

"Hey!" she shouted at him, and narrowed her furious eyes. "Be careful, will you!"

She then went into a small office just inside the entrance and reached for the telephone.

There was no question of John waiting for a tram. His confused mind believed it would be too dangerous to wait around unnecessarily. So when he reached the end of the Hospital driveway he kept on running; and ran along the main road towards the city.

He questioned his sanity over and over again. How could the German soldier from his nightmares turn up in a British Army uniform at his mother's bedside? It just couldn't be real. But he was clear about what he saw, and his fear was real. So he kept running.

The cocktail of fear and adrenaline delivered enough energy to help him run for a couple of miles into the city, which was probably further than he had ever run in his life. His legs ached and his body became increasingly heavy with fatigue, but he kept on running. Eventually his knees began to buckle and he staggering slowly on, until the point where he was barely at a walking pace. And then a taxi appeared, travelling out of the city. Breathless and exhausted, John almost fell into the road as he hailed it.

"What the..." exclaimed the driver when John opened the door and tumbled into the taxi, his cap skidding across the floor and coming to rest by the far passenger door.

"Help a stranded sailor, mate," panted John. "Emergency recall."

"Where to?"

"Can't tell yer," John rasped. "Careless talk costs lives."

"I mean, where d'you want taking?"

"Oh. Station."

"Yer look knackered. How far d'you run?"

"Uh? Dunno. Far enough." The taxi turned around and drove off towards the station. John's breathing began to return to some sort of normality and soon John had regained his physical composure. The taxi driver glanced at John through his rear view mirror.

"Surprising how many emergency recalls I pick up," the driver said, casually. John was instantly suspicious and a mild paranoia crept upon him. He frowned slightly, but the taxi driver explained with a grin. "So whose husband was chasin' yer then?" John realised the driver was making light conversation, and so he relaxed a little. He even felt the involuntary growth of a modest smile.

"Sorry, mate. Genuine recall this time," John lied.

"Oh. I hope things'll be alright for yer."

"Me too, mate. Me too." John reflected on his visit to his mother and, though not able to rationally explain his encounter, he inwardly berated himself for running away like a coward. He then berated himself for being suspicious of the taxi driver, but most of all he was disappointed with himself for not following his orders and for jeopardising everything. He decided he was not going to make the same mistake again.

JOURNEY NORTH

The taxi pulled onto the cobbled area at the front of the station and John paid the driver. Inside the station, John examined the timetables and collected his kitbag from the station office before crossing the enclosed footbridge that spanned the many platforms of the station.

He arrived at the platform at the rear of the station and waited for the arrival of the express train that he needed to catch to Edinburgh. The train pulled in a few minutes later, and John climbed aboard. He was placing his kitbag onto a seat when he glanced out of the window towards the station entrance. Six military policemen had entered the station. One of the MPs directed the others to the various corners and platforms of the station. They were obviously looking for something or someone.

Instinctively, John knew that that someone was him. He quickly removed his cap and tried to make himself as invisible as possible by pushing himself back as far as he could into his seat: sitting bolt upright, he pressed the back of his head firmly into the headrest and looked straight ahead. Three of the MPs climbed the footbridge and crossed over the platforms. One of them descended onto John's platform and, starting at the front of the train, the MP began to walk the length of the train, pausing at each of the windows of the carriages to scrutinise the passengers within. He had reached only the second carriage when the guard's whistle sounded, signalling the train's imminent departure. John paused for a moment and then cautiously leaned over to the window to see where the MP was. The MP, on hearing the whistle had walked to the door of the carriage nearest the engine. John watched him board the train.

John replaced his cap, grabbed his kitbag and opened the internal door that connected the compartment to the passageway that ran the length of the carriage. John dragged his kitbag down the passageway, and headed towards the rear of the train. At the end of the carriage he considered hiding in the toilet, but discarded this idea as a bit obvious, and in any case the toilet was so small he'd have to leave his kitbag outside. He decided that his best chance would be to head for the rear of the train and hope there was a mail-coach or something of the sort, where he could deposit his kitbag and hopefully hide himself amongst the cargo. It was at this point that John resolved, for the first time ever in his life, to resort to physical violence. He was determined to do anything, if necessary, to escape the MP and avoid arrest.

John was about two-thirds of the way down the length of the train when he entered the first class area. The carriages looked very similar to the others, a corridor along one side of the carriage, with several compartments down the other: but it was a lot cleaner, with carpeted flooring and nice lace on the headrests and armrests.

John carried on through the first class carriages and was almost at the rear of the train when the door to a compartment ahead of him opened and the head and shoulders of a naval officer peered out and glanced up and down the corridor before returning to the compartment, closing the door behind him. John stood stock still and was suddenly overwhelmed by a wish to turn himself invisible: he recognised the naval officer as his former commanding officer, Lieutenant Commander Ambrose. A few seconds later, the same door flew open again, but this time with a bang which made John flinch. Philip Ambrose stepped into the corridor and stood silently facing John. Philip stared thoughtfully, his eyes narrowed and his brow furrowed. John's face betrayed anguish and embarrassment. The silence seemed eternal to John, during which time his imagination caught fleeting images of the malign military policeman checking identities and moving nearer by the minute. Philip broke the silence.

"This is First Class, Chief," he said, tersely, "but as we are both travelling alone, you may join me." He indicated to John to enter the compartment. John muttered a simple thank you and dragged his kitbag into the compartment. Philip followed and closed the door behind him. They both sat and stared at each other for a moment. John was suddenly struck by the thought that his unmasking may actually provide him with the slimmest of opportunities for escape. This was no time for the timid. He steeled himself.

"What?" John heard himself say, involuntarily.

"I said, Popplethwaite," Philip replied, completely ignoring the lack of deference in John's voice. "You are Popplethwaite, aren't you?"

"Aye."

"So you're not dead."

"Nope."

"A telegram was sent. Your name was listed as missing-presumed-lost."

"Oh aye? Well, in that case I am dead," John replied. He scrutinised Philip's surprised reaction and then noticed that Philip was looking at his new uniform.

"I also recall that you were listed as a Leading Hand. And during my time as your commanding officer I don't ever recall your promotion to Petty Officer, let alone promotion to Chief."

"Nope."

"Explain yourself."

"Well," John took a deep breath and began to ramble, "now, I know this is going to sound right daft and a bit far fetched – well a lot far fetched – but I were trapped down the Tiller Flat when we got bombed, but I were rescued by going down some tunnel of fire with this bloke – well I think he's a bloke – who works for some sort of secret department. Then I went to some secret house in the country, but we had to hide from some sort of flying demon things on the way. Anyway, when we got there his gaffer told me that I'm dead but not really dead, if you get my drift: just my name's dead." Philip looked impassively at John, who continued, defensively. "So they gave me a new one – name, that is – made me up to a Chief and told me I had to go to Scotland to be a bodyguard for some kid who seems to be really important to the war effort for some reason. Anyway, there are loads of baddies – some sort of devil worshipers called Maligns. They want to kill the kid, I think. And they want to make the war a lot worse for everybody. I think they're linked up with Hitler's lot, but I'm not really sure. And now some of them are after me, there's one dressed as an MP, and he's on the train. I need you to help me escape from them."

A moment passed before Philip calmly spoke.

"So, to summarise, you're actually on the run."

"Only from them," John pointed towards the front of the train.

"The military policeman."

"Aye."

"Because you're actually a deserter?"

"No!" John's defensive tone increased in pitch.

"No, *Sir*!" Philip raised his voice.

"Look, *Sir*." John felt a wave of anger flush his cheeks and grip is stomach, and so he stood up to leave. He should have known that his old Captain wouldn't help, and he was wasting precious time. "You can believe me or not, but I am not stopping for nobody. I'm not a deserter. I've got a job to do." And with that he made for the door.

"Popplethwaite," Philip calmly reached up and grabbed John's arm, "I want to help." John turned and looked at Philip.

"Oh aye?"

"Really. Now sit down." John sat back down and they stared at each other for a few moments. The wave of anger slowly ebbed away, although it left an indelible trace of obstinate determination that was obvious in John's attitude. John noticed that his little outburst had done nothing to rouse any outward appearance of anger from his old commanding officer. Either nothing could anger this officer, thought John, or he was a bloody good actor.

"My new name is Drummond," John eventually said.

"What?"

"Chief Petty Officer John Drummond. The new name they gave me." John fished out his new identity papers and passed them to Philip who opened them and gave them a brief examination. "Deserters don't normally get issued with new identities, do they?" continued John, "and even if they did they'd hardly try for promotion would they? They'd probably go for some civvie identity and pretend they were medically discharged – y'know, wounded or whatever."

"Maybe," replied Philip, sceptically. "Remind me, what was your action station on board?"

"Tiller Flat."

"Did you sustain any damage down there?"

"A few ruptured pipes, I think. Caused a bit of flooding; nowt really that serious if the hatch had been lifted for me. But it were them bastards up top that went and left me trapped down below." Philip blushed slightly and looked away, momentarily embarrassed. Nonetheless, his interest was fully engaged by John's story. John continued, "Couldn't get the hatch open by myself, could I? And I'd have gone for a Burton if Marcus hadn't rescued me."

"So you escaped; and without injury?" Philip asked.

"Sort of. Well, I banged my head. And my wrist is still a bit stiff. But no broken bones or owt like that."

"You said you were trapped, and yet you escaped death," Philip remarked.

"It were Marcus and his Pathway that saved me. He said there was a 'tin fish' goin' to finish off the ship, so I had to go with him if I wanted to live. To be honest, I thought I was already dead – 'thought he was an angel or something. But they came later, o' course."

"Really?" replied Philip, thoughtfully stroking his chin.

John held an index finger and thumb very close together.

"Y'know, Sir, I've been about *this* close to death loads of times in the last few days." John sounded strangely proud of his achievement.

"Haven't we all?" Philip replied, flatly.

They stared at one another again, considering their next move. John had expected his old commanding officer to blow into a rage, or at least show some anger, but he seemed remarkably calm.

"John – it is John, isn't it?" Philip asked. John nodded in reply. "Times have changed a lot over the years, John. Doctors can treat shell shock, quite effectively these days."

"Shell shock?" John was a little puzzled by this statement.

"You'll probably still be court-martialled," continued Philip, "but I can get you seen by the right doctors…"

"You think I'm mad!" John angrily stood up and reached for the door. This time Philip made no move to stop him.

"I think you need help," Philip said.

"Yeah, but not that kind of help." John opened the door and dragged his kitbag into the corridor. His stomach once again felt tight in the grip of nervous anxiety, and he felt his hands and knees begin to shake slightly. "Tell you what, if you want to help; when that MP checks your papers just say 'Malign the Lord, His end is near' and see what response you get. If he admits to being a Malign you pull rank on him and tell him to go back to the front of the train and to get off at the next station." And with that, John slammed the door shut and stormed off down the corridor towards the rear of the train.

Philip remained seated. He sighed and muttered, "Bloody War." He closed his eyes but kept his head facing straight ahead, which made him look like he was in meditation rather than asleep. But then the train lurched, and Philip opened his eyes and looked around. His attention was momentarily drawn to the window, and to the distant landscape, where emerald hills were being showered by a curtain of rain that hung beneath a single, dark cloud in an otherwise clear sky.

Then, suddenly, this view was abruptly interrupted by a sneering red demon that appeared in full view outside Philip's window. It was flying above the track that ran alongside the train. Philip gasped and physically recoiled at the terrible sight. The demon raised a fist and moved as if to punch at Philip's window, but it did not get the chance to complete its punch. A speeding express train, travelling in the opposite direction, thundered past and the demon was swept from view by the blur of the passing carriages. Within a short moment the express train had passed, and the view from the window was once again unbroken countryside. The demon was gone.

Philip was shocked. He tentatively stood up and leaned towards the window to see if there was any trace of the demon. He could see none.

The door to the compartment opened behind him.

"'Scuse me, Sir," a voice asked. Philip swung round. It was the military policeman. Philip gave the MP a hard stare.

"Malign the Lord, His end is near," the words seemed to fall quite naturally from Philip's lips.

"Erm..." replied the MP, momentarily taken aback, but he quickly composed himself, bowed his head and replied in a very serious and solemn tone "His end is near."

Philip continued to stare at the MP. The MP finally looked up.

"Sorry, Sir. Am I interrupting?" he said.

"Of course you are," Philip replied, curtly. "Now go back from whence you came," he pointed to the front of the train, "and get off at the next station."

"But I have..."

"You have no idea who I am or what I am doing. So, do as I order." A hint of anger could be heard in his raised voice. "NOW!" he shouted. The MP flinched and backed out of the compartment hurriedly.

"Y-yes, Sir," the MP said, closed the door and scurried up the corridor towards the front of the train, grumbling to himself.

Philip stood still for a moment, as if glued to the carpet, his body swayed slightly with the movement of the train. His eyes flickered rapidly with thought, and then he grabbed hold of the door handle and opened the door. He grabbed his suitcase from the luggage rack, stepped into the corridor and made his way towards the rear of the train.

In the rearmost compartment of the rearmost carriage he found John, alone and looking very glum. Philip opened the compartment door.

"The demons you spoke of, are they reddish in colour? They fly but do not flap their wings, have nasty expressions upon their faces, and have a penchant for violence?"

John's spirits were heartily raised before Philip had completed his description.

"Aye," he answered as calmly as he could, the crease of an emerging smile just visible in the corner of his mouth. "You met one, then?"

"Yes, and I ordered the military policeman off the train, just like you asked."

"Cheers, Sir," replied John. Philip threw his suitcase onto the luggage rack above John's head and sat himself down heavily beside John.

"Now, Popplethwaite, or whatever your name is now, this is most confusing. So, tell me everything, and spare me no detail."

And so, over the remainder of their journey north, John told an astonished Philip every detail of his incredible story; of his rescue, of his Renaissance and of his mission.

INTERCEPTION

It was a lovely, sunny, late summer's afternoon, and the sun continued to throw down its heat onto the hills of unbroken pine forest that stretched across the horizon. In the far distance, a solitary black cloud doused the furthest hill with an enviously refreshing downpour.

Along the lower slopes of the nearest hill ran a narrow, dusty lane, and along this lane a dark green staff car travelled at speed. The ruts, bumps and potholes in the uneven surface caused the car to shake and rattle.

Mr Forsyth was perspiring heavily, as usual, and he squirmed involuntarily in the hot confines of the car. Tickling beads of sweat rolled down each cheek of his face; and no doubt too between the sweating cheeks of his ample and uncomfortable backside.

"My word, Perkins, it's damned hot in here," Mr Forsyth panted, tugging at his collar, and seemingly short of breath. "This must be one of the warmest days we've had all summer."

"Try stickin' your head out o' the window, Sir," offered Perkins. The windows were already wide open, but it had very little cooling effect. "It might help a bit." But Mr Forsyth cast Perkins a scolding look.

"I'm not a dog, Perkins," he answered sharply. Perkins shrugged, and allowed a smile to creep across his face.

"Works for me when I get too hot."

"Yes, yes. Well, I'm not you, and I prefer to maintain my dignity... and you should keep your eye on the road; not your head out of the window. At least whilst I'm in the car, anyway."

"Yes, Sir." Perkins struggled to conceal his amusement at Mr Forsyth's discomfort.

The high temperature in the suffocating confinement of the small staff car seemed to be turning an ordinarily uncomfortable journey into an extremely unpleasant experience for Mr Forsyth. The same could not be said for Perkins, who seemed to be handling the heat remarkably well. Mr Forsyth picked up a large buff document-folder from his knee and began wafting his sweating forehead, with questionable success. Patches of excess sweat had grown steadily outward from Mr Forsyth's armpits and now large swathes of his uniform were thoroughly soaked. He repeatedly used a soiled and soaking handkerchief to clear the sweat that was accumulating in his eyebrows.

As their journey continued, Mr Forsyth's complexion turned progressively more pallid, and his demeanour became increasingly irritable.

The car shuddered violently through one particular pothole and Mr Forsyth half-glanced over his shoulder, as if expecting to see pieces of the car scattered across the lane behind them. But nothing could be seen through the cloud of dust that they created in their wake.

"Must you aim for the largest potholes, Perkins?"

"Sorry, Sir. Thought I was missing them."

"Well, be more careful. All this bouncing and banging about is making me feel quite ill."

"Yes, Sir. Sorry, Sir. But you said..."

"I know what I said, but I also want to be conscious and coherent when we arrive."

"Yes, Sir," Perkins replied, and reduced the speed, just a little.

The lane ahead of them ran straight for about a quarter of a mile and, in the approaching distance, there was a checkpoint manned by several British soldiers. The checkpoint consisted of a sandbagged machinegun emplacement on one side of the lane, with an army truck parked behind it, just visible in the trees. As the car approached, a soldier standing in the centre of the lane held up an arm and gestured the car to stop. Perkins slowed.

"I don't recall being briefed about any encampment or checkpoints around here," said Perkins.

"Really?" observed Mr Forsyth.

"And it wasn't here when I came through the other day, Sir, that's for sure."

"Hmm. Let's wait and see, shall we, Perkins."

"Yes, Sir," Perkins replied, and pulled the car up at the side of the soldier. Perkins kept one hand on the wheel and one hand on the gear-stick.

"'Evening, Sir," the soldier said, impassively. The stripes of a corporal were on his sleeve and at the shoulder of his sleeve were the letters KOYLI. "Can I see your identification, please."

"Certainly, corporal," replied Mr Forsyth. "Go and fetch your sergeant. I want to speak to him." The corporal stared blankly in response to the request, but complied by stepping away from the car to call his sergeant. There was no reply. After a moment of waiting the corporal wandered over to the army truck, and went around the other side, calling for his sergeant. Mr Forsyth surveyed the checkpoint, whilst fidgeting anxiously with his sweaty shirt-collar.

"Bit rude aren't they, Sir?" Perkins whispered out of the side of his mouth. "Don't they see you're a Brigadier?"

"Quite, quite," Mr Forsyth replied in a quiet murmur.

Perkins allowed the car to slowly creep forward a couple of feet. The machine gunners, who were toying nervously with their weapon, took aim at the car. Perkins immediately halted the car. He craned forward to try to see where the corporal had gone, but he quickly sat back, bolt upright in his seat.

"Bloody, hell, Sir," Perkins said in a startled whisper, "they're talking to a bloody demon!" Mr Forsyth glanced uneasily across to Perkins.

"Surely not, Perkins," he replied. "Surely you're mistaken?"

"No I ain't."

"Oh, dear. So what do you propose we do?"

"Well, I don't want stay to find out what they want, Sir."

"So what do you propose?" Mr Forsyth asked, again.

"This," Perkins replied. He revved the engine and jerked his foot from the clutch. The wheels dug into the gravel and the car raced away in a cloud of dust and stones. The machine gunners hesitated momentarily, glancing at each other, unsure as to whether they should open fire. After a few seconds of deliberation, the machine gun opened fire and spat several rounds at the rapidly departing car. Fortunately for the occupants of the car, the magazine belt jammed and the gun stopped firing. The gunners began tackling the jam, but the corporal reappeared in a hurry and frantically yelled at the machine gunner not to re-open fire. It was also good fortune that the aim of the gunner seemed unprofessionally poor. Only one bullet had entered the car through a rear window, and this had exited through the windscreen, shattering it and obscuring Perkins' vision of the road ahead. Perkins kept up the speed, regardless of this handicap.

"I can't see a flaming thing," he yelled whilst trying to push out the shattered screen with his elbow.

"Slow down, then!" Mr Forsyth shouted, and leaned into the back of the car to grab his jacket from the back seat, now strewn with the shards of the shattered rear screen. He used the jacket to protect his hands as he cleared the glass from the windscreen.

"Cheers, Sir. You know, I knew there was something fishy when he didn't salute you. I bet you did, eh, Sir?"

"Yes, quite."

Perkins hurled the car almost uncontrollably along the lane. He glanced in his rear view mirror for any sign of pursuit.

"Bloody hell!" he said.

"What is it?" Mr Forsyth turned around and saw that a demon was rapidly closing in on them. "Oh, er, I see."

"My rifle is on the floor in the back, Sir," offered Perkins, "You could shoot at it."

"Bullets pass through demons, Perkins, you should know that by now."

"What shall we do, then, Sir?" asked Perkins. "What's the plan?"

"Yes, yes. The plan," replied Mr Forsyth. But time was not a commodity that they possessed. The demon soon caught up with them and flew alongside the car. It glared in through the driver's window. Mr Forsyth simply ignored the demon and stared at the lane ahead. Perkins saw the demon and simply raised the two-finger 'V' sign, which he aimed squarely at the demon in a last act of desperate defiance. The demon growled and tried to shoulder-barge the car off the lane. Perkins jumped on the brake pedal and yanked at the steering wheel, which sent the car careering down a secondary track deeper into the woods. The demon did not respond quickly enough to Perkins' sudden manoeuvre and on its next shoulder-barge, it missed the car completely and crashed into the trees. For a moment it was out of sight. Then it reappeared behind them, pausing only to remove foliage and twigs from its wings. It angrily shook its fist, and let out a howling scream that was frightening enough to make the hair on the back of any man's neck stand on end.

"He don't sound happy, Sir," Perkins said, now looking extremely anxious at the turn of events.

"Yes, yes. Thank you for that observation, Perkins. Do you know of any other ways to anger a demon?"

"Er..."

The howling stopped and the demon paused to focus itself on the car ahead. It took a deep breath and then launched itself at the car like a bullet. Neither occupant was aware of the incredible speed of the demon's approach. Suddenly, the demon burst through the rear window of the car, showering the occupants with shattered glass and debris. But the demon didn't stop there; such was the momentum of its flight that it continued through the cabin of the car and out through where the windscreen once was. The force of the demon's flight was devastating, and the energy of the impact almost tore the roof from the car.

Perkins was knocked into a semi-conscious delirium and lost control of the car, which careered off the track and into the trees. The car scythed through a swathe of saplings, and then ploughed through a patch of rough and rocky ground. Finally, the car was brought to an undignified halt when it struck a modest-sized boulder, which embedded itself under a shattered, steaming engine.

The demon flew down to the car and opened the driver's door. Perkins slumped out, his face spattered with blood. He grinned deliriously up at the demon, displaying the split lips and the bloodied gaps in his teeth that had resulted from him hitting his face against the steering wheel. The demon stared at him for a moment, and then looked around at the ground before picking up a rock about the size of a water melon. The demon stood over Perkins' prostrate body and raised the rock above its head with both hands. Perkins moaned and tried to raise an arm to shield himself. The demon howled once again and then brought the rock down violently onto Perkins' head. There was a dull crunch and Perkins' legs twitched as his life left him.

Satisfied that Perkins was dead, the demon walked around to the passenger door. He opened the door and it fell from its hinges onto the ground. Mr Forsyth was unconscious, half thrown through the windowless windscreen. The demon grabbed him and lifted him from the car and laid him on the ground beside the car. Unsure whether Mr Forsyth was dead or alive the demon sniffed around Mr Forsyth's face and listened for signs of breathing. Content that he was alive, the demon picked Mr Forsyth up, slung his limp body over its shoulder and flew off in the direction of the army checkpoint.

The demon landed a few yards from the army checkpoint. The sergeant jumped down from the rear of the truck. He was fuming; and his face was incandescent with rage.

"What were all that racket?" he yelled, pointing in the direction of the car wreck. "You trying to get us all caught?" The demon looked at the sergeant blankly and spoke in a slow, deep, nasally voice.

"Um…"

"Don't give me that 'um' crap," the sergeant said and threw his arms up in resignation. "Right. We'd best get going, then, before 'Tommy-and-his-missus' turns up." He turned to the young soldiers manning the machine gun, "Well? What yer waiting fer? A written invite?" The young soldiers jumped up and began dismantling the machine gun emplacement with remarkable speed and efficiency. The sergeant turned to the demon, "Come and give us hand with him, then." They both looked at Mr Forsyth's unconscious bulk and then the demon picked him up and gingerly placed him in the back of the truck. The corporal climbed up into the back of the truck and reached for a beige satchel with a large red cross painted on it.

"I don't think anything's broke, but I'll keep an eye on him just in case," the corporal said.

"He'd best not die or we're all for it."

"Don't have to tell me," replied the corporal, who pointed at the demon, whose back was now turned to them, "tell dumb-dust over there." The demon, sensing that they were talking about it, looked over its shoulder at them and snarled. The sergeant walked over to the demon.

"He'd better not die," he warned. "What happened to his driver?"

"Um… dead," the demon said and hung its head, subdued.

"Oh, great! You weren't meant to kill anyone!"

"Made me angry. Wouldn't stop."

"Stoopid bloody demon!" the sergeant began waving his arms about agitatedly. "And just how are they meant to find out we've kidnapped Forsyth if you go and kill his bloody driver?"

"Um…"

"Right. We need a proper doctor to have a look at Forsyth. And seen as you demolished his car and knocked him senseless you can go and tell Daephanocles… and get an ambulance while yer at it, we need one of them too."

"Um," the Demon thought about this for a moment. "Doctor. Ambulance."

"Yeah," the Sergeant said in a patronisingly slow voice, "an Army one. And tell Daephanocles what *you* did to Forsyth. I'm not getting blamed for this mess."

"Um. Meet here?"

"Bloody hell, no!" the Sergeant said, and pointed down the lane towards the late afternoon sun. "At the end of this lane there's a main road that runs along the edge of the forest. On that road is a pub. Travellers Rest, I think. Get the ambulance to meet us there. We'll be round the back keepin' out o sight."

"Um. Travellers."

"Yeah. Travellers." The sergeant shooed the demon away, "Go on. Get a move on, we haven't got all day."

The demon sneered and began grumbling as it took to the sky and flew off just above the tree tops.

The sergeant shouted after the demon, "And try to keep out of sight!" And as the sergeant walked back to the truck he muttered under his breath, "Stoopid bloody demons…"

The machine gun emplacement was now completely dismantled and everything was packed onto the truck. One of the soldiers, who had broad shoulders and a muscular build, came over to the sergeant.

"All packed and ready to go."

"Good lad. Remember that pub we went to last night?"

"What about it?"

"We need to go back there and wait for orders… and hopefully a doc and ambulance. God knows how we're meant to get him onto a bloody train for Scotland in this state." The soldier nodded and climbed into the driver's seat of the cab. The sergeant climbed into the back of the truck. The truck rumbled into life and proceeded cautiously down the lane.

The sergeant placed a gentle hand on Mr Forsyth's forehead and turned to the corporal.

"Do you think he'll make it?" he asked.

The corporal shrugged.

"Just knocked unconscious, I think."

An hour or so later, a military ambulance pulled into the courtyard behind the Travellers Rest pub. The soldiers helped Mr Forsyth, who had regained some level of consciousness, to stagger into the ambulance, which then departed, under escort, towards the nearby village railway station.

JOHN AND AGNES

John had been watching the cottage for quite a while, and his backside was now quite numb from sitting for so long on the cold kerbstones outside the churchyard at the top of the street. So, John stood up, stretched his legs and slowly paced a couple of yards either side of the churchyard's gate to relieve the numbness. The cottage was only about thirty yards away, and at no time did his gaze leave it. He'd not seen anyone enter or leave the cottage the entire time he was watching, and he'd almost convinced himself that there was nobody at home.

A grocer's delivery boy cycled past with a fully laden cycle-basket, which John presumed was destined for the vicarage just around the corner. At the sight of the food that was piled up in the delivery basket, his stomach rumbled, loudly. John was very hungry, and he reached into his pockets in search of something to eat. But there was no food left: he'd long since eaten the few biscuits that he had brought with him from the WRVS catering van at Edinburgh railway station. Nonetheless, his hunger demanded that he check his pockets anyway, just in case.

It would be dark very soon. And the late evening sky began to darken. Some rain-clouds drifted across the fading sun, and the churchyard and streets were left overcast and cool. A brief feeling of chilliness swept over him, and he shivered involuntarily. He knew that he was simply delaying the inevitable and was allowing his apprehension to get the better of his judgement.

It was the right cottage, number 12, and he saw no evidence to suggest that any Maligns were around. He'd done his best to make sure that nobody had followed him from the station, so there was no credible reason for him not to at least knock on the door, if only to see whether there was anyone at home.

But something intuitive had prevented him from walking the last few yards to the cottage. It was a peculiar kind of apprehension that he couldn't quite explain. Maybe he was just being over-cautious, making sure that the coast was clear. Maybe he was just scared of the unknown. But, whatever the subconscious reasons for his procrastination, John was aware that entering that cottage would mark the beginning of his mission in earnest, and his instinct warned him that things were about to get a whole lot more dangerous.

In the end it was hunger and the prospect of an imminent Scottish soaking that finally propelled John into approaching the cottage. He made no conscious decision to do so; and he realised he was approaching the cottage only when he reached the neighbouring house.

John's hearing was on a razor sharp alert and he listened for any noise that might be out of the ordinary. But it was a fairly quiet part of the village and nothing struck him as being out of the ordinary. He crossed the front of Number 12 and peered through the front window, but he saw nothing other than the blackout curtains drawn across the window. He didn't think this was unusual, for the time of the evening.

The front door had two frosted glass window panels in the upper half, and John looked closely to see whether there was any movement within. But there was none. John grasped the small black knocker, took a deep breath and knocked firmly three times. He stepped back from the door and studied the cottage for any sign of movement within. Nothing stirred within the house for several minutes. He was about to give up and return to the kerbstones at the top of the street when… he saw movement. Through the frosted glass he could see the faint silhouette of a short, slender, feminine figure slowly approach the door. The door chains were fastened on, the bolts were drawn back and the door was unlocked. The door creaked slowly open and Agnes's head peered cautiously around the edge of the door to view her visitor. She took one look at John and her eyes widened with shock and surprise. Her complexion drained of colour and her face betrayed the wave of sickening embarrassment which had suddenly engulfed her.

"Oh, my God!" she cried and slammed the door shut.

Seeing Agnes's face again, and under these particular circumstances, was just as big a shock for John. Her sudden, aggressive exclamation, and the slam of the door, sent him reeling into the street. He was speechless with the shock. Agnes's silhouette could still be seen through the glass. She remained behind the door, and stood with her back against the hallway wall. After a few agonising moments she leaned over to the door, slipped off the chain and slowly re-opened the door until it was wide open. And for the first time in six, long years, John saw the beautiful figure of his beloved, and supposedly dead, wife. She didn't look quite as skinny as she did when she was younger. The years had made her look somehow more mature and grown-up, rather than older, and John thought this made her look all the more attractive for it. She wore a knee-length dark blue skirt, a white blouse and an unbuttoned, dark blue knitted cardigan. Agnes stood with her back against the hallway wall and stared intently at the linoleum flooring.

The butterflies that were taking flight from John's stomach caused a sickly feeling, and his legs began to weaken a little. He stepped up to the doorway.

He thought he should say something.

"Agnes?" he said, quietly.

"You'd best come in," she said flatly, and then pointed down the hallway towards the rearmost rooms of the house. John stepped over the threshold without taking his eyes off her and then paused momentarily beside her. She would not meet his eye; instead she stared firmly at the floor. Suddenly, he was consumed by a wave of embarrassment and humiliation, which caused his butterflies to fall silent. His face flushed briefly, but then his embarrassment turned quickly to rejection and, like a rebuffed child, he marched indignantly down the hallway, past the staircase, and into one of the back rooms of the house. Agnes leaned out of the doorway and glanced warily up and down the street before she closed the door, locked it and bolted it firmly.

When the door closed, a giant of a soldier, dressed in British Army uniform, emerged from the shadows behind a large marble monument that had concealed his presence in the churchyard. A heavily waxed moustache partly obscured his pale and greasy complexion. The soldier stepped forward until he reached the gate of the churchyard, where he paused to survey the view of the street below. He sneered with an ugly, self-satisfied smile that exposed his half-filled rows of crooked yellow teeth.

"Can I help you?" said a polite voice behind him. It was the vicar, a slight, balding man in his early sixties, who had just appeared out of the vestry door of the church and was now in the process of locking it.

The soldier cast a scornful glance in the direction of the vicar and continued to observe the empty street. When the vestry door was locked, the vicar merrily crossed the grass to the soldier, whilst expertly swinging the medieval-sized ring of heavy keys in his fingers.

"Hello, my son," he called cheerfully. "Is there something I can help you with?"

The vicar was initially startled when the soldier suddenly spun around upon him, but then became strangely transfixed by the soldier's dark eyes, which gradually turned a fiery shade of scarlet. A dawning realisation crept across the vicar's face as the soldier's eyes began to blaze with a malevolence of volcanic ferocity. The keys slipped from his hand and he stumbled backwards.

"God have mercy!" he gasped breathlessly, but it was too late. The soldier growled menacingly and advanced upon the helpless cleric. Before the vicar had time to react, the soldier grasped the vicar savagely by the throat and with just one of his large grimy hands he mercilessly strangled his victim until all signs of life had departed. The vicar finally stopped struggling and the soldier dragged the limp corpse into the shadows behind the large marble monument. He then returned to his surveillance of the street.

Meanwhile, inside number 12, Agnes followed John into one of the back rooms. It was quite a large room, and probably part of a ground floor extension built sometime over the long life of the property. John first thought he was entering the dining room, or was it the living room? He couldn't quite decide because the room had both living room and dining room furniture in it. The dining table and four chairs were placed nearest to the doorway. Further along the room, beyond the ceramic tiled fireplace, there was a dark leather settee and a matching leather armchair. At the side of the armchair, there was a lamp standard that softly illuminated the room. And next to this was a small table upon which there was a big, heavy-looking, wireless that was quietly playing some sort of big band music.

John pulled out a dining chair and sat down. Agnes crossed the room, switched off the wireless and sat down on the settee. Her posture was upright and tense; her hands grasped her knees and she stared at the floor, mortified. John attempted to make eye contact, but Agnes was having none of it.

After this further rebuff he resolved not to be the next to speak. He was no longer angry with her; after all she looked far more shocked than he was. Instead, he would let her speak when she was ready to.

He leaned back into the chair and allowed the surreal circumstances of their reunion to wash over him. He could not resist admiring the beauty of the woman now sat before him. She looked lovelier now than she did when he bade her farewell at the end of his leave all those years ago. He noted that her hair was shorter than it used to be, but her figure was still very... well, very attractive. His thoughts wandered to more sensual matters and, when he realised the insensitive direction of his thoughts, he suddenly felt awkward and embarrassed, particularly when he could see how shocked her expression remained. He broke off his gaze and instead stared at the table top, and distracted himself by using his index finger to slowly trace out the grain of the wood.

"They never told me," Agnes eventually said in a tense, matter of fact tone. John glanced over. She was still staring at the floor, "They should have told me."

"Aye?" he replied softly. "Well, they never told me, either." There was a pause. "Why's that, do you reckon?" he asked, but she just shrugged in reply. John naturally speculated on what might have led to Agnes's own 'Renaissance' and her assignment to this mission. He unexpectedly heard himself say, "I never thought for a minute you might have been chosen as well."

Agnes fidgeted awkwardly, but she remained silent.

And then another thought suddenly struck him.

"Bloody hell! Does this mean we're still... married... or what?" he blurted, without even realising the words had passed his lips. John was wholly unprepared for the possibility that he was somehow probably still married, and he wasn't sure whether she would still love him after all these years apart. Agnes looked up at him. They stared into each other's eyes and, for one fleeting moment, he thought he recognised that look that told him that deep in her heart she still carried a love for him. Maybe, just maybe, she still thought of herself as his wife. He hoped.

And then John's stomach decided to unceremoniously interrupt them. It rumbled, hungrily. Agnes tried to suppress a smile. Maybe it was wishful thinking on his part but her smile made him feel warm. It gave him an adolescent-like feeling of light-headedness that he had not felt since he had first fallen in love with her, all those years ago. He grinned at her. This unexpected ice-breaker relieved some, but not all, of the tension from the moment. Agnes relaxed her posture.

"Sorry," he said, "bit hungry."

"You'll be needing some tea, then," she said and rose from the settee and crossed the room to the door. John stood up and gently took her hand. She paused and looked at him, without making eye contact. The softness of her skin and the proximity of her breath made his heart race and his mouth go dry. He swallowed, nervously.

"Do you believe in second chances?" he muttered. Agnes smiled weakly, looked away and continued with her own conversation.

"Sausage and mash do you? It's the boy's favourite," she said.

John, disappointed, let her hand slip from his and she went into the kitchen. 'And it's my favourite too, remember,' he wanted to tell her. But, of course, he knew that she already knew it was.

Suddenly, he remembered the boy. Of course! How could he forget! John rapidly refocused his mind on the purpose of his mission. He smacked himself gently on the forehead. He'd not seen the boy, yet, and so he called after Agnes.

"Where is he, anyway?"

"Upstairs. Told him to stay up there 'til it were safe to come down."

"And is it?"

"'suppose so."

And as if the boy could hear them talking, there was a short thunder of feet on the staircase as the boy hurried downstairs. He jumped the last few steps.

"Did you say bangers and mash?" he called, as he swung off the banister at the foot of the stairs.

"Yes, love. Do you want some?"

"Yeh-eh!" he replied, excitedly, and ran down the hall into the kitchen to Agnes, who was by this time busily preparing the meal.

"Aren't you going to say hello to your new guardian?" she asked.

"Oh. Yeah," the boy replied in a voice that sounded suddenly drained of enthusiasm. He popped his head round the door of the dining room and looked at John.

"Hello," the boy said.

"Hello," replied John. He stood up and offered a handshake. "My name's John. What's yours?" The boy frowned and cast John one of those 'are you being thick?' glances. The boy returned the handshake.

"Boy," was the eventual reply. "They call me Boy."

"What, don't you have a first name?"

"Boy."

"And what about your family name?"

"Not got one."

"Well, what was your dad called?" John asked, but the boy simply shrugged.

"Dun't know," he replied and trotted back into the kitchen and asked Agnes, "are we having onion gravy with it?"

"If you like, love."

John reflected on his first encounter with the boy and smiled. He wondered what on earth all the fuss was about with this boy. He seemed just like any other ordinary boy; nothing particularly special. Probably an orphan, but then that was hardly uncommon these days.

The sound of Agnes's voice in the kitchen, the sizzling of the sausages in the pan and the wafting aroma of fried onions, revived warm memories of their early married life. John took in a deep breath and relaxed. He felt the warmest and most relaxed that he could remember in a long time. He felt strangely content, and the painful memories of Agnes's terrible drowning seemed somehow less raw, now. In fact, they now began to fade like an unhappy dream from which he had finally awoken.

ARRESTED

John and the boy enjoyed their meal. It was only a simple affair, but it was nonetheless devoured with the enthusiasm of a hearty banquet. Hardly a full sentence was spoken whilst they ate, although there were many grunts of gratitude, and half-intelligible compliments to the cook. John, as always, was the first to finish, and mopped up the remnants of his gravy with a crusty chunk of bread. He pushed his empty plate forward an inch or so, pushed his chair back an inch or two and relaxed with all the nourished contentment of an indulged medieval monarch. He patted his full stomach affectionately.

"That were a right drop o' good," he said.

"Glad you approve," Agnes replied. John leaned over to the boy and whispered, loudly.

"She were always a good cook," he said and glanced across at Agnes for her reaction. She did not react, and so he continued, "Made some right lovely pies an' all, at one time." The boy looked thoughtfully at John and Agnes whilst he chewed on a chunk of sausage. Eventually, he swallowed it and spoke up.

"'That when you were married, then?" he asked.

Agnes almost choked on a mouthful of mashed potato, at the boy's remark. She quickly pulled a handkerchief from her sleeve and dabbed away the gravy that was running down her chin. John smiled and leaned over the table to her.

"Missed a bit," he said and gently wiped away a tiny drop from the side of her mouth with his finger. "You've got good hearing, eh, Boy?"

"Did you fall out, then?" the boy continued.

"Nope," John replied, firmly. He had no intention of discussing how he became a 'widower' with the boy, particularly as he and Agnes could still be married. "And we're still good friends," he added. The boy opened his mouth to speak again but Agnes raised her finger to interrupt him.

"Ah-ah," she said, quietly but firmly, "come on and finish your tea, love." The boy glanced across at John for support and was about to protest when, suddenly, there was a knock at the front door. The three of them froze.

"Expecting anybody else?" John whispered as he rose from the table. Agnes shook her head. She had a worried look on her face. The knocking continued, so John cautiously approached the doorway of the room and glanced carefully around the edge of the door frame to see down the hallway. He could see several silhouettes through the frosted glass of the front door, but couldn't decide whether they were friendly or not. He slipped across the hall and tip-toed silently up the stairs and crossed an upstairs bedroom to take a look at the darkened street through the side of the drawn curtains. He saw a car parked at the other side of the street. And then a military truck pulled up, out of which jumped several soldiers wearing ammunition belts and carrying riffles. John immediately recognised it as some kind of patrol, possibly attached to the police. John's stomach tightened and he reflected on the disadvantages of eating such a large meal before vigorous exercise, especially as he would probably have to fight them in order to defend Agnes and the boy.

But then, of course, he knew fighting would be pointless. For a start he was outnumbered, and they had guns. John had nothing other than his wit to defend Agnes and the boy with. He muttered something akin to 'bugger' and slipped back downstairs. The banging on the door intensified, with an urgency that caused John's heartbeat to quicken. He began to feel sick.

"Army patrol. Loads of 'em," he said. "We've got to get out. Get yer things, quick."

"No time for that," Agnes replied, "they'll be in any second. Come on, boy." She jumped up from her seat, grabbed the boy and dragged him into the kitchen and to the back door. "You keep 'em busy," she called back to John and then pulled the kitchen door closed behind her. John heard the back door of the cottage open and close as Agnes and the boy fled.

He couldn't recall Agnes ever behaving as decisive or as focused as she did then. He felt a small swell of pride rise inside him, and this gave him just enough encouragement to begin the slow walk towards the front door.

As he approached the door, he steeled himself for a struggle, but then the banging ceased and there was a sudden crash as the door was violently kicked open. The glass shattered and splinters of wood from around the lock and bolts were flung along the hallway. John stared mutely down the barrel of a rifle and, at that moment, he realised that there was nothing more he could do but wait for the inevitable crack of the bullet that would kill him.

But to his surprise and relief, the soldier aiming the weapon simply maintained his aim and shouted, "Get your hands up, NOW!" John immediately obliged. Another soldier, a private of rather muscular build, slipped past the first and grappled John to the ground, face down.

John lay prostrate and helpless, with the weight of the soldier's knee digging painfully into the small of his back. The linoleum felt cold on his cheek and he thought it most curious that, at a time like this, he should note the considerable build-up of dust and fluff along the edges of the hallway floor, which must have accumulated over a considerable period of time. It then bothered him that he'd allowed himself to make such a trivial observation when his thoughts should have been more concerned with the escape of Agnes and the boy. He then imagined them scurrying along neighbouring streets and alleyways, keeping their heads down, and hiding behind dustbins, fences, and garden walls until eventually the streets would became clear enough for them to make a dash for the countryside.

The muscular private harshly fastened some handcuffs around John's wrists, and this induced an excruciating level of pain in his sprained, but recovering, wrist. The private then grabbed John's collar and dragged him along the floor. A small shard of window glass cut into John's cheek as his head was dragged along the linoleum. He managed to scramble to his feet just as he was bundled into the back room where he was flung onto the settee. The soldier with the rifle followed them into the room and took up position next to the dining table, casually pointing his rifle in John's general direction. John could hear soldiers pour into the other rooms of the house, presumably searching for other potential occupants. He glared angrily at the soldier with the rifle. The stripes of a corporal were on the soldier's sleeve and at the shoulder of his sleeve were the letters KOYLI. John was unfamiliar with what the letters meant and he heard himself repeat them out loud.

The corporal glanced at the letters on his shoulder and then eyed John suspiciously.

Then, a tall, slim, clean shaven man in a smart civilian suit and a trilby hat, breezed into the room. He removed the hat to reveal the receding hairline of a man in his early forties. The man held his hat behind his back with both his hands, whilst he briefly surveyed the scene in the room with his intense, ice-blue eyes: the remains of the meal on the table and John's handcuffed figure on the settee. Finally, the man introduced himself.

"Inspector Wrynne," he said. His gravelly accent contained a slight trace of a Scottish brogue.

"Oh aye?" replied John, "Inspectoring what?" A smirk spread across his face. But the inspector had clearly heard this one-liner many times and simply ignored the remark.

"Murders," the inspector replied, and the smirk instantly fell from John's face. He was confused by the inspector's remark and realised that he should have reason to worry about the direction of the conversation. The inspector paused to observe a droplet of blood trickle down John's lacerated cheek. The droplet hung for a moment from John's jaw and then dripped onto his shirt. "What business do you have at this house?" the inspector continued, "do you live here?"

John shrugged.

"And do you have a name, Chief Petty Officer? If that is indeed what you are."

"Aye."

"And can you provide the papers to evidence your identity, Chief?" the inspector asked, and then glanced at the muscular private who was now slouched against a wall. The inspector nodded to the private, and a couple of seconds elapsed before the private realised what he had been ordered to do. An ominous, cruel grin spread across the private's face and he proceeded to vigorously empty John's pockets, retrieving both wallet and identity papers. He passed them to the inspector, who briefly examined them.

"Well, well, Chief Petty Officer John Drummond. You seem to have rather a lot of money in your wallet. There must be upwards of forty or fifty pounds, here."

"Aye."

"All yours is it?"

"Aye."

"Hmmm. Anyone..." the inspector eyed the table, "...been to visit? Or are you the visitor?"

John focused on a chair leg, determined not to give anything away through eye contact.

"So, tell me about the Reverend Petrie."

"Who?"

"The Reverend Petrie, the vicar of this parish. The man of cloth you so mercilessly murdered in his own churchyard this afternoon."

"What?" spluttered John, and cast the inspector a look of utter disbelief.

"I have a witness who saw you this afternoon… hovering around the churchyard… for maybe several hours."

"Yeah, but…"

"Robbery was it?"

"What?"

"Your motive."

"No!"

"Fifty pounds is a lot of money, after all."

At that moment there was a murmuring of voices in the hallway and a sergeant entered the room and whispered into the inspector's ear.

"Ah," he replied, "bring them in, please."

The sergeant disappeared out of the room and into the hallway, where there was a minor scuffle and a struggle.

"Gerroff, yer big lump!" shouted Agnes as she was pushed, stumbling, through the door into the room.

"Agnes!" John jumped to his feet, but the muscular private pushed him effortlessly back onto the settee. John and Agnes flashed sheepishly apologetic looks at each other. A moment later the boy shuffled in, subdued and silent. Agnes grasped the boy's hand, pulled him close to her and wrapped a protective arm around him.

"And baby makes three," said the inspector. "So, where were you two going in such a hurry?"

"It's me you want. Not them," barked John.

"Is it, now?" the inspector turned slowly and approached John. "Is it really, just you?" He leaned down until his face was only a few inches from John's, "Perhaps we should all go down to the station to straighten things out, eh?" John stared defiantly back and was about to speak when, quite unexpectedly, the inspector's ice blue eyes turned a volcanic shade of red. This lasted for only a few brief seconds before they returned to their original blue. A shiver ran down John's spine and his mouth and throat became suddenly dry. He tried to call out to Agnes but the dryness in his throat induced a coughing fit. The inspector sniggered, slowly, and callously, "Careful, now, Chief. Save it for your statement."

The sergeant entered the room again. This time he seemed a little agitated.

"Inspector Wrynne, Sir," he said and pointed to his watch, "we need to be going…"

"Take them away, then," the inspector replied, dismissively, "but make sure the boy and the woman ride with me in the car."

"Yes, Sir," the sergeant answered and turned to Agnes. "Come on, then," he said, "you heard the inspector."

Agnes held the boy close to her and shuffled out of the room and down the hall, closely followed by Inspector Wrynne.

"And you," the corporal said to John, reinforcing the order with a jab from the rifle. John struggled to his feet and the muscular private encouraged him to leave the cottage more quickly, by shoving him robustly all the way along the length of the hallway. John finally tripped out of the doorway and stumbled awkwardly into the street, where he landed on his knees.

The humiliation and pain of his undignified exit outraged John to such an extent that it stoked a determination to retaliate regardless of the consequences. As John struggled to his feet, he feigned weakness. The muscular private stepped forward ready to inflict further humiliation, but John was ready. He jumped up and swung his right foot up into the private's groin. The impact of the kick looked like it lifted the private off the ground, but this was probably the private's painful reaction as he tried to avoid the kick and protect his manhood. The private collapsed to his knees and let out a long, deep, exhausting groan. All the other men who were witness to this moment of male pain inwardly flinched, including John himself.

Another soldier, who was standing behind John, stepped forward and struck John across the back of the head with the butt of his rifle. John collapsed to the ground. The shock of the blow knocked all sense from him and his vision slowly faded into darkness as he succumbed to unconsciousness.

"NO!" screamed Agnes and she struggled and kicked and punched her way through the soldiers to John's limp body. She flung herself over him, protectively. "Leave him alone!" she snarled, venomously, at the surrounding soldiers.

Some of the net curtains in the street twitched, as curious neighbours observed the commotion in the street. Others pulled their net curtains wide, and a couple of neighbours even ventured to open their front doors in order to get a better view of the spectacle.

The sergeant cast a disapproving look at the soldier who'd inflicted the blow.

"Oh, great! Nice one," he said, sarcastically. "Just knock him bloody silly why don't you." But the soldier who dealt the blow simply sauntered off to the army truck and casually climbed aboard. The sergeant now noted the growing interest from the neighbours and so he felt at John's neck for a pulse. "He's not dead," he said. "Look, we'll get a doctor to him as soon as we can. Now, please get in the car." He glanced nervously at his watch and then at the neighbouring houses.

Agnes looked over to the car and saw the boy standing quietly by a rear passenger door, which was being held open for him by a stocky, pimply young female driver clad in a khaki-military uniform. Agnes stood up, quickly smoothed her skirt and hurried over to the boy.

"Come on, love," she said to him and they climbed into the car.

John drifted in and out of his stupor as several of the remaining soldiers manhandled him into the rear of the truck. They then climbed aboard, after him. Inspector Wrynne climbed into the front of the car. The truck rumbled into life and the two vehicles trundled slowly down the street. They passed several neighbours who had by now ventured out into the street.

Unseen by Inspector Wrynne, Agnes leaned against the car window and scanned the faces of the neighbours. She made eye contact with a middle-aged woman of careworn appearance, whose facial expression revealed that she recognised Agnes. Agnes traced out an imaginary picture on the window to her. The woman immediately recognised its significance and meaning. She nodded an acknowledgement to Agnes and then quickly disappeared back indoors. The vehicles reached the bottom of the street, turned left and shortly afterwards, they had driven out of view

.

REPAIR AND PREPARE

The rust-streaked vessel that was HMS Kiveton loomed large alongside the jetty, and the destroyer's dull grey superstructure cast a long shadow along her berth. Philip paused for a moment at the foot of the gangway and looked at his new command. She was an older ship than his last command, with slightly fewer crew. He didn't mind, though. He would be content so long as she fought well and was manoeuvrable and reliable.

The Officer of the Day, the Quartermaster and the Bosun's Mate all hurriedly assembled at the brow of the gangway. Philip waited for them to "fall-in" and stand to attention, ready for his embarkation. He then climbed the gangway when he heard the Bosun blow his whistle to 'pipe' the Captain aboard. Philip reached the brow, stood to attention and saluted the White Ensign that fluttered from the head of the flag staff at the stern the ship. His thoughts briefly wandered to the circumstances that led to the end of his last command and he silently prayed that this command would have a happier ending for both himself and his crew.

Philip glanced around. The evidence of paint kettles, brushes, and patches of freshly painted steelwork, along with tool-rolls and half-assembled anti-aircraft guns, all suggested that repairs were well under way and nearing completion. Several crewmen were occupied in carrying out this work, but for the moment they were stood to attention. Some of them, brush in hand were spattered with the grey paint that they were applying. Others were part covered in the grease of the half assembled guns.

Philip had expected a larger official reception party: one containing more senior officers; and the ship's second in command at least. But these officers were noticeable by their absence.

"Is the First Lieutenant not aboard?"

"No, Sir," replied the Officer of the Day, a young sub-lieutenant. "He's expected back on board at any time... Sorry Sir, we were expecting you to arrive much later... Sir."

"And my engineer?"

"Down below, Sir."

"Up to his arms in grease and bilge no doubt."

"Sir?" The sub-lieutenant's confused face reddened slightly with embarrassment, but before he could say anything else the head and shoulders of an officer in overalls appeared through an open hatchway in the deck. His overalls and his cap seemed a little careworn and were dusty with soot. His hands and face were also grimy.

"Apologies, Sir," he said as he struggled to his feet, "Inspecting the repairs to the for'ard boiler when I heard the pipe." He stood to attention and saluted Philip, who returned the salute. The two men then smiled at each other and shook hands with the warmth and familiarity of old friends.

"Hello Richard. Good to see you again. How are you?"

"Busy, Sir. But winning."

"Good. I'll need briefing on the state of repairs. In my cabin in about ten minutes?"

"Yes, Sir," Richard replied, and then sauntered off to his cabin to clean himself up and change out of his filthy overalls.

Philip turned to the Officer of the Day.

"Inform the First Lieutenant, when he returns on board, that he may join us in my cabin and that I would also like to address the Wardroom at some point later this evening."

"Yes, Sir."

"Oh, and my suitcase is on the jetty. Have it taken to my cabin."

"Yes, Sir."

Philip stepped through a door in the superstructure and walked along the passageway to his cabin. The hum and vibration of machinery had a familiar and reassuring feel about it. The ship's interior appeared quite tatty and seemed to be in need of a general refit. It wasn't particularly dirty, just well-worn. His cabin wasn't too bad, though. Clean and functional was probably how best to describe it. But, after all, it was wartime and the pre-war soft furnishings had long since been removed. He glanced through one of the scuttle portholes and then settled himself at his desk to examine the paperwork and signals that had accumulated there.

A few minutes later Richard, the Engineering Officer, knocked on the open cabin door.

"Come in Richard," Philip said without looking up. "Sit down."

"Thank you, Sir," Richard said as he entered the cabin. He was by now scrubbed up and wearing his usual uniform, shirt and tie. He made himself comfortable in the only other chair in the cabin, by slouching and reclining his legs out straight.

"So, my old friend, what action damage repairs do you have left to complete before we are seaworthy again?"

"None, Philip. It's all done, now: subject to successfully raising steam and tidying things away," Richard glanced at his watch. "And a flame was established in the for'ard boiler room about fifteen minutes ago."

"Good. I want the ship at one hour's notice for sea as soon as we can."

"Impatient as ever, eh, Philip?"

"Impertinent as ever, eh, Richard?"

Both men laughed. Philip relaxed a little. It felt good to be in the company of an old friend. The two men spent the next hour catching up on old times; even sharing a small hipflask of whiskey, courtesy of Richard. But even in the relaxed atmosphere of his friend, Philip did not dare relate the experiences of his recent train journey. Their conversation circled around their shared reminiscence of life in the Royal Navy before the war; and they avoided talking about the unpleasantness that the war had visited upon the two men.

During the hours that followed, a steady stream of officers and men returned to the ship, and by nightfall all the crew were present and correct. Philip had briefings in his cabin with each of his senior officers and, once he was satisfied that the ship was fully repaired and operational, he ordered a signal to be sent to the Flotilla Captain announcing that "action damage now repaired and ship in all respects ready for service."

He formally introduced himself to the rest of the Wardroom, and raised a glass to the health of His Majesty King George. Then, using the ship's broadcast system, he made a short, introductory speech to the whole crew. He congratulated them on the speedy repair of the action damage and he informed them that that the ship had been signalled to remain at four hours' readiness for sea whilst they awaited further orders.

Philip then had a very short informal walk around the ship. Ostensibly, this walk-around was to familiarise himself with the layout of his vessel and view the repaired action damage, but it also enabled him to gauge the morale of the crew, which was reassuringly high.

After the walk around, Philip retired to his cabin, pulled off his shoes, let out a large sigh and laid on his bunk. His mind was contemplating the events of the day, particularly the encounter on the train with John Popplethwaite and the red demon. Had it really happened? It seemed such a dream to him now. Popplethwaite had definitely been on the list of missing. But could he really have survived? Or had the entire incident on the train been imagined; a hallucination induced by the stress of the loss of his ship? After all, there were no witnesses to what took place on the train. Philip rolled onto his front and tried to dismiss such unwelcome thoughts. He decided to instead fill his mind with other, happier thoughts: like his family and children. But these happy thoughts were suddenly interrupted by a voice he did not recognise.

"Awake, Philip Ambrose," the voice commanded. Philip was non too pleased with the abruptness of the interruption, or the clear lack of deference in the tone of voice. And he was irritated by the fact that someone had the audacity to enter his cabin without invitation or even knocking. He lifted himself into a sitting position in order to see the man to whom he was about to give an almighty reprimand. However, he momentarily froze with surprise at the sight before him. It was a White Angel: a large, incandescent apparition of celestial serenity. Outwardly, Philip seemed his usual calm self, but inwardly his heart beat rapidly. He quickly composed his thoughts.

"Do you mind? I'm trying to rest," he said, flatly.

"Philip Ambrose," the Angel continued, "awake and prepare, for you have much to do."

"I'm sorry?" he replied, "who are you?"

"She was once Majestic, but now she is humbled by Maligns. They must be stopped."

"Are you drunk?" Philip folded his arms as he asked. But the Angel slowly raised a finger and pointed to one of the scuttle portholes and the darkened river beyond.

"Hurry!" it said, "They gather strength."

"What, in the river?"

"John Popplethwaite is in grave danger. You must help him."

"Ah. Popplethwaite, again." Philip rose from his bed, lifted the deadlight cover of the scuttle porthole and looked out. He could see very little because of the blackout and the reflection of the incandescent light from the angel. He concentrated hard. Out in the river, faintly illuminated by the muted light of a cloud-covered moon, he could see the vague silhouette of a solitary old hulk. What had this hulk got to do with John Popplethwaite?

"Is he out there?" he said and turned to the Angel, but the apparition disappeared, plunging the cabin into darkness. Philip harrumphed at the abruptness of the departure and the scantness of the information provided. For a moment he wondered if he had imagined this encounter too.

Then, there was a knock on his door. He opened it and a young signalman was standing in the corridor holding a piece of paper. "Yes?" Philip demanded sharply.

"Signal, Sir," the signalman offered the piece of paper. Philip snatched the signal and read it. The ship was ordered to sail and rendezvous with a convoy that was assembling the following afternoon.

"Wake the First Lieutenant, Engineer, and the Navigator. I want them in my cabin in five minutes. Then come back here for a reply to that signal."

"Yes, Sir," the signalman replied and scurried away to attend to his errand. Philip slipped on his shoes, sat at his desk and began the task of compiling a signal. Obviously, he had his orders, but he desperately wanted to reassure his own sanity. There was only one thing for it. He had to check out that hulk. But first he needed permission. He carefully pondered over a suitable form of words that would be unlikely to raise suspicion. But he was too confused and couldn't bring himself to write anything. Maybe he was being too hasty. He needed to know more about that old hulk before he committed his ship to a test of his sanity.

The Navigator was the first into Philip's cabin. He was a short ferrety-looking man with a particular quickness about his movements.

"Escort duty," Philip offered the signal to the Navigator, whose arm flicked out quickly to accept the signal, "Convoy assembly position and time is there."

"Yes, Sir," the Navigator replied.

"Oh, and we may be making a short stop to inspect that hulk in the river on our way out."

"Hulk?" Richard interrupted as he entered the cabin. He'd obviously only heard Philip's last few words. "What about it?"

"What do either of you know about that hulk in the river?"

"You mean the old Caledonia?" the Navigator replied.

"Ah," said Philip, with a note of recognition in his voice, "is that what it is?" He recalled that the old HMS Caledonia was a boys' training ship before the war.

"Yes, Sir," the Navigator said. But she's not long been raised."

"Raised?"

"Yes, Sir. She sank early in the war but they managed to raise her not long ago."

"They must be desperate for the scrap," observed Richard. "Wasn't she completely gutted by a fire?" Philip looked at Richard and the Navigator blankly. "During that air raid wasn't it? Remember? Just after war was declared."

"Not personally, Richard. I was in Gibraltar when war was declared." Philip then fell silent and began to slowly pace around his cabin. His thoughts wandered back to the words of the angel. What did they mean? What could they mean? Was John Popplethwaite really aboard the old Caledonia? He heard himself mutter, "So, what's so majestic about her?"

"That's right, Sir," the Navigator said, "she was the Majestic." Philip stopped pacing and stared at the Navigator.

"What?"

"The Caledonia, Sir. She used to be called Majestic. Blue Ribband winner as well, I think." Philip felt his stomach start to turn cold and become tense. What was waiting for them on that old hulk? Popplethwaite? Demons? Germans?

"Are you alright, old chap?" Richard asked. "You've gone a little pale."

"Perfectly fine," Philip replied, firmly. His initial fears, and then Richard's observations, had an instant, galvanising effect on his mood. He hated fear. And so, with a huge mental effort he wrenched himself away from the path of fear and focused his mind on what he knew must now be done. "Where's Number One?" he called out, sharply. The First Lieutenant appeared in the doorway at that very moment.

"Here, Sir."

"Right, Number One. We've a convoy to escort. Rendezvous tomorrow afternoon. Navigator has details." Philip drew breath and addressed them all. "When we sail, I want a boarding party ready and armed. We'll be making an unofficial stop at the old Caledonia." The Navigator and Richard exchanged worried looks. The First Lieutenant simply looked bemused, but Philip continued, "There's something of concern about that hulk. And I want to check it out." Richard opened his mouth to speak but Philip cut him off.

"Those are *my* orders."

"Of course, Sir," replied the First Lieutenant. "May I ask the purpose of this additional evolution? For briefing the men, I mean."

"It will still be dark when we sail. So we should find the vessel deserted. No breakers yard workers. Nobody. But I have reason to believe there are undesirable elements aboard that hulk. Probably criminals. Possibly the enemy. Maybe fifth columnists. I just don't know for sure, so we're going to find out."

"So the men need to be prepared for a bit of a scrap, then, Sir?" the First Lieutenant asked.

"Yes."

"Very good, Sir. I'll get right to it," replied the First Lieutenant and disappeared out of the cabin to attend to his orders. Philip turned to Richard and the Navigator.

"Between getting steam up, high tide, and making the rendezvous with the convoy, how much time can you give me for the Caledonia?"

"Erm," replied the Navigator and looked at Richard. Richard thought for a moment.

"Well, the boilers are still hot and have some pressure in them. Give me two hours and we'll be ready to sail."

"Good." Philip said. He turned to the Navigator, "And?"

"Erm," he said, "in that case I could give you at least a couple of hours, I'm sure. I'll need to look at the charts and make a few calculations but I think a couple of hours would be reasonable."

"Good. Get them done and get back to me with an accurate window of opportunity."

Richard and the Navigator left Philip alone in his cabin. He sighed deeply. He knew that he was likely to get into serious trouble for an unauthorised boarding of this nature. He may even lose his command. But he also knew that he had to find out whether he was losing his sense of sanity and reality. He sat at his desk and began to compile the signals that he would need to send to the Senior Naval Officer on the Forth, and his Flotilla Captain. The signal implied that there was an apparent rumour of inappropriate activity on the hulk in the river. He requested permission to briefly stop and inspect the hulk on the ship's departure in order to dispel the rumour. Philip knew that he was unlikely to obtain permission, but he felt that he needed to at least tell his superiors what he was doing, whether they approved or not.

The signalman returned shortly after Philip completed his signal.

"Here," said Philip. "And be quick about it."

"Sir," the signalman replied.

Philip's career and sanity now rested on the events fixed for the next few hours.

INCARCERATION

John groaned. He was groggy and had a terrible headache. Slowly, he ventured to open his eyes. Thankfully there were no bright lights to aggravate his throbbing head. The room was dark, only a narrow shaft of very dim light entered through a keyhole. He dragged himself, gingerly, into a sitting position, but a whooshing sound in his ears and a flush of hot nausea washed over him, and this induced him to lie back down on the thin, grubby mattress.

"You alright?" the boy asked. John simply breathed deeply.

"Where are we?"

"Dunno," replied the boy.

"Agnes. She here?"

"Dunno. Want some water?" the boy said and reached for a metal jug on the floor. He poured some water into a small tin mug, and placed the jug back onto the floor with a clang. He then offered the mug to John.

John propped himself up on one elbow and groped in the semi-darkness until his hand came into contact with the mug. He slurped the water down and put the empty cup onto the floor. The side of his hand came into contact with the cool metal of what he assumed was a ship's deck, corroded and covered in a thin layer of damp, slimy filth. He knocked on the metal deck to confirm his suspicions.

"On a ship then."

"Yeah. Really old one. Everything looks burned and rusty."

"Oh, aye?" John tried again to drag himself into an upright sitting position, this time more successfully. Another wave of nausea briefly swept over him and he placed his head in his hands.

"You sure you're alright?"

"Aye. Not right good at getting up after a sleep at the best of times, never mind when I've been thumped." John breathed in deep, slow, deliberate breaths to try to control the nausea, which eventually waned. He glanced across at the boy's slight and skinny figure crouched in the dimness on another mattress. "Anyway, you alright, son? They didn't hurt you or owt?"

"No, I'm alright. Bit cold, but alright."

John hadn't noticed the obvious chilliness in the compartment. The hot and clammy flushes of nausea had inhibited much of his senses, but as his senses gradually returned to him he became aware of the coolness of the compartment. He liked it, for the moment, because he thought it helped him not to vomit.

The quality of the air was poor: heavy, smelly and not conducive to his fragile state. He couldn't quite define the smell. In one breath he could smell the salty, seaweed smell of a harbour when the tide was out; in another breath, there was the smell of smoke and oil. And in each breath he tasted the sense of decay that permeated the whole environment of his incarceration.

"Is there nowt in here you can use to keep warm?" he said, finally, and looked around the compartment. But there was nothing. They were in an empty metal box, stripped bare of its fittings. The only things in the room were the filthy mattresses upon which they were sitting, the jug of water and tin mug, and a metal bucket in the corner near the door; which presumably had been provided as a rudimentary toilet.

"Hmm." John said. "How long we been here?"

"Dunno. Ages."

John clumsily grasped the tin cup and jug and helped himself to more water, spilling some of its contents as he did so.

"Was it still dark when we got here?"

"Yeah. They had some right trouble getting you up that rope ladder from the boat; they could hardly see what they were doing."

"Boat? We came by boat?"

"Yeah. A couple of 'em. Don't you remember shouting at 'em?"

"No," answered John. "Did everybody come, then?"

"Er, yeah. I think so."

"Even Agnes?"

"Yeah."

"And the inspector?"

"Er, dunno," the boy said, hesitantly.

"Right," said John slowly, struggling to digest this new information. His mind still felt a little fuzzy. "So much for him taking us down the station."

"What we going to do, then?" the boy asked. John slowly climbed to his feet.

"Escape, I suppose," he said and tried to open the door. It was metal, and the wood or bakelite trim of the handle had either been burnt away or removed, leaving the stubby piece of rough metal that was now sticking out from the door handle mechanism. John grasped it as best he could and tried to turn it to open the door. But it was no good. It was too stiff and simply wouldn't budge. John crouched and spied through the keyhole. The boy stood up and inquisitively approached John.

"It's not daylight," said John as he turned to the boy.

"No." the boy said and helpfully added, "I think we're a long way down. There were loads of ladders."

"Oh aye? Can you remember how many?"

"Er, dunno. Two, three? Not sure."

John turned his attention back to the keyhole. Suddenly, it went completely dark as a key was inserted into the lock and blocked out all light. John and the boy quickly shuffled back a few paces. The boy threw an arm around John's waist and John placed a protective arm around the boy's shoulder.

The door creaked slowly open and the dim glow of light from the passageway flooded into the compartment. John squinted and blinked. He glanced around the compartment to gain his bearings, and guessed that the compartment could have been an old cabin of some sort, possibly second class. He noticed there was a porthole, now sealed up from the outside with a large wooden bung. So John at least knew that they were above the waterline.

The door had been pushed open by the muscular private, who now stood to one side in the passageway in order to allow the corporal to step into the compartment.

"We can do it the easy way or the hard way," the corporal said. "Easy way – come quietly with no struggling."

"Oh aye? And the hard way?" enquired John.

"These and a good slap," the corporal replied and held up a pair of handcuffs.

"Mmm," John looked down at the boy. "Shall we give 'em a break and go with the easy way?" But the boy looked confused and frightened. John felt suddenly responsible, and slightly embarrassed by his misplaced flippancy. He looked back at the corporal. "Aye, we'll come the easy way."

"Not the boy. Just you."

"Eh?" John said, irritated by the corporal's attitude. He could sense a stubborn confrontation was brewing. "But it's pitch dark in here! The boy's frightened enough as it is. I'm not goin' if you're goin' to leave him on his own in the dark. We go together or we go the hard way." John clenched his fists and raised them defiantly in front of the corporal.

Either the corporal was not in the mood for a confrontation, or he was under orders to avoid one.

"He can go in with the woman, then," he replied.

"Right," John agreed and relaxed his clenched fists. "Come on, lad."

John and the boy shuffled out into the passageway, followed by the corporal. The muscular private closed the door behind them. The passageway was a blackened, filthy shaft of corrosion which was illuminated for a length of ten or fifteen yards by the glow of a crude, makeshift string of underpowered light bulbs. Beyond the furthest light bulb the passageway disappeared into unfathomable darkness. John could only speculate on the length of this passageway or what could be found in the darkness beyond, but he guessed that it was probably very long and very empty. It was then that he realised the ship was eerily quiet and still. There was no noise or vibration from machinery or ventilation systems. This was a truly dead ship.

They shuffled down the passageway, which was punctuated on both sides by several other doors. The party halted at one particular door on the same side of the passageway as the compartment they had just left. The muscular private unlocked the door and opened it to reveal Agnes, sitting in a similar sized compartment and on a similarly filthy mattress as used by John and the boy.

Agnes looked up. Her eyes were bloodshot and sore with crying. She sniffled and did her best to quickly hide her recent emotional outpouring. She stood up and cleared her throat.

"The air in here is terrible," she stammered and snittled again, "giving me a terrible cold and making my nose run shockin'."

The corporal invited the boy to enter the compartment. John released his protective arm from around the boy and allowed him to go in to Agnes. Agnes, in turn, shuffled over to greet the boy, with her arms open wide. The boy flung his arms around her.

"It's alright, love. I know," she said. The boy turned and looked over to John, who smiled weakly at both of them. The corporal abruptly closed the door, shutting out the light. By the time the key had been turned in the lock John was seething with a deep sense of outrage at the inhuman treatment of these helpless captives. And from this moment of outrage, emerged his total, absolute determination to prevail over all obstacles. He was going to destroy this Malign unit by whatever means necessary.

The corporal shoved John, who irritably complied, and trudged further along the passageway. John was halted at another door, this time located on the opposite side of the passageway.

The door was opened and John was thrust into a larger compartment which was thankfully illuminated, if only by a single makeshift electric lantern that hung loosely from one of the girders that ran the length of the deck-head ceiling. The compartment was similarly blackened and corroded, and John expected that most of the rest of the vessel would be. The door was closed behind him, but it was not locked, which he thought unusual. But maybe it just couldn't be locked; or his gaolers were just plain lazy; or maybe he just hadn't heard the key in the lock. John assumed the corporal and the muscular private would probably be stationed outside the door to prevent any attempt at escape.

John viewed the compartment. At the other end of the compartment was another door, which John presumed to be locked. In the centre of the compartment there was a rickety-looking old table and several metal-framed chairs placed around it. And sitting upon one of these chairs was…

"Mr Forsyth!" exclaimed John and rushed across the compartment. Mr Forsyth slowly rose from his chair and John vigorously shook his hand, in an almost surreal moment.

"Got you as well, Sir," John observed, solemnly.

"In a fashion, John. In a fashion," replied Mr Forsyth, without a smile.

John noticed a number of tiny cuts and grazes on Mr Forsyth's head and hands. He was about to enquire after them when Mr Forsyth brushed off the concern with a wave of his hand.

"Fine, fine. Just superficial. And you, John?"

"Aye. Bit dizzy still from another crack on me head, but I'm alright."

There was a momentary pause as John reflected soberly on the unfavourable turn of events. Eventually, he shrugged apologetically.

"Sorry, Sir. Only ten minutes into me first mission and it all went belly-up."

"No need to apologise, John. Please. Sit down," Mr Forsyth replied and shuffled round to the other side of the table. He then gestured with a sweep of his arm for John to view the compartment. "And how are you finding your father's handiwork?"

"Eh?"

"Your father's handiwork. This vessel." John hadn't a clue what Mr Forsyth was talking about. He looked around but saw nothing that he thought was of significance, other than maybe the ship itself.

"What, the ship?" he said, slowly.

"Yes, yes," replied Mr Forsyth, "the destruction of this vessel was entirely your father's own handiwork. His seminal... and, as it turned out, his terminal... achievement."

John frowned as he contemplated the potential meaning of the words 'terminal' and 'achievement'.

"You mean it was just his last mission, or do you mean he actually died on this mission?" Mr Forsyth's solemn expression seemed to have the answer written all over it. "Oh. Right," said John.

"I'm very sorry, John. The fire certainly did consume your late father, along with a major part of this vessel."

John pulled a chair to him and sat down.

"Aye? Well, I bet he took loads of Maligns with him," he said, with a hint of hope in his voice.

"Mmm," said Mr Forsyth, thoughtfully, "in a fashion."

"What's 'Mmm, in a fashion' supposed to mean?"

Mr Forsyth sighed, leaned forward to John, and spoke in a low voice.

"I suppose... I had hoped to protect you from the awful truth... less it adversely influence your performance on your maiden mission. You do understand...yes? But seen as we are now where we are; and as you will probably find out from sources less sympathetic than I..."

There was a long pause.

"Aye..." John said in as encouraging a tone as possible without sounding too impatient, because Mr Forsyth was beginning to irritate him.

"You see, the thing is... Well the truth of the matter... Your father was... well actually, he was a Malign. There, I've said it."

John recoiled at the words and was almost as stunned by this news as he would have been if he'd just been punched on the nose.

"And an important Malign at that. He was only exposed last year."

"But..."

"Yes, yes, I know, no one ever suspected a thing. We all just thought he was bit of a maverick. You know: the lovable rogue; but always with his heart in the right place."

John didn't know, of course, because he had never met his father.

"Maverick?" he repeated, quietly.

"Indeed, yes, in many ways he played by his own rule book. You know, your father used to visit your mother frequently over the years, even though such visits are strictly forbidden; but of course, you probably already knew about that from your mother."

John frowned and was bewildered by what Mr Forsyth had said. Had he heard correctly or was that extra bang on his head muddling his sense of perception?

Mr Forsyth appeared emboldened enough to continue.

"And he rescued a certain person whose name does not appear on the List of Chosen?" he said. "He knew it was *expressly* forbidden, yet he went ahead and co-opted your own wife without any due regard for the wider consequences. But you probably knew that already too." Mr Forsyth closely watched John for any sign of reaction.

"Er, No." John said, perplexed by this statement, too.

"Oh?"

John felt a growing sense of unease at these revelations. He mentally grasped at the flood of facts and tried to hold one steady enough in his mind to understand it more clearly.

"You mean Agnes wasn't chosen like the rest of us?"

"Goodness, no."

"Oh," John replied. He was sure that she had told him that she had been chosen. But if she wasn't on the List of Chosen, why say she had? Why had she left him all those years ago? Why the fake suicide? And what had his dad said or done to convince her to leave if she wasn't chosen?

"Ah. Should I assume that she led you to believe that she was on the List of Chosen?" Mr Forsyth asked, but the brooding silence from John contained all the answer necessary.

John felt a horrible knot of betrayal grip his stomach. Was Forsyth lying to him? Why should he lie? Why should Agnes lie? Surely she'd told him back at the cottage... or had she? John couldn't remember clearly, and hoped it was because of the extra thump to his head. He felt very confused, and sighed deeply.

"And this vessel was the scene of his last desperate stand," Mr Forsyth continued, but John was hardly listening, now.

The door opened and the sergeant entered the compartment. Mr Forsyth rose from his chair and walked towards the door. John's thoughts returned to the here and now and he stood up with the intention of following Mr Forsyth.

"Not you," the sergeant said. John sat back down, and Mr Forsyth left the compartment, escorted by the sergeant. The door was closed behind them, and then locked, leaving John alone to dwell on his confused and unhappy thoughts.

A FIGHT ON THE FORTH

The First Lieutenant climbed the short ladder up onto the bridge.

"The boarding party's ready, Sir," he said to Philip. "Thirty men, two senior rates and two officers, all volunteers. Sub-lieutenant Shaw is in overall command of the party."

"Good, thank you, Number One," Philip acknowledged this information without looking at the First Lieutenant. He was observing the crewmen who were preparing to 'single up' the ship's hawsers and remove the gangway in readiness for sailing. "I expect we shall leave the wall in the next ten minutes or so."

"Very good, Sir," replied the First Lieutenant.

"Good," Philip said to himself as he viewed the activity below him. He glanced at his watch, and noted the time. He called after the First Lieutenant, "On second thoughts, Number One, I think I'll speak to them before we sail." Philip grabbed his tin hat and turned to the officer of the watch, "I'll be five minutes," he said and followed the First Lieutenant down the ladder.

The boarding party was mustered amidship, next to the ship's torpedo tubes. They were standing 'at ease' in a squad formation two deep, and on first impression they seemed an improbable collection of fighting men: a motley mixture of men from different branches of specialism. Some were stokers, still dressed in their overalls, others were stewards, torpedomen and signalmen. All wore their tin hats and carried a rifle slung over their right shoulder. There were also two gruff-looking senior rates standing beside the main squad: a Chief Petty Officer and a Petty Officer. Two young officers, both sub-lieutenants, were standing facing the boarding party. The senior of the sub-lieutenants, Sub-lieutenant Shaw, saw Philip descend a nearby ladder and was about to bring the mustered men to attention when Philip waved his hand and shook his head.

"It's alright, Sub-lieutenant Shaw. At ease, men. At ease," he said, and then he addressed the boarding party. "In the next few minutes we shall leave the wall and head out into the river. You men are going to board and search a hulk in the river. A hulk formerly known to some of you as HMS Caledonia. Some of you may have noticed when you steamed past her recently, that she is in the process of demolition. Much of her superstructure has been removed; and the quality of the decks, ladders, internal layout, etcetera, are likely to be in a poor condition and potentially hazardous, particularly in the darkness. So, particular care needs to be taken." Philip then paced in front of the party as he spoke. "So, why are we boarding her? Surely the vessel is deserted at night: there should be nobody on board? Well, that is exactly what we are going to find out. She should be deserted at this time of night. But if she is not, then criminals, deserters, Fifth Columnists or even the enemy may be on board. Don't shoot anyone unless you have no alternative, and take prisoners wherever possible. Any questions?" Several of the men exchanged looks of surprise and bewilderment. Philip waited for a moment, but there were no questions. "Good."

Philip turned to Sub-lieutenant Shaw.

"There is the possibility that one or more persons are being held hostage on board; so make sure the men are mindful that we may need to cut them out the old-fashioned way."

"Yes, Sir," the sub-lieutenant replied, with an expression that implied he was not entirely sure of the meaning of that last statement.

"Good. Good luck men and God speed," Philip said and turned on his heels and sped off up the ladder back towards the bridge.

When Philip returned to the bridge he was briefed by the officer of the watch, who informed him that the ship was ready to put to sea. Once completely satisfied that this was indeed the case, Philip glanced at his watch, and then ordered the ship's moorings to be slipped.

HMS Kiveton drifted slowly from her berth. Her propellers began to turn and the water astern of the ship churned and frothed, and the ship glided away from the jetty and out into the river. And with the Navigator close beside him at all times, Philip sailed his ship across the glassy estuary and towards the solitary rusting hulk anchored out in the darkness.

The boarding party moved forward and mustered on the forecastle. Some of the men nervously carried out last minute weapons checks whilst other, more seasoned veterans calmly began unfastening the guardrail along the port side of the forecastle in readiness for the boarding. They then tied several fenders over the side in order to protect the ship from any contact with the hulk.

The ship approached its destination and slowed almost to a stop; and Philip carefully manoeuvred the Kiveton so that her port bow came within a few feet of the wreck's rusting, rivet-plated hull. Throughout this manoeuvre, the Kiveton's searchlights scoured the deck of the Caledonia for any signs of occupancy, but they illuminated none.

When the vessels were almost touching, Sub-lieutenant Shaw shouted the order to board.

Unfortunately, the edge of the Kiveton's forecastle deck was several feet below the deck-edge of the Caledonia, and so the boarding party had to give each other a 'leg up' from the deck of the Kiveton. They frantically scrambled up blistered paintwork and corroded platework, and after a few tense moments the entire team had clambered aboard the Caledonia. Philip pulled his ship back to a more comfortable distance to observe proceedings.

On the deck of Caledonia, Sub-lieutenant Shaw quickly dispersed his party into six smaller teams, with orders to swiftly investigate the hulk, and to specifically determine whether there were any signs of unauthorised habitation or occupancy below-decks.

The moonlight offered a faint illumination of the hundreds of feet of rusting upper-deck, and its light revealed the dozens of pitch black holes that punctured the dangerous deck. Some holes were old hatch openings just a few feet across; others were several square yards in size, cut specifically to remove machinery.

The six teams silently moved across the decks and identified eight significantly sized holes that had wooden ladders lashed to them; where the ladders led down below to other decks or into machinery spaces. The torches the sailors had were weak, but gave sufficient illumination during these below-decks investigations. However, the brilliance of the occasional searchlight beam that passed across the decks was dazzling and momentarily impaired the night vision of any team member naive enough to look into the beam before his descent below.

The teams discovered that each hole and deck that they investigated was eerily quiet and in pit-shaft darkness. The hulk appeared to be deserted, as the teams reported their observations to Sub-lieutenant

Shaw, who co-ordinated the progress of their tasks from a makeshift command post near to their point of embarkation.

Sub-lieutenant Shaw looked at his watch, impatient to complete the search and to leave the vessel. He turned to his Chief.

"Well, Chief," he said, "I think the rumours were baseless, after all. This old wreck is well and truly deserted. Five more minutes of this and we'll be done."

But as he spoke, a sailor from one of the teams near the forward part of the Caledonia emerged from a large hatchway. He vaulted the last few rungs of the ladder and, with an agitated and excited expression he hurried across to Sub-lieutenant Shaw.

"Sir, Sir!" the man whispered excitedly, "Over here."

Sub-lieutenant Shaw called over two additional teams that were returning from the aft section of the Caledonia and, with an enlarged team, he followed the man back down the ladders. Two decks down, the sailor guided Sub-lieutenant Shaw into a passageway where a large heavy black curtain was drawn across it. Around the edges of the curtain seeped a dim yellow glow: there was light beyond.

The team shuffled towards the curtain as silently as they could, their ears straining to detect any sounds of life behind and beyond it. A faint murmuring of voices could be heard. Sub-lieutenant Shaw, who had obviously not expected to encounter anyone on board the Caledonia, dithered for a moment. But the chief petty officer of the boarding party moved to the front of the team.

"Come on, Sir," he said, and slowly drew back the curtain to reveal a deserted passageway: a blackened, filthy corridor of corrosion that was illuminated for maybe fifteen yards by the glow of a crude, makeshift string of underpowered light bulbs. Beyond the furthest light bulb the passageway disappeared into darkness.

The team cautiously shuffled along the passageway. The chief petty officer paused in front of a door and listened attentively. He indicated to the team that the voices were coming from behind it. He motioned to two men behind him to search the compartments on the opposite side of the passageway; and to two more men he indicated that they were to continue along the corridor and to listen at the other doors further along. The second pair shuffled past and made their way down the passageway.

Then, the handle of the door in front of the chief turned and the door creaked open. The chief's immediate reaction was sharp and aggressive. He kicked open the door and stormed into the compartment followed by a rush of sailors. Sub-lieutenant Shaw, was swept along by the tide of his men.

"Royal Navy! Get yor 'ands up!" boomed the chief, and pointed his rifle in the general direction of four startled soldiers, who were in various stages of undress. They were sat around a rickety old table and seemed to be playing a game of cards. The soldiers, each with a smoking cigarette loosely hanging from half opened lips, slowly raised their hands in surrender. They were still clutching their cards, such was their surprise.

A fifth man, who had been opening the door, had been knocked spread-eagle from the force of the chief's kick. A sailor launched himself toward the soldier and aimed his rifle square in the man's face.

"Don't move!" spat the sailor.

Sub-lieutenant Shaw surveyed the smokey compartment, which appeared to be some kind of makeshift mess-room-cum-sleeping-quarters. In addition to the rickety old table and chairs, there were four sets of creakingly old, rust-streaked, metal-sprung bunk-beds with thin dirty mattresses on them. Strewn across the beds were several dark coloured blankets and several items of discarded army uniforms. Beside the beds were piles of discarded uniforms from all three services.

"Excellent work, men," Sub-lieutenant Shaw said. "And well done, Chief."

"Sir," replied the chief before turning to his captives. "Right, then, you lot. Over to that bulkhead, with yor 'ands on yor 'eads." The spread-eagle man scrambled to his feet and joined the other captive men, who obediently shuffled over to the bulkhead.

Meanwhile, the other members of the boarding party began to robustly search the other compartments along the passageway. Suddenly, a rifle shot rang out and then an almighty gunfight erupted along the passageway. The chief pointed to two sailors.

"You men. Watch this lot. If they make any sudden moves, don't muck about. Just kill 'em. Rest of you, with me." The captives turned pale and one gulped noticeably. Clearly they had no appetite to test the sailors' resolve.

The chief approached the doorway and crouched down. Sub-lieutenant Shaw stood close behind with his hand on the chief's shoulder.

"Careful, Chief."

"That's the plan, Sir," the chief replied and poked his head into the passageway to glimpse what was happening. A ricocheting bullet pinged against a bulkhead and whizzed past his head, and he quickly withdrew. "Bloody hell, that was close!"

"What did you see?"

"One of our lads is down. Smithson, I think. Looks like he's trying to crawl towards us. Didn't see where the firing's coming from, though." The chief leaned towards the door again and shouted out, "Moorlands! Nichols! How many of them are there?"

"Two, I think," replied Nichols.

"Yeah, probably," added Moorlands.

"Where from?"

"Four or five doors down; left hand side," Nichols said.

"Keep up the pressure. And mind you don't hit Smithson." The chief turned to Sub-lieutenant Shaw and smiled, thrilled with the action. "Might be here a while, Sir."

Sub-lieutenant Shaw harrumphed and folded his arms in frustration. He then paced the compartment, glowering at his captives.

"Chief!" a voice called out from the direction of the curtain in the passageway.

"That you, Rattler?" asked the chief.

"Yeah. Keep 'em busy. We'll go round 'em and cut 'em off further for'ard."

"Good, Lad."

But then the rifle fire, which had initially been furiously intense, abated quite abruptly, and soon it was evident that the only rifles being fired were those of the boarding party.

Sub-lieutenant Shaw went over to the chief at the door. They exchanged glances. The Chief shrugged. Sub-lieutenant Shaw shouted out of the door.

"Cease firing, men!" The passageway fell silent. "This is Sub-lieutenant Shaw of the Royal Navy. You are surrounded by forces of the Royal Navy and I demand that you lay down your arms and surrender!"

Whilst Sub-lieutenant Shaw spoke, the chief crouched as low as he could and scurried out of the door and down the few yards of the passageway to the wounded Smithson.

"Yor alright, lad," he whispered, grabbed Smithson by his collar and began dragging the subdued casualty back towards safety and medical help.

During these moments of ceasefire, the accumulated smoke of battle began to disperse a little and the corpse of a soldier was revealed, slumped in a doorway further along the passageway. Several of the boarding party saw the corpse, and then saw their chief toiling over their wounded comrade. Without any order from Sub-lieutenant Shaw they slowly emerged from the safety of their own doorways and cautiously paced down the passageway towards the corpse and to shield their chief. Their rifles remained aimed steadily at the doorway where the corpse lay.

The fighting on board the Caledonia seemed to be over, at least for the time being. Other sailors now emerged from other doorways and gathered up their wounded shipmate, relieving their chief, who was now free to examine the corpse. However, he was distracted by a furious banging from a nearby door. There was shouting coming from behind it.

"Let me out!" the voice called.

The chief tried the door handle but it was locked. The chief leaned against the door.

"Stand back, mate, and yor'll be out in a mo," he said, and then signalled to one of the sailors to help him. The two men soon forced the door open with a few well co-ordinated kicks. The occupant of this small cell-like compartment was a fellow mariner. He was filthy from the greasy soot that covered every surface of the cell, and he had dried blood caked across a cheek.

"Boy... Agnes..." John spluttered, frantically. "Where..."

"Ease to five, mate," the chief said as he tried to calm John, "we'll find 'em."

John wrestled past the chief, stepped over the dead malign, and began kicking open the remaining closed doors of the illuminated passageway.

"Got to find the boy... Got to find the boy..." he repeated aloud.

Each time he wrenched a door open to reveal an empty compartment he became more animated with desperation. Soon every door was wide open and all the remaining compartments along the passageway were confirmed as empty. The boy, Agnes and Mr Forsyth, were nowhere to be found.

"They've got to be somewhere!" John snapped angrily. "They can't have just... just... disappeared!"

"Chief!" called a sailor from further down the passageway. He pointed into the darkness just beyond the lights. "There's another door just here."

John pushed past the sailor and grasped hold of the door handle, but it was locked. John and the sailor then kicked the door open with a single combined kick.

CONFRONTING THE PAST

The policeman sauntered past the deserted shop fronts along the darkened high street as if he hadn't a care in the world, which he probably hadn't, given the lateness of the hour and the quietness of the streets that night. However, when he heard the local church clock chime a quarter past the hour he stiffened up, increased his pace and smartly marched the last few yards to the police station. He marched beneath the wrought iron archway upon which a blue police lantern was mounted. It was not illuminated because of the blackout, and the darkened entrance to the police station looked slightly forbidding and intimidating. He vaulted the few stone steps and was about to push open the large, heavily glossed door when the door opened. A man in civilian clothes emerged, silhouetted in the doorway by a very dim light from within. The policeman tugged his forelock and exchanged simple pleasantries as he allowed the other man to leave the station. The man quickly descended the steps before the policeman stepped across the threshold into the station. The heavy door closed with a clunk.

The man emerged from under the archway and into the moonlit street. It was Inspector Wrynne, and he seemed in a rush. He hurried along the footpath and stopped at a parked car. He fumbled in his pocket for the car key, jumped into the car and sped off up the street as soon as the engine turned. The car's headlamps, heavily shielded because of the blackout, came on after the car had travelled a dozen or so yards. They did little to illuminate the way ahead.

A few moments after Inspector Wrynne had driven away, another car which was parked on the opposite side of the street, started into life and followed the inspector at a considered distance.

The journey was of short duration, partly because of the short distance and partly because of the reckless speed at which Inspector

Wrynne hurled the car around the streets of the town. The car eventually came to a halt outside a two-storey stone-built building, which on first impression looked like it may once have been a wealthy merchant's home. Now, however, it was run down and scruffy. The litter-strewn path to the front door, lined by six dirty, overflowing metal dustbins, indicated that the building had long been converted into squalid, bed-sit style apartments.

Inspector Wrynne produced a key, slipped through the front door and up the staircase. A few moments later a light came on in one of the upstairs rooms and this briefly illuminated the second car, which had pulled up behind Inspector Wrynne's. But the illumination was short-lived, because Inspector Wrynne appeared at the window and closed the blackout curtains, plunging the street back into darkness once again.

A door of the second car opened and Tobias climbed out. He slammed the door shut, pocketed the car key and crossed the street to the bed-sits. He paused by the front door and then dragged two of the brimming bins, carefully and quietly, onto the path in front of the door. This had the effect of obstructing the doorway. Tobias then produced a set of key-sized tools from a pocket, which he then used to unlock the door. When the door was partly opened he slid quietly into the building and up the staircase. When he reached the door of Inspector Wrynne's bed-sit he paused again. He took a deep breath and knocked firmly at the door. A few moments later, the door was unlocked and flung open, which made Tobias flinch. The inspector filled the doorway.

"Yes?" the inspector demanded sharply. Tobias simply stared back with a look of intense concentration, his head cocked very slightly to one side as he studied Inspector Wrynne's face. A moment passed before Tobias eventually spoke.

"Hello, Daephanocles."

The Inspector seemed taken off guard for a second before he replied.

"I beg your pardon? My name is Wrynne and I am a police inspector. What is your business at this ungodly hour?"

"Ungodly hour? Ironic, don't you think, Daephanocles?" remarked Tobias. But Inspector Wrynne frowned, and so Tobias continued, "That your *undoing* should occur during an hour which you describe as *ungodly*." But Inspector Wrynne simply folded his arms and stared blankly.

"Is that so?"

"You may dispense with the pretence, Daephanocles," continued Tobias. "Remember, I can see you. Remember what I am."

The inspector flashed an angry stare at Tobias.

"You're a filthy half-breed," he hissed, then shoved Tobias backwards across the landing and made a dash for the stairs, which he descended in a single leap. He pulled open the front door and, as he tried to hurdle over the dustbins he tripped and stumbled forwards. The bins crashed over and flung their contents along the path. Inspector Wrynne tumbled over amongst the grime, then staggered to his feet. He ploughed through the scattered rubbish, kicked a bin out of his way in a fit of frustration and then careered off down the street.

"You'll never conjure me!" he yelled over his shoulders as he pelted down the street as fast as his legs could carry him. Tobias jogged after him.

Inspector Wrynne ran past several shops and businesses. Then he saw that a pair of large solid wooden gates to a timber-merchant's yard had been left slightly ajar. He made his way to them and forced the heavy gates apart just enough to slip through, then he forced them closed behind him. However, the bolt mechanism was damaged and unusable, and for a moment he frantically searched for the way to secure the gates. He cursed, and then left the gates closed but unlocked.

The inspector turned and quickly surveyed the yard. The gate was at the end of a long rectangular yard, with wooden buildings on the three other sides. At the far end of the yard was a machinery workshop where a large circular saw could be seen through an open door. Along one side of the yard was a single storey office and an ironmongers; and along the other side was a two storey, open-sided timber storage building. This particular building had two wooden staircases, one at each end, and these led up from the yard to a balcony-style walkway that ran the entire length of the open-sided upper floor.

The inspector disappeared into the darkness behind the various stacks of timber stored on the ground floor of the storage building.

The gates creaked open and Tobias entered the yard. He pushed the gates closed and looked for a way to lock them. Eventually, he noticed several long and heavy timbers that were stood on their ends at the side of one gate. Tobias pulled at them until they fell to the dusty ground, landing at the foot of the gates and obstructing the gates from being opened much more than a couple of inches.

Tobias slowly strolled around the yard. He glanced in through the windows of the office and into the shadows surrounding the stacks of timber. He peered into the workshop but it all appeared deserted.

"You cannot escape, Daephanocles. Your time has come," he said.

"No it's not," shouted a reply from behind. Tobias whirled round just in time to see the inspector hurling several blocks of wood at him from the timber storage building. He ducked and raised his hands to protect his head. One of the blocks struck him on the back of his hand, causing it to bleed. Tobias quickly recovered his composure and, ignoring the pain, he darted over to the timber storage building. At the foot of the nearest staircase he extracted a club-sized chunk of wood from a rack of off-cuts before he entered the shadows of the ground floor.

Tobias cautiously explored the avenues of timber stacks, ready to defend himself with his makeshift club. A brief clunking sound from the upper floor attracted his attention, so he made his way to a staircase in the yard, and slowly climbed to the upper floor. "You were seen, by one of our agents," he said. "You were helping the Maligns, Daephanocles. You could have remained hidden from us, as you have done for centuries. But you chose not to. Why was that? What was so important about the boy that compelled you to break your cover? Or might it be appropriate to ask '*who* compelled you'?"

Suddenly, the inspector appeared from out of the shadows and lunged at Tobias, who stumbled backwards, his club raised in defence.

"You are mortal," snarled the inspector, "and alone." He wrestled Tobias to the floor and fought for possession of the club. Tobias would not yield and so the inspector struck him across the face several times. The inspector appeared to be getting the upper hand and was tugging at the club with increasing ferocity. Tobias let go of the club just as the inspector gave one particular heave and the inspector, now clutching the club, rolled backwards away from Tobias. Tobias quickly jumped to his feet and darted along a gap between two stacks of timber planks, where he sheltered in the shadows at the far end of one of the stacks.

The inspector now swung the club, menacingly, and paced up and down the walkway, scanning the lines of stacked timber in search of Tobias.

"You are trapped, my friend, and now I have the upper hand," the inspector said and paused at a stack of timber planks, which he tapped with the end of the club. At the far end of the same stack, Tobias peered over the top and glimpsed the inspector, who was looking the other way. Tobias placed his hand against the ends of the top two planks and shoved them as hard and as fast as he could along the top of the stack. At the other end of the stack the planks shot out and struck the inspector on the side of the head, toppling him over the edge of the walkway.

"Woah!" exclaimed the inspector as he fell.

Tobias emerged from behind the stack and peered over the edge of the walkway.

The inspector had landed in a broken heap on the dusty concrete below. The awkward, motionless tangle of limbs; the grotesquely twisted neck; the vacant, unblinking eyes, they all indicated that the inspector was dead.

"Blast!" muttered Tobias, "Blast! Blast! And Blast again!" he repeated as he bounded down the staircase to the body. He felt at the neck for a pulse. "Blast!" he said again and stood back from the body, nervously scooping up the fallen club as he did so.

The body began to flinch and shiver as a red glow slowly enveloped the corpse. Wisps of ethereal mist appeared to seep from the inspector's body and accumulate in the air above it in a slowly revolving vortex. Tobias stepped further back, anxiously tapping the open palm of one hand with the club. He glanced around and behind him, appearing to be uneasy with the situation; and looking for support that wasn't there.

The vortex slowed almost to a stop and the body fell limp. Then the vortex ceased spinning and it revealed the demon, Daephanocles, in all its terrible, demonic reality. Daephanocles stepped away from the corpse, glanced down at it and then looked over to Tobias.

"I never did like that man," the demon said in a deep nasally voice. "He was proud, arrogant, envious and greedy. Pity, though. He was a good host."

"Your sentiments are immaterial, Daephanocles. Your time is over, whatever occurs; your captivity remains at hand."

"Captivity?" snorted the demon, "but you have just released me." Daephanocles stretched his arms and fluttered his wings. The demon sneered, raised itself above the ground and drifted the few paces over to Tobias. It stopped only when its face was inches from Tobias's. "See," Daephanocles said, "I can even fly, now." Tobias stepped back, and gulped nervously.

"Nonetheless, I intend to dispatch you to your rightful captivity in Raquia."

"Ha!" Daephanocles scoffed, "you think *you* can conjure me into captivity?"

"Yes."

"Ha!" Daephanocles paced menacingly in front of Tobias. "You! A half-breed without proper celestial powers. You! Your father was a freak; and your mother a goat herder."

"Actually, I think she was a maid."

"Whatever," Daephanocles dismissed the correction with a wave of his hand. "You'll have to try harder than that little performance."

Tobias was provoked by the demon's ridicule and insults.

"We 'half-breeds' always work hard for our redemption," he said stubbornly.

"Redemption? Ha! A fool's errand," scoffed the demon, who seemed perversely entertained by Tobias's faith in redemption. "Redemption is for the weak and powerless. But, of course, you *are* weak, *and* you lack the celestial power to see redemption for the folly that it is." Daephanocles snatched the club from Tobias. "Power. Now, that's what really counts," and the demon effortlessly snapped the club like a dried twig. "Power is something I have plenty of. And you, my friend, do not." Tobias stared thoughtfully at Daephanocles for a moment.

"So it was a more powerful demon, was it?" he asked. Daephanocles reacted defensively.

"No!" the demon insisted. But Tobias continued.

"You were told by a creature more powerful than yourself, to break your cover and help those Maligns."

"He's not more powerful!" Daephanocles snapped. "But, anyway, what if he did? You're too late to stop him now. The boy *will* be separated by fire; your precious headquarters *will* be destroyed; and you will die this very night. Why? Because *you* and your little friends have no power."

"You forget that I had the power to see you when you were in possession of the inspector."

"Ha! And you forget that you are mortal... and alone."

The demon raised the broken club, menacingly, ready to strike Tobias down.

"Ah," Tobias added, as he raised his arms to shield himself, "but when we conjure and capture demons, you forget one important fact about we 'half-breeds'."

"And what's that?"

"We never work alone," whispered a voice from behind the demon. Daephanocles whirled round in complete surprise and was horrified to see Marcus standing a few feet away, next to the open doorway of The Pathway.

Swirls of spinning flame leapt from the Pathway and flung an invisible, celestial grip around Daephanocles.

"No!" wailed the demon, but it was too late. Tobias launched himself at the distracted demon and used every ounce of his strength to shove the demon at The Pathway. Daephanocles desperately clawed at Tobias, but the demon was substantially weakened by the power of The Pathway. Tobias easily overcame the struggling demon and stepped away.

Daephanocles sobbed and pleaded for mercy, but The Pathway relentlessly tore the demon apart, piece by demonic piece, wisp by ethereal wisp, and sucked it down the long fiery corridor. The wailing demon faded away steadily until the last wisps of its existence finally disappeared down The Pathway and the doorway closed abruptly behind it.

The yard fell silent.

"Impeccable timing, brother," Tobias said.

"You're most kind."

"For a moment, I had considered the possibility that you had been unable to locate our whereabouts."

"A potential outcome not altogether lost on me. I visited many varied streets of this town before I eventually secured your location," replied Marcus. "Was it absolutely necessary for you to pursue this demon without waiting for me?"

"Brother, as you well know, over half a century has passed since you and I were previously presented with the opportunity to conjure and capture a possessing demon. I was somewhat reluctant to concede the opportunity for Daephanocles to evade captivity."

"Daephanocles?" Marcus said, "that was..."

"Yes, brother, Daephanocles."

"I had not recognised him..."

"No, brother. Recognition is my gift," Tobias sagely observed. "Now, I would be obliged to you if you could utilise your own gift and summon The Pathway. We must return to Overbank Hall with great haste. I believe our comrades could be in mortal danger."

"Certainly, brother," Marcus replied and then glanced at his watch.

"However, I must first attend to the List, and the small matter of a rescue that cannot be postponed. Under the circumstances, you may wish to accompany me."

"Of course, brother," Tobias said, "particularly if it enables our speedy return to Headquarters."

"Absolutely."

The Pathway reappeared and the brothers sauntered over to it.

"I am pleased that The Pathway is, once again, a secure method of transportation," Tobias remarked.

"Thanks to you, brother, for it was you who correctly suspected the breach in our security," Marcus replied as they stepped up into the flame-filled doorway.

"Indeed, it is regrettable that we failed to consider the possibility any earlier than we did."

And with those words The Pathway closed and the timber-merchant's yard was plunged once again into darkened silence.

ESCAPE AND EVASION

Agnes and the boy were sitting in the dimly lit compartment where John had earlier met with Mr Forsyth. They had been locked in there a few minutes before the gunfire had first erupted outside in the passageway. But now, after several minutes of gunfire, the fighting had subsided and Agnes and the boy now waited, quietly and anxiously holding hands.

"Be alright, love," she reassured him, patting his hand gently. "They must know we're in here. It won't be long, now."

The boy slipped his hands free and tip-toed over to the door that was nearest to where the fighting had taken place. He cocked his head slightly and strained to listen for movement outside the door.

"Come here, love," Agnes said, "they'll come for us soon enough."

"But I can here voices," he said.

Suddenly, they heard the rattle of keys in the lock of the *other* door to the compartment: the door that was behind them. The boy scurried over to Agnes and flung himself on her lap and wrapped his arms around her. The door creaked open and the sergeant and Mr Forsyth entered the compartment.

"On yer feet," growled the sergeant, and waved his rifle at them. "Come on, haven't got all day," he added and forcibly ushered them towards the door, where they followed Mr Forsyth out into the passageway. It was a similarly lit passageway to the one where their original cell was, and was totally deserted except for a soldier, a docile-looking private who was standing sentry outside the compartment. The private locked the door behind them and then followed the small group as they all trudged by torchlight along a network of dark, derelict passageways until they arrived at a huge, wooden door in the side of the ship's hull. The door was about six feet across and was crudely made from what seemed to be old railway sleepers. The sergeant and Mr Forsyth switched off their torches and plunged the party into total darkness. Then, the sergeant yanked on a rope that was hanging from a bulkhead. This released a chain hoist mechanism which rattled as the door swung effortlessly open to reveal a floating wooden pontoon tied alongside the hulk.

Agnes and the others peered out of the door and saw a small motorboat tied alongside the pontoon. And less than a mile away from the hulk there was the silhouetted outline of a village and small harbour, half-hidden in the moonlit night.

"Told you I'd get this door workin' eventually," the sergeant said with a smile.

"Yes, yes. Very impressive," replied Mr Forsyth rather agitatedly. He turned to Agnes and invited her to climb down onto the pontoon. "Shall we?" he said.

"After you," she replied firmly, holding the boy close to her.

"No, no. After you, my dear." Mr Forsyth gestured with a flourish of his arm, which he then extended for Agnes to hold herself steady on the few steps down onto the pontoon. She ignored Forsyth's hand. Instead she held the boy's hand tightly and they stepped slowly down and shuffled across the pontoon. Forsyth and the rest then followed.

The party paused at the edge of the pontoon, and neither Mr Forsyth nor Agnes seemed willing to be the first into the boat. The sergeant rolled his eyes and huffed.

"Look, can we just get on with it?" he said firmly, "they'll be onto us in a minute."

Mr Forsyth offered a hand to help Agnes. She released the boy and took hold of Mr Forsyth's outstretched hand. The sergeant put down his torch, slipped his arm beneath Agnes's other arm and helped her into the boat.

"You know I said the time for escape would present itself eventually?" she said, looking at Mr Forsyth. He frowned in puzzlement.

"My dear, I haven't the faintest idea what you are talking about…"

But Agnes turned away from Forsyth and spoke to the boy.

"That time is now, boy," she said and with immense effort she locked her arm with the sergeant's, grasped Mr Forsyth by the sleeve of his jacket and dragged both the men down into the boat with her. They landed in a tangled heap and she yelled, "Run! Boy, run!" as she struggled to keep the two men in the bottom of the boat.

The boy did not need telling twice. He grabbed the torch from the pontoon deck and darted back into the darkness of the Caledonia, like a rat down a gutter. The private, who had been stood beside the boy, stepped forward to help the entangled men, oblivious to the boy's departure.

"Get 'im, yer bloody idiot!" yelled the sergeant. The sudden realisation that the boy had escaped had the private spinning around several times as he chased his imagination around the empty pontoon, and he then almost fell over himself before he eventually started running after the boy down the dark passageways.

The boy flew fearlessly down the passageways, retracing his steps along the network of dark and dirty passageways. He frequently skidded on the greasy filth beneath his feet, particularly when he approached and rounded the many corners, but this did not faze him, nor delay him. The private thundered relentlessly after him, clumsily sliding into bulkheads as he careered and floundered around the slippery corners. Unfortunately, though, the private easily out-ran the boy on the long straight sections of passageway. And he was almost upon the boy when they emerged from the darkness and into the section of illuminated passageway near the compartment where the party had set out from. The boy glanced over his shoulder and saw that the private was about to pounce.

"Leave me alone!" he screamed. Panic was evident in his voice, and this outburst attracted the attention of a sailor who happened to be searching nearby compartments. The sailor stepped cautiously into the passageway to see what was happening and he saw the private soldier pursuing the boy. He raised his rifle and called at the private to halt. The private either ignored the sailor or was oblivious to his presence. And this ignorance cost him his life as in the next second the sailor shot him cleanly through the base of his throat. The soldier fell to the floor like a marionette whose strings had just been cut, and the boy slid to a collapsed, gasping heap at the sailors feet. The sailor looked down at the boy.

"'s'all right, mate. He can't get you now," he said and helped the boy to his feet. He wrapped an arm around the boy and held him close, so that the boy could not see the soldier's gurgling death throes amid the pulsing scarlet shower that squirted from the neck wound. "Come on, let's get you up top, eh?" he said and flashed a weak smile down at the boy.

They turned and started their walk to the safety of the upper deck, when a clenched fist suddenly appeared from a doorway and struck the sailor squarely on the side of his head. He was knocked unconscious by the sheer force of the blow and he slumped to the deck, his tin helmet pushed awkward across his face. The boy was pulled to the deck by the collapsing sailor and, as he struggled free, the owner of the fist stepped into the passageway, grabbed the boy by the scruff of his collar and lifted him cleanly into the air with one hand. It was the muscular private.

"Where d'yer think you're goin'?" he sneered, and put his other hand across the boy's mouth to prevent any further screams. He then stepped over his dead colleague, taking care not to slip on the pool of blood, and sauntered off down the passageway toward the escape boat.

Moments after the boy and the muscular private had disappeared into the darkness, two sailors came stomping into view from a connecting passageway, in response to the gunshot. They saw their collapsed shipmate, who was now groaning and reeling on the deck.

"Nick!" one of them called out and ran over to the groaning man. He helped Nick into an upright sitting position, whilst the other sailor scanned nervously up and down the passageway. He saw the dead soldier and turned to Nick.

"Bloody, hell, mate. Hope you don't think I'm helping you clean that lot up," he said, flatly.

"Never mind that, just give us hand," said the other sailor as he struggled to drag Nick to his feet. Seeing that their shipmate had no apparent bullet wounds, the two sailors propped Nick up, with an arm over each of their shoulders, and carried the delirious sailor back along the criss-cross of passageways. They carried him past the makeshift mess-room and the curtain at the end of the main passageway. At the foot of the ladder that led back up to the upper deck, they paused for their commanding officer, who was descending the ladder.

"Sir," they instinctively mumbled a greeting.

"Thank you, men," Philip said. Nick had by this time regained some level of consciousness, but was babbling incoherently.

"That the Skipper?" he suddenly slurred.

"Yes, it is, er…" Philip looked to the others for help.

"Nichols, Sir. AB Nichols," offered one of the men.

"Don't worry, Nichols, we'll have you right as rain in no time," Philip said.

"Boy, Sir. A boy… I saved him… and then…" slurred Nick. Philip's ears pricked up.

"Yes..? And..?" he demanded. But Nick slipped back into an incoherent mumbling. Philip looked at the two men, who seemed completely bewildered by Nick's ramblings.

"Didn't see no boy, Sir," said one of the men.

"Found him knocked out next to a dead Jerry, Sir," continued the second man.

"Killed the bugger, too. Shot 'im right in the gullet," added the first man. Philip grimaced at the thought, and the sailors tried to suppress a smirk at Philip's reaction. Philip flashed a disapproving look at them and their faces quickly became serious again, neither of them willing to incur the wrath of their new Captain.

"But no boy?" Philip asked.

"No boy, Sir," confirmed the second man. Philip nodded an acknowledgement.

"Carry on, men," he said and strolled on through the curtain and along the passageway, where he found the chief petty officer in the makeshift mess-room. The chief was supervising several sailors who were securely restraining the prisoners ready for transfer ashore. He glanced over at Philip and, recognising his Captain, stepped smartly over to him.

"Sir. Just restraining the prisoners."

"Good," replied Philip as he surveyed the compartment. His eye was drawn to a pile of military uniforms and caps beside one of the bunks. There was a wide variety of kit and Philip recognised the red trim of a military policeman's cap, the grey of the RAF and even the jacket of a Royal Navy petty officer. The chief followed his captain's gaze.

"There's more stuff like that in one of the other compartments further down the flat, Sir," he said.

"Mmm…" replied Philip as he approached one of the prisoners, whose arms were securely restrained behind his back. Philip drew very close, his nose almost touching the prisoner's. "I presume that you are not in regular full time service with the forces of His Majesty King George." The prisoner scoffed in reply. Philip turned to the chief, "Carry on the good work, Chief," he said and drifted out into the passageway.

Further along, he came across the blood-soaked corpse of a malign, slumped in a doorway. The deceased appeared to have died of a chest wound. Philip paused momentarily, for there seemed to be something vaguely familiar about the man; so he used his foot to lift the corpse's head in order to get a better look at the face. To his astonishment he stared straight into the face of the military policeman whom he had challenged on the train! Philip let the head fall free and peered into the compartment, which was larger and better illuminated than the other compartments he had passed.

Inside, Sub-lieutenant Shaw was struggling to placate a frustrated and animated chief petty officer, who was filthy and had dried blood smeared across a cheek.

"Don't speak to me in that tone of voice, Chief! You will do as you are told!" demanded the sub-lieutenant.

"Look, Sir," replied John, "You've got no bloody idea why I was held here so just let me..."

Philip interrupted their heated conversation.

"Sub-lieutenant Shaw," Philip called out. The sub-lieutenant swung around as Philip entered the compartment. "An extremely well executed boarding. I congratulate you."

"Thank you, Sir," was the flattered reply, and a small smile formed across the sub-lieutenant's face.

"And you, Chief Popple... I mean... Chief Drummond." Sub-lieutenant Shaw's jaw dropped open in disbelief.

"You know this man?" the sub-lieutenant asked, incredulously.

"Of course I do, Shaw," Philip replied, slightly irritated. "How are you, Chief?"

"Where's the boy? Where's Agnes? And the others," John asked with a note of desperation in his voice.

"It seems that one of my men briefly liberated the child but was then overpowered. I'm sorry."

"And what about Agnes?"

"Agnes?" Philip asked, "who is Agnes?"

"Never mind," John sighed. Philip turned and spoke to the sub-lieutenant.

"How close are we to completing the search?"

"Erm," the sub-lieutenant replied as he gathered his thoughts. "A team's sweeping the last few compartments and flats up for'ard, Sir."

"Good."

"Apart from the prisoners and this chief petty officer," the sub-lieutenant continued, "the other finds of material value were hoards of stolen property: jewellery and cash mostly, and lots of it. And forged identity papers; dozens of them in bundles."

"Really?" Philip raised a surprised eyebrow. "Excellent work, Shaw. I am impressed."

"Thank you, Sir," the sub-lieutenant replied, and then leaned closer to Philip and whispered, "Sir, how on earth did you know that this man would be here?"

"A rather large white bird came and told me," Philip answered in a patronising whisper. Sub-lieutenant Shaw realised he was being mocked and his cheeks reddened.

A petty officer then entered the compartment.

"Sir," the petty officer said, "for'ard flats and compartments 'ave been checked and secured."

"Good," Philip said, and glanced at his watch. "Time is upon us already, men; and we have a convoy to meet."

"Sir," the petty officer continued. "But we did find a big door in the side of the ship. Wide open. It leads down to a pontoon. Couldn't see any boats or anything, but we think some of 'em might have got away."

"And with Agnes and the boy too, no doubt," Philip observed, and placed a hand of consolation on John's shoulder.

John sighed heavily.

"But let's get you showered and changed, first, eh?" Philip said and led John out into the passageway. "We can't let you go after them looking like this, can we."

"Aye," muttered John, "but where am I going to find 'em? I don't know where they could have gone."

"I have no idea either, John. But you mustn't give up," Philip said. They then climbed the ladders to the upper deck. "And, I think," Philip continued when they were finally stood on the upper deck, "you should go back to your headquarters, or whatever it is you call it. Get help. Get reinforcements, get intelligence, and get winning again."

The two men crossed to the edge of the upper deck and looked at the waiting destroyer.

"I'm sorry we didn't get them all, Chief. I just wish…"

"'s all right, Sir. You did your best."

"I just wish I could do more."

There was a pause.

"Well, you could get me ashore, Sir. It'd save me swimming back to headquarters." The two men looked at each other for a moment and then smiled. The chase was on.

REGROUPING

It was lunchtime when John emerged from the railway station in the small town near to Overbank Hall. He hailed a taxi from the rank outside the station and headed for Headquarters. Conversation during the ride was dominated by the driver's complaints about an air raid that had happened the previous night. It was the first on the town.

"Bleedin' Jerries," he muttered, "why did they have to go and drop 'em on us, eh?"

"Was there much damage?" John enquired politely, not so much because it interested him, but rather to keep the conversation away from questions about John's personal life.

"Well, I don't have an outside loo anymore," replied the taxi driver.

"Oh aye?"

"And no glass in me back windows."

"Oh, dear."

"The wireless said they might have been heading for one of the bigger cities, Liverpool or Manchester, but got lost and dropped 'em on us instead." John detected a note of anger creeping into the driver's voice, so he chose not to pursue the conversation any further.

The taxi slowed down as it went round a bend in the tree-lined country lane as it approached Overbank Hall, and it was then that John caught his first glimpse of the wisps of smoke drifting up from behind the trees. His heart sank.

"Don't tell me, they got the Hall as well," the driver remarked, darkly.

The taxi dropped John at the gate at end of the driveway, and headed back towards the town. John showed his identity papers to the soldiers guarding the barrier. They examined them without a word and allowed John through. He trudged past the screen of trees along the gravel driveway and approached the smoking ruin of a once proud country home. It was now a pile of smashed stone and smouldering, broken beams; with fragments of furniture and wood protruding from the wreckage. Several staff and students, along with some auxiliary firemen were still crawling over the rubble, trying to recover bodies, whilst a lone fire-tender was being used to damp-down the few remaining embers. The faces of weary survivors, streaked with smoke and tears, painted a painful picture of the agony of the previous night.

John observed the scene with a surreal detachment that he had once described to a shipmate as 'witnessing the world turning'. He had experienced this feeling before, on every occasion that he had seen action at sea when the ship had been hit and shipmates and friends had been killed or wounded. And it was not lost upon John that on this occasion, too, there may be people he knew who were now dead or injured or trapped under the wreckage of Overbank Hall.

His natural inclination was to join in with the rescue efforts, but he knew that this was not his particular battle. He had his own to fight. So he resisted the temptation to help, and instead he concentrated on searching for a familiar face he could talk to. He found two amongst the stunned survivors that were congregated on the lawned gardens, Walter and Solomon.

Solomon was sitting on the lawn, propped against a small retaining wall that supported one of the raised flower beds. The locks of his long lank hair hung untidily, half-obscuring his face. He looked his usual frail and forlorn self; and seemed deep in thought. A sombre-looking Walter sat beside him, and offered him a drink of water from a flask. John approached them and without a word plonked himself on the grass beside them. Solomon hooked his hair behind his large ears, slaked his thirst and then offered the flask to John, but John shook his head, silently. They all gazed across at the wrecked Hall.

"We can defend ourselves against demons," Solomon said at length.

"But not Nazi bombs," John noted, dryly.

"Many more could have died had the angels not observed the bomber's change of course and confronted the demon responsible for it," Solomon said.

"So it wasn't a stray bombing raid," said John.

"Of course not," Walter said.

There was a long pause during which John waited for Solomon or Walter to enquire about his own progress. But they both remained silent for the moment. Solomon glanced at his pocket watch, which he produced from inside his leather jacket, and then rested his head back against the wall. He closed his eyes as the sun shone onto his face.

"I lost 'em," John suddenly blurted.

"I assume you are talking about your mission," Solomon said, without opening his eyes.

"Aye."

"Who exactly is gone?" enquired Walter.

"Forsyth, Agnes, the boy," he continued, "all of 'em, gone."

"Mr Forsyth?" Walter sat suddenly bolt upright. "You've seen Mr Forsyth?"

"Aye," replied John.

"Where? When? Is he alive and well?"

"He were when I last saw him," answered John. "Why all the concern?"

"We discovered his staff car, yesterday afternoon," explained Walter, "smashed alongside the body of his driver. When we couldn't find Mr Forsyth's body, we assumed he had been abducted by the Maligns."

"Don't know about abducted," commented John, dryly, "he acted more like he were one of them Maligns."

Solomon opened his eyes and looked across to John. He raised an eyebrow.

"Is that so, John," Solomon said.

"And where have they gone?" asked Walter.

"Aye don't bloody know!" John threw up his arms, "that's why I'm here. One minute I were in a safe house; next I were locked up in a rusty old wreck in 'pitch dark. Then there was a gun battle, and now they're all gone!"

Solomon gave John a hard stare. Some curious survivors suddenly lost interest in the recovery work and eavesdropped on John's tirade.

"I'm sure he's a Malign, y'know," John added, "he acted right strange. He must be running the show, or something. I'm sure of it. Anyway, the Navy somehow got wind of what were happening and they came and rescued me, thank God. But Forsyth and some of his Malign mates escaped and took Agnes and the boy with 'em."

"So, the Maligns finally have the boy," Solomon said, thoughtfully. "And yet you say they haven't killed him, despite the opportunity they've had. Interesting."

"I need to find out where they've gone but I don't know where to start looking," John continued. "And then this," he indicated the ruin of the Hall. "This is the last thing I need."

"Worry not, John. We are here to help," a familiar voice said.

Solomon, Walter and John turned around to see Tobias and Marcus emerge from the shrubbery and jump down from the retaining wall onto the grass beside the others.

"Hello, Tobias; Hello, Marcus," Solomon said, "successful mission?"

"Very," said Marcus.

"Solomon, we must continue this conversation in a more secure environment," continued Tobias.

"This way please, John." Marcus indicated to John that they should move towards the nearby chapel. "Please be so kind as to join us, Walter."

Marcus and Tobias helped the frail Solomon to his feet and half-carried him over to the chapel and into the vestry. Here they evicted a few loitering staff and deposited Solomon on the only available chair.

The room was small and drab, the decor was plain and dull, and the tiny, frosted window above the door let in a narrow shaft of daylight. This dimly illuminated the room. In addition to the chair, the only other furnishings were a dressing table and a modest wardrobe. A full-length mirror hung next to the interconnecting door that led into the chapel.

"And you say the boy was not killed, but taken with them when they fled the Caledonia," Tobias said when he was certain that they were all finally alone.

John nodded.

"Gentlemen, we have little time," Tobias said, "Daephanocles was involved."

"Who's Daephanocles?" asked Walter.

"Daephanocles was a demon of high Malign standing," replied Tobias, "formerly of the Fourth Choir of Angels. He had not been seen for centuries, and then he suddenly appeared centre stage in John's mission."

"You said '*was*'," Solomon observed, "as in the past tense."

"Conjured," Tobias replied.

"And now safely held in Raquia," added Marcus.

"Congratulations," Solomon said, and looked pleased with this particular success.

"But before I conjured Daephanocles, he informed me that the Maligns intended to separate the boy by fire."

"Oh, my word," Solomon, gasped, "we must stop them."

"What's that mean?" asked John, "separate by fire."

"It is a ritual sacrifice," replied Solomon, "through which a Malign can increase their energy and strength by stealing it from a sacrificial victim."

"Eh?"

"It is a very unpleasant sacrifice involving fire, but is rarely practiced these days, mainly because of a scarcity of suitable victims."

"And because *most* people yield very little energy to make the risks of the sacrifice worth while," added Marcus, as he exchanged an anxious look with Tobias.

"And what happens to the victim?" asked John.

"Why, the victim is consumed by the fire and dies," replied Solomon.

"Oh, aye?" said John, and then added, "but now that you got rid of that Daephanocles, they can't do the sacrifice, can they?"

"That's not quite true," replied Tobias, "Daephanocles implied that there was a Malign more powerful than himself, who was behind the boy's abduction."

"Who?"

"We don't know," said Tobias, "we just know he wants the boy and is now likely to have him."

"But why?" asked John, "I mean, why the boy? Can't they sacrifice somebody else?" Marcus and Tobias exchanged anxious glances with each other again, but said nothing. There was a brief pause.

"What I want to know," Walter piped up, "is why Mr Forsyth would become a Malign?"

"Indeed," Solomon added, "what evidence do we really have?"

"Well, for a start, he never told me that Agnes would be there," John said.

"Agnes?" asked Solomon.

"Agnes was looking after the boy when I got there. Forsyth knew she was and he never warned me! Never told her either."

Solomon raised a quizzical eyebrow.

"That is your evidence? Mr Forsyth omitted to disclose the identity of the incumbent guardian?"

"Aye," replied John.

"And why was it important to tell you who she was?" asked a curious Walter.

"Because she's my wife."

John scrutinised everyone's reaction to this revelation. Marcus and Tobias appeared mortified; Walter looked puzzled and bemused; whilst Solomon remained calm and impassive.

"Mmm…" Solomon said and stroked his chin, thoughtfully, "your wife?"

"Aye."

Marcus and Tobias glanced at each other in utter astonishment.

"When..? How..?" said Tobias, "she never spoke to me of any marriage."

"You mean *you* know her as well!" John gasped with incredulity.

"Er… yes," Tobias replied, slightly embarrassed. He turned to Solomon, "Mr Forsyth ordered me to replace the boy's incumbent guardian with Agnes on a temporary basis, until permanent guardians could be assigned. I understood that John was to assist her in this mission. I had no idea that they had any previous knowledge of each other, let alone that they were ever married."

"And does every other bugger know her as well?" John demanded.

"I don't," offered Walter.

"Right then," said John, "how long have you lot known her, then? Since she was chosen? Or just recent?"

"Well, technically she wasn't on the List of Chosen," Tobias answered, "but, yes, we've known her since William brought her here… about six years ago, I think it was."

There was a pause.

"So you knew my father as well?" John said.

"Your father?" asked Marcus, slightly puzzled.

"Yes, my father. William," John said impatiently. "He was my father."

Tobias's jaw dropped. Marcus smacked himself on the forehead.

"Of course," Marcus cried, "now it all makes sense."

"But you look nothing like William," Tobias said, weakly.

"He doesn't have to, brother, when he looks like his mother," Marcus replied and turned to John. "Mr Forsyth spoke freely about your parents when you first arrived, did he not? Your father and Mr Forsyth were acquaintances of long standing, were they not?"

"Aye, they knew each other, according to Forsyth."

"Before their Renaissance?"

"Aye."

"On reflection, it was most improper of Mr Forsyth to discuss such personal matters at length. I should have recognised the warning signs but, alas, I wasn't paying proper attention. I was too engrossed in the problems I'd had with breaches in The Pathway's security."

"Well," said Solomon, "I think it is premature to assume that Mr Forsyth's malign motives are rooted in his pre-Renaissance life. What other evidence do we have?"

"Marcus and I believe that the Pathway's security breach was Mr Forsyth," said Tobias.

"Of this you are quite certain?" asked Solomon.

"Absolutely," continued Marcus, "I was baffled by the security problem. But then Tobias pointed out that Mr Forsyth was the only other person who knew my mission destinations."

"I became suspicious," added Tobias, "and so I advised Marcus to undertake several journeys without the knowledge of Mr Forsyth."

"The problem duly disappeared," concluded Marcus.

"Is that so?" Solomon pondered, "But how did Mr Forsyth inform the Maligns of your destinations? Surely we'd have noticed?"

"I saw him," offered John, "out of the window, on my first night. I woke up and went to close the window and I saw him hand something to a soldier."

"That in itself proves nothing," Solomon said.

"In the weeks prior to his abduction," suggested Marcus, "Mr Forsyth made a number of unorthodox and secretive trips to London. All were undertaken without using The Pathway."

"But why would he want to stop you using The Pathway?" asked John.

"For his own security," chipped in Walter. "By breaching the security of The Pathway he could create the right environment needed to carryout his own abduction. And an inoperative Pathway would delay the movement of our staff during any subsequent emergency."

"Like now," observed John.

"Yes," answered Walter.

"But now we've rumbled him," said John, "and all I need to do is find out where he is so I can give him a good kicking!"

"Indeed," Solomon said, dryly. "Now, tell me, John. Tell me everything that happened on your mission." John relayed the detail of his mission; meeting his old captain; seeing Agnes and the boy; the arrest and captivity on the old Caledonia; his meeting with Forsyth; and his rescue by his old captain.

"... and now I've no idea where they could have gone," John concluded. He was confused and didn't mind admitting it to the others.

"We need more help," he added, "or this is going to take too long and it'll be too late for the boy and Agnes."

Suddenly, there was a knock on the interconnecting door. Walter opened the door, but there was nobody there. He stepped into the chapel to investigate.

"Gentlemen," he called to the others, "I think your presence is required."

The others shuffled through the door into the chapel. It was a modest-sized Victorian chapel, plainly decorated and containing around a dozen rows of plain wooden pews on either side of a central isle of black and white mosaic tiles. Above the altar was a huge, round, stained glass window depicting the passion of Christ.

In front of the altar was a white angel, surrounded by an incandescent aura of light.

Solomon, Marcus and Tobias bowed cordially to the apparition.

"Arella," Solomon greeted the angel with a smile, "it is an absolute pleasure."

The Angel Arella reciprocated by slightly bowing its head.

"Greetings," Arella replied in a quiet, gentle voice. "Congratulations to Marcus and Tobias," Arella nodded to Marcus and Tobias, who seemed slightly embarrassed by the unwelcome attention. "Your efforts in dispatching Daephanocles to Raquia have been duly noted and accredited to your redemption." Arella then turned to John. "John Popplethwaite. The solution to your problem can be found if you look into your parents' past."

"My parents' past?" John asked and glanced at the others. "What bit of their past?" he added and turned to Arella, but the angel had vanished. "Oh. Where's it..?"

"Angels never stay for long," remarked Tobias.

"So, Forsyth may have gone to somewhere in your parents' past," Solomon continued. "What did they have in common from their past?"

"Mum worked for Forsyth's family, I mean the Rotheton family. That were his name back then. They're a really rich family."

"And you know of the family?" enquired Tobias.

"Yeah, 'course."

"And where can we find them?"

"They own a big estate, Rotheton Park."

"Pathway, Marcus?" Tobias asked.

"Certainly brother," replied Marcus. "Destination, Rotheton Park. I'll take us straight into the house."

In the place vacated by Arella, the first flicker of The Pathway appeared.

"Walter, go and assemble a contingent of your men," Solomon ordered, "reinforcements may be required."

"Reinforcements, yes, Solomon," and Walter trotted off up the central isle to the main chapel door.

"And make sure they've got guns!" John added.

"Good luck, John," Solomon said. Marcus walked over to The Pathway.

"Ready?" asked Marcus. Tobias and John both nodded. Marcus looked across to Solomon. "I'll re-open The Pathway here, if we need reinforcements. We may also require the services of a number of Galearii in reserve, if that's possible, please." Solomon nodded an acknowledgement.

"I shall endeavour to arrange all that I can," Solomon replied.

John, Tobias and Marcus then stepped into The Pathway and went to search Forsyth's old family home.

ROTHETON WEALTH

Their destination was a large, grand room, possibly a drawing room, located within a substantial stately home. The room, and the house, was a statement of wealth, and there was no mistaking it. John peered into the room from the safety of the Pathway and was instantly awed by the room's opulence and splendour. He'd never seen anything like it before in his life. The highly polished wooden floor was partially covered by large, lavishly woven rugs; the walls were decorated with masterpieces; the sizeable marble fireplace was ornately carved; the bright, gold-leafed furniture was elegant and upholstered with soft velvet cushions. And on the ceiling, framed by an intricate oval of ornamental plasterwork, there was an enormous fresco, of a scene depicting four mischievous, cherub-like creatures, hiding behind bushes and undergrowth, whilst secretly watching several beautiful, naked women bathing in a river.

This, in John's mind, was clear evidence of the decadent wealth from which Forsyth had emerged. And it was in sharp contrast to the austerity and poverty that he remembered from his own upbringing.

It was all very quiet. The loud, slow 'tick-tock' of a large and exquisite, ornamental clock was amplified by the otherwise silence that greeted their arrival.

"I had expected a livelier place," commented Marcus, as he and Tobias cautiously stepped down from The Pathway.

"Aye, a bit quiet, in' it," John said, as he followed them. "Maybe a bit too quiet. Shouldn't there be some servants or something?"

"John, you wait here with Marcus whilst I take a look around," Tobias said and wandered towards the highly polished door at the opposite end of the room. "And please keep The Pathway open, Marcus. We may be required to depart in a hurry." He opened the door and sauntered off into a large, tiled entrance hall of equally splendid decor. The door closed behind him with a soft clunk, but the echo of his footsteps tapping across the tiled floor carried through the closed door. Tobias's footsteps faded from earshot as he explored deeper into the house.

Marcus stood next to The Pathway, as stiff and upright as a soldier on sentry duty. John, meanwhile, wandered around the room, gazing in wonder at the refinement of the Rotheton wealth. His thoughts wandered to the expert craftsmanship that created much of the excellent and delicate carvings that adorned much of the furniture. He slowly ran a finger along the edge of a marble table and examined his finger for any sign of dust or dirt. There was none.

"Bet they have folk dusting and cleaning all day long in a place like this," he commented. Marcus said nothing. "Do you think they'll be able to tell that we've been? Yer know: mucky finger marks, or footprints in the carpet, that kind of thing." They both glanced at the rugs for signs of footprints, but of course there were none.

The tapping of Tobias's footsteps came within earshot again, the door opened slightly and Tobias poked his head round.

"It would appear that the ground floor of the property is deserted. I shall presently investigate upstairs. It should also provide me with a suitable vantage point to survey the surrounding grounds," and he disappeared again, accompanied by his tapping footsteps.

"Where could people be?" John wondered out loud.

"I think Mr Forsyth may be able to provide some of the answers," commented Marcus.

"But only if we can find him."

Just at that moment, a servant's entrance, which was concealed in the corner nearest to John, creaked slowly open to reveal a large and forbidding demon. The demon stepped slowly into the room.

"Um..." the demon said, in a slow, deep, nasally voice. It appeared to be trying to suppress much of its fierceness. The demon hung its head in a kind of half-hearted bow as it moved forward. The facial expression seemed a mixture of discomfort, embarrassment, humiliation even, although its eyes occasionally flashed with anger and resentment. Its hands were raised in the traditional surrender pose, presumably to imply it had no intention to threaten.

John, not altogether surprised by the presence of a demon, slowly shuffled towards Marcus and The Pathway.

"Um..." the demon said, "Parley?"

A look of incredulity passed across Marcus' face.

"Parley?" he exclaimed, "You want to parley with us?"

"Um..." the demon paused and slowly thought about the question, "Yes."

"Oh, aye? What for?" asked John, a little too aggressively.

"Please, John, I'd be obliged if you would allow me to conduct this... er... this... most unusual of conversations."

"Say what you want to say, then," John said to the demon.

"Um... Forsyth... not here."

"Aye, I think we gathered that already," John said sarcastically and folded his arms. The demon flashed an angry stare at John and made a growling sound. John stared back impassively. Marcus shot a concerned glance at John.

"John, please, I implore you," he said and then turned to the demon. "Do continue."

"Um... Forsyth at Vulcan Foundry."

"What? *The* Vulcan Foundry?" John reacted with some surprise.

"You are acquainted with this place, John?" asked Marcus.

"Aye. Well, sort of. It belongs to the Rotheton's. It's where my dad worked when he were younger, when he met my mother."

"And is it correct to assume that Mr Forsyth cordially invites us to grace him with our presence?"

"Um..." the demon frowned as it thought hard about what Marcus had just said.

"He means," John spoke in a slow, deliberate, and loud voice, as if he was talking to a slightly dim, slightly deaf, elderly person, "does Forsyth want us to go to the foundry?" The demon snorted angrily and growled again, but managed to retain its composure.

"Um... Yes," it said.

"Marcus, can The Pathway take us there?"

"Of course, John," Marcus replied, "it is already prepared. All that is required is for you to step up into The Pathway and it will lead us there."

"Oh," John was a little surprised at the speed and ease with which Marcus was somehow able to redirect The Pathway.

"So, if you would be so kind, John," Marcus said with a gesture inviting John to step up through the flame-door into The Pathway, but without taking his eyes off the demon.

"But what about Tobias?" he asked as he stepped up into The Pathway.

"Tobias is perfectly capable of attending to his own affairs."

The demon was no longer able to control the anger rising within it.

"Daephanocles!" it suddenly wailed, "you conjured him? Sent him to Raquia?"

"With the help of my brother, I did, yes," Marcus replied, jutting his chin out defiantly. "And what of it?"

"Daephanocles... gone... never come back?"

"Daephanocles is now captive and will remain so until Judgement Day," Marcus answered. "And I caution you to prepare for your own inevitable captivity."

The demon briefly surveyed the otherwise empty room. John sensed that the parley was drawing to a close and that Marcus was now the one needlessly provoking the demon.

"Come on, Marcus," he muttered a warning through gritted teeth, "I think playtime's done with."

The demon drew itself up to its full height and growled menacingly.

"Brother not here," the demon then sneered. Its eyes narrowed and a malevolent glint appeared in them. "You alone."

"Erm..." Marcus shuffled back towards The Pathway; his face betraying the sudden realisation of the vulnerability of the situation.

The simmering anger and malevolence of the demon finally erupted and it flung itself angrily at Marcus, who was now only a single footstep away from The Pathway. But he might as well have been half a mile away, such was the speed of the demon. Marcus was scooped away from The Pathway by one of the demon's shovel-sized hands and thrown along the centre of the room, where he crashed into a plump and luxurious sofa that was up-ended by the force of the impact, hiding Marcus from John's view.

"No!" John yelled and tried, unsuccessfully, to jump down from The Pathway to aid Marcus and to confront the demon. But he couldn't step down, because it was too late. The Pathway had begun its slow and relentless closure and John could do nothing to stop it. As the last chink of daylight was replaced by the orange, flame-like swirls, the final image he had of Rotheton Park was of the demon stalking over to a helpless Marcus.

John just stood there, shocked by his own helplessness. He was almost certain that Marcus wouldn't be able to survive such a ferocious onslaught for very long. John remained silent for several seconds whilst he came to grips with the consequences of this sudden reversal of fortune. He was now alone and he suddenly felt uncertain and vulnerable.

However, he knew that to dwell on such feelings would not be helpful, so he took several deep breaths and considered the options that now lay before him: he could stay in The Pathway or he could travel along it to its destination. Obviously, he knew that if he stayed in The Pathway he would probably starve, and that wouldn't be helpful to Agnes and the boy, or to Marcus and Tobias. He had no choice but to continue alone.

John took his first hesitant steps and began his journey, slowly to begin with, but as his lower limbs became accustomed to the tingling sensation of The Pathway, his confidence gradually returned and he opened his stride into an enthused march. He was determined he was going to give Forsyth and his cronies a bloody good hiding when he got hold of them.

After what seemed like ten minutes of walking, John began to wonder whether The Pathway would take him directly into the foundry, or just near to it. But he didn't have to wait long to find out because the doorway of The Pathway suddenly began to open ahead of him.

The doorway revealed a blackened brick wall a few feet away. John paused. He couldn't see anything else without stepping down from The Pathway. But a cacophony of noise and smells flooded his senses: the smell of smoke, the clang of heavy metal, the whooshing of steam, and the low rumbling of machinery which shook the ground. It occurred to him that The Pathway had opened inside some kind of industrial building, but all he could see was a wall of dusty, blackened brickwork.

John presumed that he could remain protected whilst ever he remained within The Pathway. So, without poking his head out of the doorway, he peered out. He couldn't see much, so he poked his head out of the doorway, slightly, to get a better look. The blackened brickwork stretched about twenty yards either side of The Pathway door, and it reached upwards of twenty feet before it met a corrugated iron roof. The place was dimly illuminated and, apart from the glow of The Pathway, a little amount of light entered through a few small, filthy windows close to the roof. Nobody was around, so John cautiously stepped down from The Pathway and took a good look around. He was in the back of some kind of boiler house. The wall was at the back of a row of hot, steaming boilers: huge, black, ancient, riveted cylinders laid on their sides and supported by blackened brick frames. The diameter of each boiler was probably twice the height of a man, and they were arranged very close together, so that only the skinniest of men could squeeze between them.

The rumbling of the boilers was such that John would have been unlikely to hear anyone approach, so his head and eyes frantically darted to and fro, like a nervous meerkat recently emerged from its burrow. The Pathway closed, and this took with it much of the illumination.

John scurried along the dusty concrete to the end of the row of boilers. The gap between the end boiler and the side wall was wide enough for a man to walk down. He peered cautiously round the end boiler and saw, halfway down in the side wall, a door with faded blue paint flaking from it. Beyond the front of the boilers, there was a heap of coal upon which danced the flickering shadows from the furnace flames. John tip-toed over to the door and tried it, but it was locked. He went to the front of the boiler and was about to peer around the front when he felt something hard and blunt poke him in the back.

He slowly turned and saw the smug face of the army sergeant who had arrested him in Scotland. The sergeant had sneaked up behind John from the locked side-door, which was now held ajar by another soldier. Again, the sergeant prodded John with his rifle. John raised his hands and thought, rather philosophically, that at least he would now find Forsyth much sooner than he had expected to.

The sergeant ushered John out through the door. Outside, it was a little quieter, but there was not much daylight, partly because the sky was shrouded in chimney smoke, and partly because they had emerged onto a narrow, access lane that was overshadowed by the enormous, blackened, industrial structures on either side of it. John was silently shepherded along the lane and through a truck-sized doorway into a huge building situated at the very end of the lane; all the while the sergeant repeatedly prodded him. Above the door was a sign that said 'No1 Melting Shop'.

Inside this hot, grimy building a row of six massive furnaces, each as big as a house, occupied much of the interior. A huge, cauldron-shaped ladle, which John thought was probably big enough to fit ten men inside, was being carefully lifted by a large gantry crane, and ferried with its fiery, orange, molten payload, towards a huge pit containing what John presumed to be the moulds for the molten metal. Another ladle, which looked empty and unused, stood on the concrete in front of the furnace nearest to John. There were several workmen busily attending to their duties. Each one glanced briefly at John and the soldiers but said nothing. John was fascinated and thrilled by the sights and sounds, and for a moment he forgot the reason for his visit. He paused to admire the wonders of the modern industrial age, but was prodded again by the sergeant. John frowned and obediently accompanied the sergeant to some rudimentary offices that had been built into the corner of the building.

They climbed a wooden staircase to the upper floor of the offices and the sergeant knocked on a door marked 'Foreman. Knock Before You Enter.' The private stayed outside whilst the sergeant and John entered the office. Inside, John discovered the perspiring and extremely agitated figure of Mr Forsyth sitting behind the foreman's scruffy desk. He glowered at John.

"Where are they?" John snarled, and marched threateningly towards Mr Forsyth. The muscular private, who had provoked John in Scotland, was stood behind Mr Forsyth and now aimed his rifle at John. This persuaded John to curtail his intended assault and to temper his aggression. But it would only be a temporary respite, he promised himself as he seethed and huffed at Mr Forsyth.

"Rest assured, John, they remain unharmed and safe, for the moment," Mr Forsyth said. "You will be reunited in good time. But for the time being we must wait for our guest of honour to arrive."

COMEUPPANCE

"So, Sergeant, where was he discovered?" asked Mr Forsyth, making idle conversation to pass the time.

"He were spotted in the Boiler House. But we got him before he knew it. Were dead easy."

"Alone?"

"Yeah."

"And what about Marcus?" asked Mr Forsyth. The sergeant replied by making a cutting motion with his finger across his throat. The news hit John like he'd been punched in the stomach.

"Good," said Mr Forsyth, "it would appear that our trap has worked seamlessly, Sergeant."

"Thank you, Sir," the sergeant said. "Can I call the rest of my men off, now?"

"Of course, Sergeant. You may stand your men down and assemble them down in the Melting Shop ready for the ceremony."

The sergeant nodded and made to leave, but Mr Forsyth wasn't finished. "Ahem, but before you go, please restrain our guest, will you."

The sergeant looked at the muscular private.

"You heard the man," the sergeant said. "Get on with it."

The muscular private placed his rifle on the desk, produced a set of handcuffs from a drawer and approached John, but John was in no mood for co-operation and he backed away into a corner of the room and raised his fists ready to fight.

"No chance," he growled.

"John, violence is unnecessary, and won't get you to Agnes and the boy any sooner," Mr Forsyth reasoned. "But if you are absolutely determined not to co-operate," Mr Forsyth indicated to the sergeant, who aimed his rifle at John's lower legs, "then, with reluctance, we can debilitate you a little more… permanently, yes? The choice is yours."

John allowed his arms to drop to his side and the muscular private shoved him, face-first, up against a window and applied the handcuffs. Once these were fastened, the sergeant left the office.

The window provided a panoramic view of the entire melting shop. John could see the furnaces, the ladles, and the sunken pit containing the moulds; and even the raised platform at rear of the furnaces, from where the raw materials were loaded into the furnaces. Mr Forsyth joined John by the window and looked at the scene.

"The Rotheton Iron and Steel Foundry Company," Mr Forsyth said.

"Aye, I know," replied John. "Big place, in' it."

"In total, there are almost two square miles of this sprawling industrial complex," replied Mr Forsyth, almost salivating at the thought, "and all mine by birthright."

John raised an eyebrow and glanced sideways at Mr Forsyth.

"Oh, aye? I thought you lost your birthright when you had your Renaissance?"

"And so I did, thanks to your father. But soon I shall reclaim what is rightfully mine. And this time, nobody: not your father, not you, *nobody* is going to stop me getting what's mine."

"Oh, aye? And how d'you think you can do it with the world and all the angels huntin' you down, eh?"

"Why, by dying, John!" exclaimed Mr Forsyth, raising his excited eyes upwards. He was clearly relishing the prospect. "A new Renaissance! Today Herbert Forsyth dies and I shall succeed to my true inheritance."

"Oh?" John was not entirely clear as to what Mr Forsyth meant by dying, but he assumed it must mean another fake death.

"With some Malign assistance, of course," added Mr Forsyth, almost as an after-thought. He glanced at his watch.

There was a pause.

"You're mad," John observed, flatly.

"Mad? I'm absolutely livid! And why shouldn't I be? I had wealth. I had prospects. I had love. And then the cup was dashed from my lips by your bloody father. He took away everything from me."

"What do you mean? My dad took nothing. He were no thief," John replied defensively.

"Oh, maybe not in the conventional sense of the term, but he was certainly a thief when it came to the heart. Not only did he wreck my inheritance, but he took away from me the one chance I had of true happiness with a woman."

"Oh, aye?" John replied with a raised eyebrow. "Somebody important was she?"

"Yes she was, John. She was your mother."

"You what?" John thought he had misheard, "did you just say my mother?"

"Yes, yes," Mr Forsyth replied. "She was the most beautiful flower in the whole world, and I had plans for us. But then your father came along with his coarse humour and his disregard for deference; yes, he came along and plucked her petals, and it made me very, very angry," Mr Forsyth fell silent for a moment. "So I vowed to get back what was rightfully mine, one way or another."

"Go on," encouraged John, with just a slight hint of confrontation in his voice.

"That's why your father joined the army. I had to get him away from your mother, so I arranged for him to be arrested for theft."

"Theft?"

"Yes, yes. I can't remember exactly what I said he'd stolen from the estate. Anyway, we persuaded him to join the army in exchange for me dropping the charges."

"We?"

"My father and the magistrate."

"Oh."

"And, of course, once in the army it would've been easier for him to get killed, or to have him killed."

"So then you'd be free to marry my mum."

"Good God, no," Forsyth replied. "No, your mother could never have been my wife. She was just a servant. No, I'd have probably married the usual debutant. And I'd have kept your mother as my mistress, of course, but not as my wife."

The thought of his mum being kept as a mistress, like some kind of pet, stirred a deep feeling of revulsion within John. He felt his anger rising again.

"So, if you hated my dad so much, why did you go back to save him at Mons? Or was that just a story you made up?" he asked.

"In a manner of speaking, John, I suppose it was. You see, we were never actually in the same battalion. I was in the Territorials at the outbreak of war. But, during the retreat from Mons, several battalions and regiments became mixed. And that's when I came across your father, very much alive. So when it emerged that he'd been left behind, I volunteered to go back for him: but it wasn't to save him. It was to kill him."

"But before you got your chance, The Pathway turned up and spoiled your day."

"Something along those lines, yes."

"But you were rescued!" John exclaimed, thinking how ungrateful Forsyth was. "It saved your life."

"It saved my flesh, but took away my life. It took *everything*. Surely, it was the same for your own rescue?"

"I know that if I weren't rescued I'd be rotting at the bottom of the sea."

"Would you? How do you know that?" Forsyth stared hard at John. "How do you know that the hatch wasn't opened moments after you stepped into The Pathway?"

John, of course, knew that he didn't know, and would never know.

"So, I suppose you killed him, in the end, I mean, last year, didn't you?"

"He had his comeuppance," Mr Forsyth said, coolly. This provoked John into an angry response.

"Aye, and you'll get yours." But Mr Forsyth sneered and then chuckled slowly.

"And who will dispense my comeuppance? You? Marcus & Tobias? Solomon? Remember, you are the one in chains, yes? Headquarters has been destroyed, and Marcus didn't stand a chance, alone against a demon."

"I'll still have yer," muttered John to himself. Mr Forsyth did not catch what was said and continued talking.

"But worry not, John, if you remain co-operative, you will shortly be reunited with Agnes and the boy, unharmed."

John withdrew into a sullen silence.

There was a knock at the door and the sergeant entered. He strode up to Mr Forsyth and whispered something in his ear. Mr Forsyth's face fell, slightly.

"Problem?" asked John.

"'Tis but a small delay," Mr Forsyth said to John, and then turned to the sergeant and whispered something in response. The sergeant nodded.

There was another knock at the door. A workman entered the office and removed his cloth cap.

"Next lot'll be ready soon, Sir," he said.

"Thank you, Foreman," replied Mr Forsyth. The workman nodded and replaced his cap. Mr Forsyth turned to John. "It is time. Please follow the Foreman if you wish see Agnes and the boy." John walked over to the door but paused as he overheard Mr Forsyth and the sergeant begin a tense exchange of words. Their voices were mostly hushed but occasionally became heated and were audible to John above the din that flooded into the room through the open door. John managed to catch snippets of their conversation before the muscular private roughly bundled him out of the door. John thought Mr Forsyth said something like "Tell them they have about ten minutes, maximum… plans can't be delayed… don't care… ten minutes or they all get it…" and the sergeant said something like, "but the boy… too risky… what about us… don't be daft… we have to wait for him."

The private and John filed down the wooden staircase and followed the Foreman across the noisy melting shop floor to a solitary ladle that stood at the edge of the building, close to one end of the furnaces. John noticed a wooden ladder leaning against the ladle. At the foot of the ladder, they waited for Mr Forsyth and the sergeant. When they arrived a few minutes later, the sergeant indicated to John that he should climb the ladder. The noise was too great to be heard properly, so John pointed up the ladder and looked at the others for confirmation. Mr Forsyth nodded and so John slowly climbed the ladder and peered over the top of the ladle to discover Agnes and the boy huddled together in the bottom. He slung his legs over the lip of the ladle and slid down the inside, where he joined Agnes and the boy in a long and much welcomed embrace.

The inside of the ladle seemed to be somewhat sheltered from the noise, and so they were able to hear each other, so long as they spoke with slightly raised voices.

"I thought you'd never come," said Agnes, partly crying and partly laughing, whilst trying to rub away the dirty tear streaks from her face. She smiled weakly. "Thought for a minute you might have been killed."

John smiled a reassuring smile even though his insides were in turmoil at the hopelessness of the situation.

"Not yet, love," he said and raised his handcuffed wrists for her to see. The disappointment was evident in her face.

"So you didn't manage to slip in unnoticed, then," she said, almost angrily.

"Nope."

"So what's the plan?" she asked, tersely. John shrugged his shoulders.

"Get us out, I suppose," he replied. Agnes rolled her eyes, but he continued, "Forsyth's got something that isn't going quite to plan. Looks like somebody's late or giving 'back word' on a deal involving us… or the boy." He glanced down at the boy, who remained quiet.

"So we could be here a while," she observed. John shrugged, again. He was not willing to disclose the part about 'ten minutes, maximum'.

"Only if you want to," he said and nodded towards the lip of the ladle. "Tell us what you think."

"Give us a leg-up, then. Let's have a look," she said and lifted a foot up for him to hold. John crouched down, and held out his handcuffed hands for her to step up into. He then lifted her up until her head and shoulders were above the lip of the ladle. He heard the crack of a rifle shot, followed by a loud clang as a bullet ricocheted off the side of the ladle. He opened his hands and Agnes dropped suddenly back into the ladle, panting. "They bloody shot at me!" she yelled, exasperated.

"You alright?"

"They bloody well shot at me!" she repeated, which led John to believe that she was not injured.

Then, through the rumble and roar of the furnaces they heard the whining of powerful electric motors, and their attention was attracted by the lattice-metal beam of a large gantry crane that came into view above their heads. Slung beneath the beam was a heavy-duty pulley system, and on the end of this pulley was a special hook mechanism for carrying the ladle. It consisted of what could best be described as an enormous bucket-handle with large hooks attached to the ends. This bucket-handle mechanism was obviously designed to hook into the two huge eyebolts fixed to either side of the bucket shaped ladle, and then lift it. Also hung from the pulley system, but from a smaller, separate cable was a large chain and hook. This was evidently designed to fasten to the base of the ladle, and used as a means to tip the ladle so as to pour out its contents in a precise manner.

All the hooks were lowered until they hung loosely beside the ladle and then they were quickly and expertly attached to the ladle by unseen workmen. John felt an air of foreboding about this activity. Neither Agnes, nor the boy made any remark about the crane's intention, but John could see the fear building in their eyes.

The crane's motors whined and the pulley mechanism whirred as it took up the slack. It paused momentarily, which John presumed was to enable the workmen to check the ladle was correctly attached to the crane.

The crane then jumped back into life again and the ladle lurched into the air, where it swung almost unnoticeably, as if in a very gentle breeze. The ladle was hoisted up until it was perhaps ten feet from the ground.

"Must be to stop us escaping over the side," Agnes said, eventually.

"Oh, aye?" remarked John, "so why's it taking us over to that great big furnace thing?"

It was true, the ladle was now being transported slowly and relentlessly towards the furnace that was closest to the Foreman's office.

"Oh my God…" muttered Agnes, "You don't think they'll…" her voice tailed off

"Fill us up with a scalding steel soup?" he finished her question for her. "Aye, probably."

"But…" she muttered, and fell silent. She grabbed hold of the boy, pulled him close to her and wrapped her arms protectively around him. And with that pitiful image in his mind, John sprang into action. He leaped up and reached for the lip of the ladle. He caught hold by his fingertips and frantically tried to haul himself up; his legs scraping and clawing desperately for traction against the inside of the ladle. Agnes jumped to his aid, but it was all she could do to avoid him inadvertently kicking her in the face. So she shoved her shoulder up against his backside and pushed him upwards until she was on her tip-toes. Eventually, John managed to scramble that extra few inches up and take hold of the large hook with his handcuffed hands. Agnes then grabbed one of his flailing legs and placed the foot firmly onto her shoulder, so that he could stand upon it. John glanced down and realised what Agnes was doing, and then with one last push he managed to hook a knee onto the lip of the ladle and slowly drag himself up so that he was partly knelt on the lip.

There was another crack of rifle fire, and the bullet ricocheted off the hook with a loud 'ting!' Another crack of rifle fire followed quickly upon the first, but this time there was no 'ting' or 'clang'. Instead there was a grunt from John and he slumped backwards into the ladle. Blood began to appear beneath his armpit.

"John!" screamed Agnes.

"What?" replied John as he struggled to his feet. Agnes pointed to the blood.

"You're wounded!"

"Eh?" John looked at the blood and lifted his arm, slightly, to get a better look. He noticed a bullet hole in his jacket sleeve, but felt no pain. "Oh, it's nowt. Just a graze."

The ladle jerked as it approached the Tapping Platform at the side of the furnace and it bumped clumsily against the side of the platform. Above them was the tapping point of the furnace, where its volcanic load would be emptied out into the ladle.

"I think a tiny bit of bleeding is the least of our problems," he said and placed his handcuffed arms around the boy and Agnes. He then gave her what he assumed would be their last kiss before the Foreman released a deluge of molten metal upon them.

INTO THE FIRES OF HELL

In the Boiler House, behind the hot rumbling boilers, The Pathway reappeared and opened in exactly the same spot where it had recently delivered John. Marcus appeared from the swirls of the arched doorway and cautiously stepped down. He was quickly followed by a stream of British-clad troops led by Walter, who was now dressed as a British Army Lieutenant. Each one of the troops wore a thick band of pure white cotton tied around each upper arm.

Marcus glanced around the edge of the end boiler and noticed the side exit door with the blue flaking paint. The door was ajar and Marcus hurried over to it and peered into the lane. He beckoned the others to follow. Walter came over and stood close beside him in the doorway.

"See that building at the end?" Marcus said to Walter, and pointed to the building at the end of the lane. "Melting Shop Number One, the sign says. That's where they are."

"Are you quite sure the angel said the building was called Melting Shop Number One?" asked Walter.

"Of course I am," Marcus answered, defensively. "Now disperse your men out, or whatever it is you do in these circumstances, and progress to that building as quickly and as quietly as you can," he said and then slipped out through the door.

Walter turned to his men and gave them some orders regarding their approach to Melting Shop Number One.

"And remember, do not shoot at anybody unless they are threatening to attack – after all, there may be some innocent workers wandering around," and he concluded with, "Good luck, men."

Walter peered around the door and saw the lane was clear of people; even Marcus had disappeared from view. Walter drew his pistol, walked into the lane and paused whilst the troops poured out after him. They spread out and began their advance upon the melting shop. There was not enough cover for twenty fully armed troops, and it was inconceivable that they could reach their objective without being spotted by at least one of the Malign guards patrolling the streets and lanes around the melting shop. Nonetheless, working in pairs, they dashed from one place of temporary refuge to another, each man covering his partner as best he could throughout the advance. They progressed steadily and quickly from doorway to doorway and from building to building.

A Malign soldier sauntered out through the large, main doorway of the melting shop and caught the full view of the white-banded troops advancing towards him. Immediately, the soldier shouted the alarm to his Malign comrades. He then dropped to one knee and raised his rifle with the intention of opening fire. But a well aimed shot from one of the forward troops passed clean through his skull and pitched him backwards into a dead heap.

The other Maligns were stirred into action. Malign soldiers appeared at the doorway and saw the approaching troops. They then flung themselves towards the shelter of the door frame as an inevitable volley of shots from the advancing troops came their way. This marked the beginning of a fierce and frantic fire-fight.

On hearing the gunfire, some of the workmen simply fled out of the rear entrance of the building, which opened onto a scrap metal marshalling yard behind the melting shop. But to get to that entrance the workmen had to first climb up onto the raised platform that ran along the rear of the furnaces. It was a wide platform, from where the furnaces were normally loaded with the scrap metal that entered the building from the marshalling yard through the rear entrance. The short flight of steps that led up to this platform was located at the end of the row of furnaces, quite close to the main front entrance. These steps came under heavy rifle fire quite soon, cutting off the escape for the other workers. They had to find whatever shelter they could from the ricochet of bullets coming from the white-banded troops. Some hid behind a disused ladle; some behind the open staircase leading up to the office; and others hid down amongst the huge moulds in the casting pit; in fact, they hid anywhere that afforded them the slightest prospect of protection.

The Malign soldiers were outnumbered by the white-banded troops, and soon the lane and doorway to the melting shop was littered with dead and wounded Maligns. The melting shop foreman and another workman dashed over to two wounded Malign soldiers, but instead of offering them aid they took up the soldiers' discarded rifles and began shooting at the white-banded troops. As the shop foreman loosed of a round, he was shot through the chest and slumped to the ground, dead. A moment later, the second workman was shot through the head and killed, too.

These two particular workmen had not been willing Maligns. They had actually been possessed by demons. And now that the men were dead, the demons within them were free to leave their host.

A red glow enveloped the bodies, and wisps of ethereal mist seeped from each corpse. This mist accumulated to create a slowly revolving vortex above each body, and the demons gradually appeared inside the vortex. This startling display caused a momentary lull in the fighting. And then, the demons emerged, fully formed, and to the obvious astonishment of almost everyone present.

Marcus arrived at the edge of the melting shop's doorway just in time to see the two demons being released from each vortex. He muttered something, stumbled backwards and dashed out of sight again.

The released demons stepped away from their dead hosts and loomed menacingly towards the white-banded troops. The troops shot at the demons, but the bullets passed harmlessly through them. In response, the demons let out a howling scream and shook their heads and fists in a violent fit. All gunfire ceased. The white-banded troops faltered in their resolve and started to retreat from the melting shop. Some troops had to place their fingers in their ears to block out the deafening din. So too did some Malign soldiers. Then the screaming stopped, abruptly. The demons raised themselves off the ground and then floated quickly and effortlessly towards the white-banded troops, who were now retreating in droves out into the lane. The Malign soldiers did not have the presence of mind to pursue the troops. Instead, they simply stayed where they were and watched from the sidelines.

Up in the Foreman's office, Forsyth and the sergeant viewed the entire spectacle from the window. The sergeant was unmoved by the sight, whilst Mr Forsyth's anxious face betrayed a rising level of agitation and distress.

Outside the melting shop, the demons taunted the white-banded troops. One demon grasped an unfortunate trooper by his throat and lifted him almost twenty feet into the air before releasing him. The trooper fell to the ground with a crunch and a scream of agony that told everyone that his lower legs had been shattered by the impact.

"Why don't you come and try that with me, you overbearing ruffians!" a voice rang out. The demons turned and saw Marcus stood in front of a nearby building. They floated slowly towards him, but as they got closer The Pathway opened up next to Marcus and this caused the demons to hesitate. "Please, don't be shy," Marcus said, "The Pathway will despatch you safely on your journey."

The two demons, who were now only a couple of yards of Marcus, appeared confused by the invitation. They paused and glanced at each other.

"Of course, please forgive me," Marcus added. "How rude of me for not informing you of your destination. It is captivity, in Raquia."

A look of horrified shock passed across the faces of the demons and they took a step back from Marcus and The Pathway.

"Surely, you're not afraid," Marcus feigned surprise. "Maybe my associates behind you can persuade you to embark on your journey."

The demons glanced over their shoulders, curious as to the identity of these 'associates.' They were shocked to discover two huge, white angels standing behind them. Before the demons had time to react, the angels grabbed them and flung them violently towards the arched, flame-filled doorway of The Pathway, where the magnetic-like pull of the spinning flames grabbed them firmly and began to drag them, screaming and wailing, down the long, flame-filled corridor, piece by demonic piece, wisp by ethereal wisp, atom by celestial atom.

A giant of a man watched the unfolding events from the vantage of a small, grimy, upstairs window in a building across from the melting shop. He had a pale and greasy complexion, which was partly obscured by a heavily waxed moustache. His face carried an ugly, enraged grimace that exposed his half filled rows of crooked yellow teeth. When the demons had finally disappeared down The Pathway, he growled angrily and stomped away from the window and disappeared into the depths of the building.

The Pathway closed behind the demons.

"Well, men," shouted Walter to his men, "what are we waiting for?" and they resumed their attack.

Marcus leapt for the cover of a nearby doorway when bullets were once again exchanged. But this time it was clear that the Maligns were not going to hold out for much longer, and many of them retreated for cover behind the moulds in the large casting pit, situated in front of the farthest furnaces.

The Foreman's office came under fire from the advancing troops, and Forsyth and the sergeant quickly ducked away from the window. They crept out of the office, down the open staircase and then sprinted across the exposed shop floor in a desperate attempt to reach the raised platform and make their escape out of the rear entrance of the building.

As they climbed the short flight of steps, the first wave of troops entered through the main melting shop doorway, led by Walter, and opened fire. The sergeant was hit several times and he toppled backwards and landed, crumpled and bloodied, at the foot of the steps. He made a monumental effort to drag his mortally wounded body from the dusty floor but he was shot again and collapsed, dead.

Forsyth, who had just reached the top of the steps when the sergeant was first shot, was wounded in the leg and he staggered along the raised platform, and behind the furnaces; out of sight and out of reach of the troops.

Walter led some of the troops into the offices, which they stormed and secured within a matter of seconds. Inside the foreman's office, Walter sidled over to the side of the window and cautiously peered from the corner of the window to the action below. This birds-eye view of the melting shop revealed that the last remnants of Maligns had fallen back to positions in and around the casting pit. Walter also saw the ladle slung up against the nearest furnace, which appeared as if it was about to be filled with molten metal from the furnace's Tapping Point. And to his shock and surprise he saw John, with a bloodied, wounded arm, struggling to climb out of the ladle!

"Look!" he beckoned over one of his men and pointed to John, "one of our men is inside that bucket thing. We must move it away from the furnace and get him out. Molten metal may be poured onto him if we don't."

"Yes, Sir," replied the trooper. They quickly identified the whereabouts of the crane driver, who was slumped dead on the footplate at the top of the access ladder, possibly hit by a ricocheting bullet as he'd tried to escape. They also saw that a Malign soldier of muscular build was scaling the access ladder. The muscular private, with his rifle slung over his shoulder, reached the crane operator and ditched the body over the side of the footplate before climbing to the controls.

"Shall I take him out, Sir?" the trooper asked.

"Yes," Walter replied. The trooper went outside of the office and took careful aim with his rifle, supporting it on the banister rail of the staircase to steady his aim. He then fired one shot, which hit the muscular private between the shoulder blades. The muscular private fell forwards onto the controls, blood pouring from his mortal wound. The trooper sauntered back into the Foreman's office.

"Good shot! " congratulated Walter, "I didn't know it was possible to kill a man and drive a crane at the same time."

"You what, Sir?" the trooper said, slightly bemused.

"Look," Walter said, pointing to the ladle, which was now being hoisted up away from the furnace, with John desperately clinging on to the pulley mechanism.

The ladle was hoisted as high as the pulley mechanism would travel, and it came to a jolting, creaking halt beneath the latticed metalwork of the crane gantry.

Fortunately, this now made it possible for John to climb from the crane mechanism to the gantry beam, which he managed despite his shackled wrists and wounded arm, which by now was hurting a lot.

During his climb from the ladle, John had originally planned to crawl along the gantry to the crane driver's position, but seen as two men had been killed within minutes of each other at the controls of the crane, he reasoned that the crane controls would probably remain unusable for the duration of the action. He also thought that Agnes and the boy would probably now be safer inside the armoured protection of the ladle, for the time being at least.

So, rather than crawl towards the controls, he crawled to the opposite end of the gantry beam where it was supported by massive, robust iron girders that were sheltered inside the roof space directly above the furnaces.

Here the heat was stifling, and the hot metalwork burned his hands. John began to feel light-headed and a tingling sensation tickled his ears. He realised it was essential for him to climb down from these roasting temperatures if he was to remain conscious. He had no wish to expose himself again to the gunfire and the fighting in front of the furnaces, so he clambered across onto another crane's gantry beam. This gantry beam spanned the width of the raised platform behind the furnaces. As he crawled along it, away from the heat of the furnace John glanced down and saw Mr Forsyth directly below him on the raised platform. Forsyth was cowering in amongst the charging boxes close to the furnace. The charging boxes were chunky, coffin-sized containers brimming with scrap metal and they were lined up, side by side along the front of the furnace's five doors, awaiting insertion into the volcanic bowels of the furnace. There was not much room in between each charging box, but Mr Forsyth had managed to drag and squeeze his wounded, portly bulk into the tight gap separating two particular boxes. Here he was carefully examining his injuries through his torn, blood-soaked trousers.

John wanted to leap upon Forsyth immediately, but he knew he would be unlikely to land accurately, and would be more likely to land on the jagged scrap metal poking out of the charging boxes. He looked for an alternative way down, and found one in the form of the Furnace Loader. This was a peculiar looking contraption: a tower of latticed metalwork that was hung upside-down from the gantry beam that John was crawling along. Attached to the bottom of the tower, suspended two feet from the ground, was the Loader's control footplate. And reaching out from the control footplate, pointing in the direction of the charging boxes, was a long, horizontal arm of thick metal, like a battleship's gun-barrel aimed at the furnace. At the end of this arm was an odd-shaped hook. The arm was evidently used to lift the charging boxes and insert them deep into the furnace.

John reached the tower and began to climb down towards the control footplate. He glanced around to see if there were any other Maligns around on this side of the furnace, but the area seemed clear of Maligns and John presumed they had escaped from the building through the rear entrance and scrap metal marshalling yard.

Within a few seconds, John had reached the Loader's control footplate. He glanced at the clearly labelled controls, and then at Forsyth. A terrible idea entered John's mind and with a push of a button the furnace door behind Forsyth began to open. Forsyth glanced over his shoulder at the opening furnace door and began to haul his pallid, weakened body to its feet. But in doing so he did not see the Loader's massive arm start its approach. John looked down the line of the arm, as if he was taking aim, and carefully propelled the arm at a slow and steady pace down along the tight gap between the charging boxes towards Forsyth. Forsyth suddenly saw the approaching arm and yelled out in a terrified voice.

"Stop! Somebody! Over here!" He grabbed the end of the arm for support but staggered as it rammed him slowly and relentless towards the blistering blaze in the furnace. Through the haze of heat he glimpsed the Loader's footplate and was horrified when he saw John's impassive stare.

"You!" Forsyth then growled, "I hate you!" And then he tripped. For a brief second he seemed to be suspended on the threshold of the furnace, and then with screams of excruciating agony he fell into the furnace and the fires of Hell. His clothes burst into flame and tongues of fire licked at the furnace doorway. John pressed another button and the door began to close. Forsyth, the persecutor of his family; the murderer of his father, was dead.

REUNION AND REVELATION

Dan McGarret's 'yard' was at the end of a short dirt track that forked away from a narrow lane in the bottom of a wooded valley on the edge of the village. It was an oil-stained, dusty courtyard, enclosed by two time-worn stone outbuildings and an adjoining stone barn. A mass of ivy clung hopelessly to the barn's flaking stonework and grasped desperately to the cracked slate tiles along the edge of the roof. The barn hadn't been home to livestock or grain for many years and was currently used as a garage-cum-workshop for a dismantled steam traction engine. The yard looked smaller than its actual size because of the imposing presence of a pair of gleaming black traction engines that occupied most of the available space. The McGarret's home, a tiny forlorn-looking cottage, was tucked away in the furthest corner of the yard.

Dan was crouched beneath the boiler of one of the engines whilst he adjusted something with a heavy spanner. Tobias was stood beside the engine, trying to engage Dan in a meaningful conversation about the boy's potential placement with the McGarrets.

"And Mrs McGarret is happy to take the boy in?" Tobias asked.

"I told you, Lizzie's fine about it, so long as you get a ration book sorted for him. She says he can have our Arthur's old room. He's going to be at sea 'til God knows when."

"And if Arthur returns home on leave?"

"We've loads of space in there," he said, nodding in the direction of an outbuilding. "It's lodgings we have for hired hands. Arthur can stop there. Not that we expect him home for months or more. No. If the boy's got to stop with somebody, like one of them evacuated kids, he can stop with me and Lizzie. Go ask her yourself, she's in the house."

"Thank you, Dan. You and Mrs McGarret are extremely generous," said Tobias.

Chattering voices drifted into the yard and Tobias looked over to see John, Agnes, Marcus and the boy trudging up the track. They looked filthy and exhausted. Agnes and the boy were holding hands and talked as they walked. The boy occasionally pointed at the landscape as he spoke, as if explaining that he knew the area.

Tobias trotted down to greet them, whilst Dan extracted himself from under the engine and wiped his grimy fingers on his trousers in an effort to clean them up a little.

"Greetings! Greetings!" beamed Tobias. "It is heartening to see you all alive and in one piece." He then noticed the wound on John's arm and added, "You are injured, John?"

"Aye, it's nowt. Honest."

"If you insist. Please, come," Tobias beckoned Dan over and introduced him to everyone. "And of course," Tobias said when he reached the boy, "you two know each other already." The boy nodded and Dan smiled at him.

"You look tired and hungry," Dan said to the boy. "Let's see if Mrs McGarret can't sort something out to fill that stomach of yours, eh?"

As they crossed the yard, Dan called out for his wife, who came out of the house after a moment or two. Lizzie was a jolly lady, short and round with a broad face and a warm, natural smile.

"My word!" she said, her face changed to an expression of concern when she saw the filthy condition of the new arrivals. "Are you alright? Did you get bombed out of your lodgings or something?"

John and Agnes glanced at each other, knowingly, and tried to suppress a wry smile.

"Aye, something like that," John replied.

Lizzie took Agnes and the boy by the hand and led them towards the cottage. She spoke rapidly. "Well, let's get you cleaned up, shall we," she said. "You can borrow some of my spare clothes whilst we get yours washed and dried. And as for you, young man, you can have some of my son's old clothes. They're probably a bit big, but I can take them in if need be. You'll all be staying the night, won't you? Are you hungry? You must be famished. My name's Lizzie, by the way…" and they filed into the cottage.

John, Tobias and Marcus looked at each other as if wishing to speak but being mindful that Dan was present. Dan sensed that they wanted to talk privately.

"I'll, er, just…" he excused himself by showing them his spanner and nodding in the direction of the traction engine.

"Thank you, Dan," said Tobias. Dan returned to the traction engine to continue his adjustments. Tobias, Marcus and John drifted into the barn where they were out of earshot. Tobias could hardly contain his enthusiasm for news of recent events, which John and Marcus duly relayed.

"Dead, you say?" Tobias solemnly reflected upon Forsyth's death.

"Yes. And his Malign accomplices defeated," added Marcus.

"A cause for celebration. Of that there's no doubt," Tobias said.

"Aye, but we still don't know who Forsyth's deal was with," John reminded them. "And if we want the boy to be safe, we'll need to get to them before they get to the boy."

"John is right, brother," said Marcus. "We must identify the Malign who was to perform the separation by fire."

"Indeed," added Tobias, "and until we do, the boy remains in danger, regardless of where he resides."

"Do the McGarrets know the risks?" asked John. "I mean, did they have a Renaissance too?"

"No, John. Not everyone experiences a Renaissance," said Marcus.

"And you should not discuss yours with them," added Tobias. "The McGarrets are content enough to know that they are helping a vulnerable child in desperate times. As far as they are concerned, we work for a secret governmental agency and the boy is a target of the German High Command. Now, I suggest you and Agnes remain with the boy for the next few days, until Tobias and I consult with Solomon and do our best to identify this elusive Malign."

"Right, then," said John. His stomach rumbled loudly. "Enough talk for now, then," he added, "let's eat. I'm starvin'."

The three of them went into the cottage, where Dan was already washing his hands whilst Lizzie served out a simple meal of bread, cheese and fruit. Agnes and the boy were soon bathed and changed and they rejoined the others around the kitchen table.

After the meal, Marcus and Tobias thanked their hosts, and made their excuses to leave.

"We really do have to get back to Headquarters," insisted Tobias.

"Yes, thank you for the hospitality, Mrs McGarret," added Marcus, "but we really must be off. We have quite a journey ahead of us." John glanced across at Marcus, who returned a defensive look.

"Long train journey, then?" asked Dan.

"Oh, we're used to the travel," replied Tobias.

The brothers said their goodbyes and then left the cottage.

"Well," said Dan, "I've a couple of other things I need to get sorted on that engine for tomorrow."

"Need a hand?" offered John, not wishing to sit around.

"That'll be great. Thanks," answered Dan.

The two of them left the cottage and crossed the yard to the traction engines, Dan glanced down the track. It was empty.

"Your mates don't half walk quick," he said.

"Aye, you'd be surprised how quick they get about," replied John. He knew perfectly well that Marcus and Tobias would have already stepped into The Pathway and taken the shorter route back to Headquarters.

"Right," said Dan, "it's this thing under here." He pointed to the underneath of one of the traction engines. "Keeps working loose and needs tightening every day. Bloody ancient, these things. Want to swap 'em for new tractors and more modern stuff, but, you know… money's a thing… and then the Ministry's waiting lists…"

"Aye," answered John.

Suddenly, there was the sound of distant gunshots: two rounds fired in quick succession about a mile or so away. John's ears pricked up and the hairs on the back of his neck tingled. Dan saw John's stony-serious reaction.

"Don't whittle, mate. Probably just poachers, gone rabbiting or something like that," Dan said. "Don't worry about it."

"Oh aye," replied John. "You get a lot of that up here, then? Poachers, like."

"A bit. Usually down that way, though," Dan said, pointing in a different direction to where the shots were heard. "Not usually up there," he pointed to where the shots were heard. "Old man Thwaite doesn't use his gun much these days, see."

"Thwaite," John pondered, "Thwaite. I've heard that name before."

"It's where the boy used to live."

John should not have been surprised by the sound of a shotgun being used in the open countryside. But his suspicions were firmly raised. He was made nervous by the knowledge that the gunshots had come from the direction of Thwaite's farm.

"I think I'll just have a wander up and see if everything's alright."

"If it makes you feel better," replied Dan, indifferently.

"Aye, I think it will. Besides, it'll help me get to know the area better," John replied and he sauntered out of the yard.

He set off in the direction of old man Thwaite's farm, climbed the gentle slope of the valley and crossed a field containing some cattle.

At the other side of this field was a track which led him past a newly ploughed field and up a short steep incline to the back of Thwaite's farm. John then cut along the narrow path which was lined by the overgrown hedgerows, and he soon entered Thwaite's farmyard through the small gate next to the farmhouse.

It was very quiet. Not even a dog to greet him. John drifted quietly around the yard, glancing in through the windows of the farmhouse and in through the doors of the outbuildings. There was nothing and nobody about.

John noticed that the main yard gate was wide open. He went to investigate it, and it was at that moment that he saw the dog, a Border Colley, lifeless and in a pool of blood in the centre of the lane.

Several yards away, on the wall of the barn at the rear of the outbuildings, there was a splash of blood, about knee high. A trail of dribbled blood led from there to the dog. A few other, lighter splashes of blood led into the barn. John strained to hear anything, but all he could hear was the shuffling of hooves and the mooing of cows from inside the barn.

He cautiously approached the barn door and slowly peered round it into the depths of the barn. To his left was a row of cattle pens, with several animals in each pen. To his right was a long stack of neatly packed bails of straw, reaching high up to the rafters. At the far end of the barn was a pale and frail old Mr Thwaite. He was cowering, half-delirious, beneath a giant of a man in a British Army officer's uniform.

The soldier towered over old man Thwaite, and wielded an enormous, threatening fist, which was raised as if ready to strike the frail old man.

John was momentarily shocked by this nightmare apparition and audibly gasped with surprise. The soldier, on hearing the gasp, spun around and John was confronted by the officer who had recently visited his mother. This giant officer was the complete, terrifying figure from the nightmare of his youth. A sneer appeared beneath the heavily waxed moustache and this revealed the half filled rows of crooked yellow teeth that John so vividly remembered from his tormented dreams. And the soldier's eyes were the same fiery, volcanic eruptions of hatred and malevolence.

"N-No!" John spluttered, "It-it can't be." His legs felt like they had turned to lead; he willed them to move, but they simply ignored him, "You! You're a dream. You don't exist."

The soldier's interest in the old farmer was forgotten as quickly as if it had never existed. Instead, the soldier advanced with a menacing growl towards John.

John sensed that this was to be a life-defining, if not life-ending, confrontation. He glanced at the farmer, a forlorn, crumpled, shadow of a man, pallid and bleeding, and it upset John deeply to see. He had witnessed so many depressing injustices over recent days; pain, hardship and suffering at the hands of nauseatingly wicked villains like this towering example of outrageous, violent brutality that bounded towards him.

And then something in John's heart became transformed. Suddenly and inexplicably, all his inhibitions, fears and weaknesses fell away from him like the unwanted and unwelcome burdens that they were. In their place, his heart became overwhelmed by an absolute, single-minded determination; an indescribable stubbornness that meant he no longer cared for his own personal safety or survival. He just wanted that giant bastard dead!

But he couldn't move! No matter how much he willed his legs to move, they were held motionless as if gripped by some invisible hand.

And then, out of the corner of his eye he saw the boy stride purposefully past and approach the advancing soldier. John tried to reach out to the boy to protect him, but the child was beyond his limited reach. The boy ignored John's call for him to flee the giant. Instead he calmly stood and held up a hand to halt the malevolent beast.

"Stop!" the boy called out and held up his arm like a policeman halting traffic. The soldier was startled by the sudden appearance of the boy and was surprised the confidence with which the boy gave the order. The soldier stopped as instructed. Then a strange expression of demented delight slowly crept across his pasty face when he realised that he had the boy within easy reach. John couldn't see the look of concentration on the boy's face, because the boy stood between him and the soldier.

"Ferotorn," the boy said. "Your name is Ferotorn, isn't it?" The giant soldier, clearly dismayed that the boy should know his name, opened his mouth to demand how the boy had come to know it. But the boy continued before Ferotorn had chance to reply. "See the evil in your heart," the boy said and spread open the fingers of his outstretched hand. The fingers began to emit a pale blue glow that grew brighter by the second until it burned a phosphorous white. Ferotorn was surprised by the boy's action and unwillingly became transfixed by the celestial aura that had been conjured.

"Look," the boy ordered. Ferotorn tried to turn away but it was impossible for him to break eye contact with the light. John could only glimpse at what was happening, but he was mightily impressed with the effect the boy was having on Ferotorn, the tormentor from his nightmares.

"No!" Ferotorn barked. He collapsed to his knees, but could not break his eye contact with the light. "Leave me be!" he growled.

"See the nightmare of your own heart, Ferotorn? See it… feel it… they are your fears, your nightmares. You cannot hide them from me. And I show them you, now."

"No! Leave me alone!" Ferotorn boomed, and an expression of horror crept across his clammy face.

"I'll leave you alone, if you leave me and my friends alone. If I see you ever again, you'll see this again. Do you understand?"

"Yes," muttered Ferotorn.

"Now go," the boy said, "and never return." He closed his fingers and the light vanished. The hold on Ferotorn was broken and he fell to the floor, exhausted. "I said go!" the boy reminded him. Ferotorn scrambled to his feet, and careered angrily, and clumsily, out of the barn and out of sight.

The hold on John's legs was released. The boy turned and threw his arms around John. They stood in silence for just a couple of seconds before John finally spoke.

"I think we need to get Mr Thwaite to a doctor."

A NEW BEGINNING

Mr Thwaite was asleep in his own bed, in his own bedroom. It was a neglected, untidy room, with untidy piles of discarded clothes draped across an old dressing table and strewn across the floor. A pile of grimy bed linen, desperate to be laundered, waited in the corner by the door.

Agnes watched over him as he slept. It was a difficult and troubled slumber, broken by bouts of restlessness. He kicked off the bed clothes, again, and Agnes leaned over and carefully pulled the sheets neatly back over him. She then sat down in the only chair in the room, an old, hard, wooden dining chair.

Mr Thwaite had broken no bones in his encounter with Ferotorn, and the few lacerations he had received from a glancing shotgun wound were all superficial and were all now cleaned and bandaged. Nonetheless, Mr Thwaite was not a young man, and he had been shocked and roughly treated by Ferotorn. Everyone remained concerned for his recovery.

John knocked gently on the door and quietly entered the room. Agnes felt at Mr Thwaite's forehead and looked over to John.

"He should be in hospital, you know," she said.

"Oh, I don't know," replied John. "The Doc from Overbank Hall says he just needs lots of bed rest."

"But he still needs looking after, 'til he recovers," she said.

Mr Thwaite began snoring loudly, like a hog, and this made John smirk, childishly, just for a moment. Agnes cast him a serious look that said 'behave.' John then crossed the room and stood beside her. He placed a hand on her shoulder. She folded her hands on her lap. A long silence passed between them.

Agnes eventually broke the silence.

"I am sorry, you know," she said, without looking up at John. John didn't know what to say, so he said nothing. "It's just that... It were such a shock," she continued, "seein' you after all this time. I mean..." her voice trailed off.

"Aye?" John said, quietly.

"I was goin' to tell you what had happened to me. Honest. But, I couldn't. Not in Scotland... not in front of the boy. Wouldn't have been right. And then, well, I couldn't bring myself to face it."

"Face what?"

Agnes sighed.

"Face what?"

"I were ashamed."

"Ashamed of what?" John asked.

"The truth."

"Because you weren't chosen? I know you weren't. Forsyth told me."

"Did he tell you that it were your dad... who saved me, I mean, when he came to see me after the baby..." her voice faltered as if the words themselves refused to be spoken. She paused and sniffled. John affectionately squeezed her shoulder and pulled her closer to him.

"You mean, after our daughter died," he completed the sentence for her.

"Yeh," she said, weakly.

"Go on," he whispered.

"Well, he saved my life. Your dad..." Agnes said, slowly, "'cos... Well, I weren't thinking straight, you know. I blamed myself about the baby. You were away at sea. I'd got no family. I'd got your mum to look after as well... I'd got nobody to talk to. Nobody to help me... I felt it were all my fault. I just thought everybody would be better off without me..."

"You mean, the note were real, then?" John said, slightly surprised. "You mean you were actually goin' to... you know... jump off that bridge?"

Agnes nodded slowly.

"You must really hate me," she said, "for puttin' you through all that. And then not really being dead, after all that grief."

"God, no, love. I don't hate you," he replied, honestly. He considered his next question carefully, and was not entirely sure how much he wanted to know. But he felt he had to ask. "So, if Dad stopped you jumping, what did you go with him for? I mean if you weren't chosen?"

"Maligns. They turned up and we had to run for it. Probably Forsyth's doing. Anyway, I couldn't go back... I'd already left the note... and, well... your dad wouldn't let me anyway. He said I knew too much, you see. And that the Maligns would have only come back and killed me, later. I didn't get chosen, but I didn't go willin', either."

John felt an embarrassing flush fill his cheeks when he recalled the period shortly after her death. When she had died, he had been angry with her because, by killing herself, she had 'run away' from her responsibilities, and run away from him. He'd thought it cowardly. But soon afterwards he'd become angry and guilt-ridden for letting her down; for allowing things to get so desperate for her. This was why her last letter had meant so much to him.

He wasn't angry with her now. He couldn't be even if he wanted to. He was just glad she was alive, and was part of his life again.

Any trace of anger that he might still carry, deep down, was not directed at her, or at his dad. It was directed at the Malign's. It was they, and Mr Forsyth, who had denied him six years with his wife. And it was they, and Mr Forsyth who had killed his dad.

John was glad Mr Forsyth was dead. He was also glad to have been on the List of Chosen; and to have avenged his father's murder and to have saved the lives of his wife and an innocent child.

But there was one final question he had on his lips: one that could close that lamentable chapter of his life and, hopefully, signal a new beginning for himself and Agnes. In the silence of the moment, he summoned the courage to ask her if she still loved him.

But, suddenly, there was a knock at the door, and the boy poked his head into the room. John felt a sudden wave of adolescent angst sweep over him.

"Is it alright to come in?" the boy asked.

"'Course it is. Come in, Love," Agnes replied, wiping away a tear from her cheek. The boy entered, followed by Mrs McGarret.

"He's been pestering to come up all morning," explained Mrs McGarret.

"Oh, you should have let him," Agnes smiled weakly, and added, "we've just been talking, that's all. You didn't have to wait."

"Dan not with you?" asked John, feeling suddenly claustrophobic.

"No, he's up the fields. They don't plough themselves, you know. Tobias is here, though. He's downstairs. Had a good long chat with him about this lovely lad, haven't we boy?" The boy's cheeks reddened slightly with embarrassment at the attention.

"Aye?" John said, "well, don't let me get in the way of your visit. I'll be downstairs if you need me." And he left the room.

Tobias was sat down at the kitchen table with a fresh cup of steaming hot tea when John entered the kitchen.

"Tobias, I want to ask you a personal question," John said. "It's about me and Agnes." Tobias instantly looked uncomfortable.

"I'm not really the appropriate person, John," he replied, hastily, "to discuss personal questions. I'm here to focus our efforts on the situation at hand."

John felt rebuffed by his friend and so he poured himself a cup of tea, in a childish, heavy handed manner. Tea splashed from the pot as he poured, and the lid rattled when he plonked it heavily on the kitchen side. Tobias winced when John banged his cup on the table, spilling some of its contents.

"Fine," John remarked, childishly. "Tell me about this Ferotorn bloke, then."

"Well, firstly, he is not a 'bloke'," Tobias said, "he's more of a demon."

"Oh, aye? You mean he's a demon, like that one that possessed that Scottish copper?"

"Not in so far as possessions. A more accurate description would be to say he's a demon that takes on the actual physical form of a human, rather than possessing one."

"That's clever."

"Yes. Ferotorn is a very high ranking Malign, and an extremely dangerous demon, too."

"Come across him before?"

"I know of him. Although, I must say he has not been seen or heard for… well… centuries."

"Because he gets other folk, like that copper and Forsyth, to do his dirty work for him?"

"Possibly. It could explain his elusiveness."

"D'you reckon he were the other half of that deal that Forsyth were on about."

"It is a real possibility that should not be ignored."

Tobias and John slurped at their tea.

"You know, the boy scared him off all by himself, and did something to my legs so they wouldn't work."

"I know. You've already told me twice."

"So, how is it that he needs us around? I mean, he didn't look like he needed protecting much if you ask me."

"The boy's powers are growing, blooming like a flower as the boy comes of age," replied Tobias. "Ferotorn was not aware of this. And he is unlikely to make the same mistakes again."

"You mean he'll have another go for the boy?" said John, surprised.

"Ferotorn now recognises that his window of opportunity is shrinking rapidly. If he does not separate the boy by fire soon, his opportunity will be lost forever. He will probably try different tactics next time."

John slurped from his tea.

"Tobias," John began, slowly, "ever since I were a lad, I had this nightmare. Regular, like. Ferotorn was in it. He killed me with a bayonet, every time."

Tobias was surprised by John's frankness. He paused to consider this revelation.

"Every time?" Tobias asked.

"Aye," replied John.

"Interesting. Mmm. It may be appropriate to re-examine your order papers. Well, that is, if we are able to find them under the rubble of Headquarters."

"Why?"

"It may well be that your mission orders from Forsyth were fraudulent. Remember, Forsyth was corrupt, after all."

"But what's that got to do with my dream?"

"Well, it is my understanding that there are some associations between the dreams of the Chosen and the dreamer's celestial duty."

"Oh, aye?" John raised an eyebrow. "You mean my real mission is to get killed by Ferotorn?"

"Of course not. No."

"But you think it's something to do with Ferotorn?"

Tobias was about to reply, when Marcus arrived outside the cottage and cheerfully rapped on the kitchen window as he passed it on his way to the door. Tobias was pleased to see his brother.

Marcus pushed open the stiff wooden door and entered the kitchen. He was carrying a bundle of clothes similar in style and colour to those that he and Tobias wore: dark green trousers, dark green woollen pull-over, a small brown leather jacket, and a small crumpled hat. A pair of small, heavy boots hung from his arm. The clothes were too small even for Marcus and Tobias's diminutive frames.

"Just in time for tea, I see," Marcus observed, as he dumped the clothes and boots on the table, and poured himself a cup of tea. He sat down next to Tobias.

John picked at the pile of clothes, placed the boots on the floor, and held up the pair of child-sized trousers.

"Bit small for you, eh?"

"They're for the boy," Marcus said with a proud smile.

"Oh, aye? But this lot'll make him look like you two."

The brothers grinned like moronic schoolboys and nodded excitedly. John then realised the significance of the clothing. A smile of amused astonishment spread across John's face

"You're jokin'!" he exclaimed and laughed. "He's one of you?"

They nodded again.

"How long have you known, then?"

"Just recently," answered Marcus, vaguely.

"Does this mean you're going to take him away?"

"No, of course not," said Tobias. "He will remain with the McGarrets."

"However," added Marcus, "it will be necessary for him to attend certain… tutorials. Once a week I will take him to Headquarters to be tutored by Solomon."

Just then, Marcus and Tobias noticed something over John's shoulder and they both became very solemn and stood up.

"What?" asked John, turning to look behind him, "Oh…" his voice trailed away when he saw the majestic presence of Arella, the white angel, who had appeared and filled an entire corner of the kitchen. John, too, stood up.

"Greetings," the angel said, and revealed a small, ancient-looking roll of papyrus and unrolled it. "The List of Chosen," the angel read, "for you, Marcus." Arella rolled the papyrus back up and passed it to Marcus. "You shall be responsible for the List until your new commanding officer is assigned. Mission order papers and further orders regarding new headquarters will be delivered to you at Overbank Hall, tomorrow morning at daybreak."

"Thank you, Arella," Marcus said and unrolled the papyrus. He briefly examined the List of Chosen. He raised an eyebrow and glanced at John.

"John, I would greatly appreciate it if you would return to Overbank Hall with me," he said, "I have to rescue the man who is to become our next commanding officer, and I would be grateful for your assistance when I return with him."

"Aye, if you want," replied John. "But what about Tobias? Don't you want him to help?"

"I have other duties to attend to," replied Tobias.

"Like, the boy?" John asked.

"Yes."

"You want to go now?" John asked Marcus, who glanced at his watch.

"Not immediately. We have sufficient time to finish our tea before we need to depart."

"In that case," John said and turned to Arella, "Arella, can you answer me a question. It's a personal one."

"John," Tobias interrupted, "it is not appropriate to divert angels from their tasks by asking them personal questions." But John continued regardless.

"Me and Agnes were married, once upon a time. Then she got brought to Overbank Hall, years ago. Now that I'm here as well, does it mean we're still married? And if we're *not* married, can we still *get* married?"

John was unaware that Agnes had come downstairs and was stood in the kitchen doorway, listening to the conversation.

"Do you wish to be married to Agnes?" Arella asked.

"Of course I do," replied John, without even considering the question, "I love her, don't I. That's why I married her in the first place."

Agnes drifted into the kitchen and went over to John, who was surprised to know she had been within earshot. She placed her arms gently around his neck and kissed him tenderly on the lips.

"I do," she whispered to him and his heart leapt for joy. He wrapped his arms around her, lifted her from her feet and they kissed for several more seconds. Marcus interrupted them with a deliberate cough.

"Excuse me please, Agnes," Marcus said.

"Yes?" she answered, without breaking eye contact with John. They were now both ginning at each other like Cheshire cats.

"Your husband and I have duties to attend to this evening," Marcus continued,

"Oh, it's just that…" she began. But Marcus glanced at his watch, again, and interrupted her.

"And, I'm afraid, John and I have to depart, now."

"Oh," Agnes and John said, together, slightly disappointed.

"I'll try and get Marcus to bring me back, tomorrow," said John.

"He's got to bring the Doc over for Mr Thwaite, any road."

"Right," she said, trying to hide her disappointment. She then assumed her usual stern, business-like attitude; the attitude that Marcus and Tobias had become accustomed to over the years. "Tomorrow it is, then."

John turned to Arella, to say thank you, but the apparition had disappeared.

Marcus drained his tea and ushered John to the door. They said their goodbyes and left for Overbank Hall. Agnes closed the door behind them. She looked at Tobias and then at the pile of clothes on the table.

"Either you've shrunk your outfit in the wash," she said, "or this lot's for the boy."

Marcus and John travelled, via The Pathway, to the chapel vestry at Overbank Hall. Here, Marcus said goodbye to John, and then disappeared down The Pathway to undertake the rescue their new commanding officer.

John emerged from the chapel and saw that a temporary community of green canvas tents, large and small, had sprouted up on the gardens and lawn around the ruins of Overbank Hall.

He saw a large sign, made from wood salvaged from the hall, which had been hammered into the ground at the edge of this 'tented village.' The words that had been daubed in white paint read 'Phoenix Village.'

"John!" a familiar, friendly voice called, and John was warmly greeted by Walter.

"I'm just finishing my rounds, inspecting the temporary services. Care to join me for a drink?"

"Aye, as long as it's not too far from the new Commanding Officer's tent," replied John, "I've got to meet him and Marcus when they arrive."

"Let's wait for them by the chapel, then."

And so they sat on a couple of old chairs beside the chapel, at the edge of the path that led into the wood, and they indulged in a few single malt whiskeys, courtesy of Walter's ever resourceful contacts, whilst they waited.

A short while later, John and Walter heard voices drifting out of the wood. John instantly recognised the pompous tone of Marcus. The other voice sounded vaguely familiar, too.

Marcus trotted into view, followed by Philip Ambrose. Philip was soaked through and was smeared in a thick, black slurry of oil. Walter jumped to his feet, darted into the chapel, and emerged a few seconds later holding a large grey blanket, which he threw around Philip's shivering shoulders.

"Eh-up, Sir," said John and offered out his hand to Philip, "Welcome to your Renaissance."

A note on the Caledonia.

The *Caledonia* was, in fact, a real ship. She was originally built as the liner *Bismarck* for the Hamburg-America Line of Germany, during the First World War. She was acquired as reparations by the British after the war and sailed under the White Star and Cunard flags as the *Majestic* until the mid 1930s. The Royal Navy subsequently acquired her for use as a training ship in Rosyth, renaming her *HMS Caledonia*. Alas, she was gutted by fire whilst being converted for troop transportation in September 1939, and sank in the Firth of Forth. *Caledonia* was eventually salvaged and broken up, allegedly yielding 40,000 tons of quality metal to feed the British War effort.

A note on the Vulcan Foundry.

Vulcan was the Roman god of fire and volcanoes, and a manufacturer of iron, arms and armour for gods and heroes. As such, *Vulcan* is a name commonly associated with ironworks, and foundries. It was not uncommon to find a *Vulcan Foundry* in many of the towns and cities of the industrial revolution. Amongst the more well known examples were the *Vulcan* foundries in Sheffield, Warrington and Newton-le-Willows, Lancashire. The *Vulcan Foundry* in the story, home of the fictional Rotheton Iron and Steel Foundry Works, is entirely fictional.